LOVE MEANS EVERYTHING

The Sisters of Rosefield Book 3

EMMA EASTER

Love Means Everything
by Emma Easter

Paperback Edition

CKN Christian Publishing
An Imprint of Wolfpack Publishing

6032 Wheat Penny Avenue
Las Vegas, NV 89122

Paperback ISBN: 978-1-64734-492-4
Ebook ISBN: 978-1-64119-882-0
Library of Congress Control Number: 2020931398

LOVE MEANS EVERYTHING

To my dear daughter, Natalie.

ONE

Trisha passed a grove of trees while pushing Ruby in her stroller. She looked up and saw a couple holding hands. The woman had a bag of groceries in her other hand while the man pushed a stroller with a baby. Trisha's heart twisted with envy and she looked away quickly.

She had started to take weekly strolls through Rosefield a few months after Ruby was born. She took a different path every Saturday, enjoying the morning air and exploring different parts of her hometown. Or, at least, she had enjoyed exploring Rosefield, until a month ago when Ruby had turned one. Suddenly, she started noticing things she hadn't before, like couples taking strolls with their babies.

The dissatisfaction had started then, and again, she had begun to fret about Ruby not growing up with a father. She had not seen or heard from Stan since he'd disappeared months before Ruby was born. At first, she had been happy about that, as the thought of even being near him had made her feel literally sick. But gradually, as the months progressed, she'd started to wish he was in his daughter's life.

Sometimes, when she looked at Ruby while feeding or bathing her, the uncanny resemblance to Stan would suddenly startle her. After that, memories of her time together with Stan would flood her mind, followed by the grim thought that Ruby might never come to know her father. She would know what it was like to have a father one day, and then lose him the next. She held close to her heart the memories of the years she'd spent with her own dad. Those memories were very precious. Losing her father as a teenager was bad enough. Ruby growing up without a dad would be far worse. Trisha didn't want her daughter to grow up without her father.

Every day, she whispered a prayer to God, asking that Stan would come back—not for her sake, as she certainly wasn't interested in restarting a relationship with him—but for Ruby's.

Trisha walked on, passing the fire station and the police station. She smiled as she saw some officers in front of the station. She made a mental note to call Audrey, now partly living in Miami with Ken, when she got home.

As she walked by the city hall, she turned and saw a man on the other side of the road, holding his daughter who looked about three years old. She sighed heavily as the man and the child crossed the road and walked by her. Looking down at Ruby, she whispered, "I'm so sorry, my darling. I wish I could give you a dad. I know what it feels like not to have one."

Ruby chuckled as though she clearly understood what had been said to her, and Trisha smiled sadly.

She crossed the street and kept walking until she came to a building under construction. She sharply sucked in her breath as the face of the owner of the building suddenly appeared in her mind. It was Frank's. She hadn't seen him for almost a year, as he lived in Boise now, but he had called regularly. He'd told her on the phone some months before that he was building a new restaurant in Rosefield, but she had never seen it since she had not walked or driven by this area in a long time.

She frowned as she walked on. Frank's face had taken residence in her mind and refused to be pushed away. This wasn't the first time she'd thought about him with such deep longing. Since she began to yearn for a father for Ruby, she had started to think about Frank a lot.

She turned Ruby's stroller around and began to make her way back home while still thinking about him. It was more than a year since her divorce, but she wasn't ready to date anyone. Yet Frank's image hardly ever left her mind. Plus, she constantly recalled the awe in his voice when he talked with her, the sparkle in his eyes every time he looked at her.

It's been over a year since you got divorced, for goodness' sake! She scolded herself silently. Why won't you just start dating again? Why don't you just tell Frank how much you miss him the next time he calls?

But she knew why she couldn't start dating now or call Frank. She was scared. After what had happened with Stan, she never wanted to experience anything like that again. She pursed her lips.

But you know that Frank will never treat you the way Stan did. You know he will cherish you.

She knew that was true. Frank had loved her for so long. Still, she wasn't completely sure she wanted to be with him. Besides, she didn't want to let her desire to have a good father for her daughter influence her decision to date Frank. From what she saw the last time Frank had visited her and Ruby, she instinctively knew he would be a good dad. But that was not enough reason to date him.

Or was it?

You like him, Trisha. Admit it. What is wrong with also wanting him to be a father to Ruby, knowing he is great with kids?

She sighed in frustration at the conflicting emotions in her mind. Even though she had tried not to let Frank into her heart for so long, she had to admit that she liked him. He had said he would wait until she was ready to date again, but surely he wouldn't wait forever. Maybe it was time to call him and let him know she was ready to give him a chance. She wanted to feel loved and cherished again. It was time she was proactive about it.

Her heart drummed as she neared her house. She would call Frank once she entered the house and tell him she missed him. He would be ecstatic… unless he had given up on her or found someone else.

She reached the two-story brick house she had shared with Stan until they'd gotten divorced and put Ruby in her playpen in a corner of the living room. She smiled at Ruby as she picked up the phone and dialed Frank's number. She held her breath as the phone rang. Her heart rate increased as Frank's deep voice came on the line.

"Hello," he said.

"Hi, Frank. It's Trisha."

The excitement in his voice was clear as he asked happily, "Trisha, how are you?"

"I'm good." She suddenly felt lost for words.

"I've missed you," he said.

She shut her eyes. She envied the fact that he could say so easily the exact words she was finding so hard to utter. But this was her chance to say it back.

"Trisha, are you still there?"

"Umm… yes, I've… umm… I've missed you too, Frank. When are you coming to Rosefield again?" There, she had said it.

There was silence on the other end of the line for a while and she thought he had hung up. "Frank?"

"Yes… Trisha. I'm here. I'm just surprised… and happy that you said you have missed me. You don't know how long I have been waiting to hear those words from you."

"It's not so weird though, Frank. I haven't seen you for so long and we are friends, aren't we?"

"I wish we could be more," he said. He sounded sad.

She wanted to tell him she would like that too… but she held back. She still wasn't totally sure it was what she wanted. Instead, she said, "I know you do. For now, I don't know if I am ready for that… but I just called to let you know I've been thinking about you."

"Trisha," he said solemnly, "I think about you every single day… no, every minute of every day. What you said just now is music to my ears." He suddenly yelped and she laughed.

"Are you okay?" she asked, chuckling.

"Never been better. You know what? I'll come to Rosefield as soon as possible. Actually, I'll be there tomorrow to see you and Ruby. Would that be good?"

"Oh… no, Frank! I know you are very busy there with your restaurant. You don't have to leave…"

"I want to. Besides, I have to check up on my restaurant in Rosefield." He paused for a second and then said firmly, "I'll be there tomorrow."

She nodded and said, "Okay. I'll see you then."

"I can't wait!" he said.

They talked a bit more about Audrey, Sienna, and Faizan, and then the call ended.

Trisha sat down on the sofa and grinned at Ruby, who was examining her new toy, a pacifier in her mouth.

"What do you think, Ruby? Frank is coming tomorrow. You don't remember him, but he held you in his arms when you were just a tiny baby."

Ruby smiled at her, and Trisha continued. "I know he isn't your dad, but he is a very nice guy, and he has loved me since we were kids. I'm doing the right thing by giving him a chance now, aren't I?"

Ruby went back to playing with her toy, and Trisha took a deep breath. She wasn't completely sure she could let Frank in now after her bad marriage to Stan, but it would be great to see how things went. Perhaps she would finally be able to move away from the memories of her dreadful marriage to Stan to more pleasant ones with Frank—if she could let Frank in.

*****

Frank stared at his phone for a long moment after his call with Trisha ended. He just couldn't believe what she had told him—that she missed him and was thinking about him. He sighed deeply. He wanted to shout for joy, but he controlled himself. His chefs were in the restaurant's kitchen with him, and there were guests in the front of the house, eating.

"Chef, are you okay?" Leon, his sous chef asked, looking up from the reduction sauce he was making. "You are smiling as though you won the lottery."

John, the pastry chef, laughed and put down the wooden spoon he was using to stir his bowl of syrup. "I hope you did. I need a raise badly."

Everyone in the kitchen laughed.

Frank shook his head and grinned, "Okay, guys! You have all had your laugh. Now get back to work!"

The chefs soon went back to their cooking, trying to keep up with the orders. Frank called out the orders while his chefs responded, made the dishes at lightning speed, and plated them. Some waiters came in regularly to get the dishes, while others came to submit orders for guests that needed to be cooked immediately. Frank was happy for the nonstop work, or he would have boarded a flight to Rosefield that very night.

From time to time, he went out to greet guests, but mostly, he kept cooking. The grueling pace in which they had to prepare the food didn't slow down until hours later when it was time to close the restaurant.

He stepped out into the moonlit night, took a deep breath as he usually did after a long day at work, and locked the doors of the restaurant. He looked up at the words 'FRANKLY EATING' engraved on top of the single-story building and smiled with pride. He turned away and only then did he allow his mind to return to Trisha and their call earlier in the day. His heart soared as he recalled again what she had said to him.

Nick, his good friend and business partner, came alongside him and they both headed for their cars together.

"I have to go to Rosefield tomorrow," Frank said trying not to let his excitement show.

Nick frowned. "So soon? But Angelo called just yesterday. The restaurant isn't ready yet and you are needed here. I could go and check it out so…"

"No, Nick. It isn't really about the restaurant, though I will definitely take the opportunity to personally see how far the workers have gotten."

Nick's frown deepened. "Then what is it about? You just visited your parents there not too…" He suddenly stopped and raised his brows. "No, Frank! Tell me it's not because of that Trisha girl."

They reached Frank's black jeep, and he leaned against it. He looked at Nick. His friend knew how crazy he was about Trisha but had always been against the relationship because Trisha had never reciprocated his feelings. Nick had told him on several occasions that he was wasting his life waiting for a woman who didn't care about him, but Frank couldn't help the way he felt about Trisha. At least he could tell Nick now what Trisha had said. Not that that would impress him, but still…

"She told me over the phone that she missed me and was thinking about me," Frank said.

Nick sighed loudly, a frustrated expression on his face. "She did that because she saw you were beginning to pull away, Frank. She hasn't seen you in months…"

"I've been calling her."

"You have? And you didn't tell me!"

"I knew what you would say if I did. You know how much I love her, Nick. She said she misses me. I can work with that."

Nick raked his fingers through his hair. "You can't just up and leave the restaurant just because some girl…"

"She isn't some girl!"

"Okay… just because Trisha says she misses you. I need you here." Nick placed his hand on his chest and made a face. "What about me? I'll miss you if you go."

"Stop it!" Frank laughed. "Seriously, though, you can handle things here while I'm gone. Leon will act in my stead as head chef. You know he's very capable. I can fully rely on him to not let things slip in the kitchen until I return."

Nick stared at him. "I don't understand why you can't get over this girl, Frank. There are so many other pretty girls…"

"Nick!"

"Okay… okay. I'm sorry. You have made up your mind, haven't you?"

"Totally."

"Alrighty then! When do you plan to return?"

"I intend to stay there for a month."

Nick's eyes grew wide. "A month! What on earth will you do in Rosefield for a month?"

Frank shrugged. "It will take at least that long to win Trisha's heart fully."

"And if you don't win her heart by then?"

"Then I will come back."

Nick shook his head. "Wow! I knew you loved this girl, but I didn't know you loved her this much." He smiled at Frank and added, "You are crazy, do you know that?"

"Crazy about Trisha."

Nick laughed. "I knew you were going to say that. Anyway, do try to protect your heart while you woo your one true love, okay?"

"Yes, sir. I will."

"And since you will be on the ground, I'm hoping you will also have time to oversee the building?"

"Definitely." Frank put his hand on Nick's shoulder and smiled. "I will be fine and the restaurant will be too. I have to do this. You know that."

Nick shrugged.

Frank got into his car. "I have to pack. I have an early flight to catch. I promised Trisha I would see her tomorrow so I have to leave early." He started the car, waved to Nick and then backed into the road.

As he drove home, he pictured Trisha, how she would look when he saw her. His heart kept soaring until he couldn't hold back his excitement. He let out a roar and then clutched his steering wheel. "Lord," he prayed, "please help me win Trisha's heart this time. She's the only girl I have ever wanted and I love her with all my heart."

He lifted up the same prayer over and over again

even as he got to his house and packed his things. As he lay in bed, they were the last words on his lips before he slipped into a deep sleep.

*****

Faizan woke up with a start and then took a deep breath. Darkness surrounded him. He sat up and shook his head as an overwhelming sadness settled in his chest. He had been dreaming about Zainah… again. These days, he dreamt only about her or about his past life as a terrorist. Each time, he woke up full of regret. He switched on the light and touched his cheeks. They were wet with his tears.

"I can't do this anymore," he groaned. "I have to see her. I need to talk to her."

But what is the point? he thought. We can't be together because of her vow.

He put his hand on his forehead and moaned. "Still, I have to see her." Rising from the bed, he put on his robe and went to the kitchen. He poured himself a glass of water from the sink and, without thinking, began to pace the floor. Someone opened the kitchen door and he looked up. Audrey came into the kitchen in her light blue robe.

When he'd come to live in the United States about a year before, he'd lived alone in the house that had formerly been his father's but that Audrey had lived in for years. Audrey had mostly moved to Miami. She came to Rosefield often for work and stayed in the house. He'd never really felt at home in that house. It had felt strange living in the house of a father he had never known. Also, the fact that the woman who had been married to his father hadn't known he'd cheated on her and had a love child only made matters worse.

After Audrey and Ken bought a bigger house to stay in whenever they were in Rosefield, he'd immediately moved in with them when they'd asked him to. He loved this new house. It was big enough to live comfortably without getting into Ken or Audrey's way. Still, he loved when Audrey was around. She was such great company, and it felt like he'd known her all his life.

She smiled at him. "Hey! What's up, Faizan? You look worried about something." She opened the fridge, brought out a half-eaten sandwich, and put it in the microwave. She looked up at him. "Do you want to talk about it?"

He exhaled. "I would. Unfortunately, there is nothing anyone can do to help."She smiled sadly. The microwave began to ding and she opened it and brought out her sandwich. "It's about Zainah, isn't it? The girl you've been telling me about. You miss her."

"Every single day," he said.

Audrey took his hand and led him out of the kitchen. "You'll feel better if you talk about it," she said to him. They entered the living room together and she sat on the couch. He sat next to her.

"Now, tell me how you are feeling, Faizan."

In spite of himself, he smiled at his sister. Even though he was older than her, she had a way of speaking to him as though he were the younger sibling; as though it was her duty to protect him, instead of the other way around. And he indulged her. He'd lived a life of violence—constantly protecting himself while hurting others. She, on the other hand, had lived most of her life protecting others while putting her own life in danger.

She tucked her legs under her and turned to face him fully.

"I dreamt just now that Zainah had been captured by some very bad people and was calling out to me to help her, but I couldn't. I know she's not really in physical danger. I think it's because I want to be her hero. I want to feel like she needs me even though she doesn't." He sighed sadly and looked down at the carpeted floor. He looked up at Audrey again and said, "What tears me apart is knowing that she loves me too, but we will never be together because of the vow she made to God."

Audrey touched his arm. "I'm so sorry, Faizan. I know I can't say I understand how you feel, but I can only say you should pray and ask the Lord to help you get over her. There might be some other girl out there for you. If you meet her now, you will not be able to let her in until you completely let go of Zainah."

Faizan shut his eyes briefly and opened them again. "I don't think I want to meet some other girl."

"You don't have a choice, unless you want to be alone for the rest of your life."

"Maybe that will be for the better."

"No… I think the Lord will soon bring someone into your life. You have so much love to give, Faizan, because you are such a passionate person. Any girl you end up falling in love with will be truly lucky. She'll definitely feel well loved."

He smiled widely. "Well… thank you, sis. But I guess you are supposed to say that because you are my sister."

"No… I said it because it's true."

He ran his hand through his hair. "Still, I just don't think I can forget about Zainah." He looked away as an idea came to him and then turned back to Audrey. "When will Ken come to Rosefield?"

"In a few days. Why?"

"I'm going crazy thinking about Zainah every day. Even though I said the best thing for me would be to stay away from her since we can't be together, I just can't. I need to see her now. I don't want to speak with my handler, Jake, directly. Since Ken is somewhat friendly with him, I want him to help me find out if I can be provided with certain things I would need in order to go visit Zainah."

Audrey frowned and looked up, her face thoughtful. "Umm… I guess you could ask him."

Faizan nodded.

"And how long are you planning to stay when you go?"

"Not long. I'll probably not be allowed to stay past a few days to a week. That was the agreement I made with the CIA."

Audrey smiled at him and took his hand. "Are you sure going to see her is the best decision?"

"Yes," Faizan said, looking quizzically at Audrey. "I am."

"I know how difficult it can be to be apart from the one you love," Audrey said. "But your case is so heartbreaking since it seems you have no hope of ever being with her. I think I understand why you need to see her, but I am afraid of what will happen when you do see her again."

He frowned. "What do you mean?""All the feelings you have for her will be multiplied once you see her face to face. It will be really hard not to be able to act on those feelings." She paused for a second and then continued. "Ken and I went through something like that, except we knew we would get to act on our feelings one day. You, on the other hand, never will."

His heart twisted with pain at her words.

"I'm sorry," Audrey said. "I know how painful it all sounds. I just don't want you to be hurt, that's all. If you believe that going to see her is what you have to do, then by all means, go and see her."

Faizan sighed wearily. Audrey was right. Zainah had made it clear that she couldn't break her vow. And he would never ask her to. However, he had to see her and hear her voice. And maybe she would let him hug her. If his heart got broken more than it was now, then so be it. He reached out and hugged Audrey briefly. "Thanks for choosing to sit and talk with me instead of going back to sleep."

"You are welcome." She rose up. "I have to be at the station early tomorrow."

After she left the living room, Faizan exhaled. He would tell Ken about his request once he'd arrived in Rosefield. Hopefully, it would be granted quickly so he could prepare to leave for the Middle East as soon as possible.

A thread of excitement went through him as he imagined the look on Zainah's face when she saw him. He had missed her terribly and he was sure she had missed him too. Even though he would not be able to declare his love for her in the way he might want to, hopefully he would find the right words and actions that would let her know he still loved her. He would try to make sure she knew that she would stay in his heart forever.

TWO

Sienna left the tiny bungalow she shared with Bryan and got into her car. Since it was a Saturday and she didn't have classes at the Bible College, she decided to go to the pharmacy. She got there in less than five minutes, bought the pregnancy tests she wanted, and left. She got into her car and placed the tests on the passenger seat. As she drove back to the house, she prayed earnestly that the tests would prove what she'd been hoping and praying for.

She nervously gripped the steering wheel as she drove. The month before, she'd been upset, just like the months before when her monthly period had come on the exact date it was supposed to. This month, it hadn't. Even though she had only missed her period this month, she'd been praying so hard for a baby, she could only believe that God had finally answered her prayer. If it wasn't so, she would be terribly disappointed... again.

She finally parked her car in front of the bungalow, entered the house, and immediately went to the bathroom with the pregnancy tests. She was glad Bryan was still at the campus, as she wanted to keep whatever results she got from the tests to herself for now. If it was good news, she wanted to surprise him with it. If it wasn't, then she wanted to mourn on her own.

Quickly, she followed the directions on the test packet and peed on the stick. Nervously, she laid it aside and waited, her heart drumming.

Her mind went back to Bryan. They'd been married for over a year and it had been the best year of her life. She loved him more now than she did when they got married. She was still in the Bible College, but he had graduated a month before. He still wasn't sure what he wanted to do. He went to his office at the chapel almost every day to pray and seek God's direction for his life. As for her, she knew exactly what she wanted to do now and for the years to come. She wanted to be a mother.

Her dream was to have half a dozen kids with Bryan, and raise them in a big house in Rosefield. She had already started to look at several properties and actually had two in mind that she really loved. If she was pregnant, she and Bryan could begin to house hunt until they found the perfect house they both loved. Hopefully, by the time she graduated the following year, they would have found one, so they could move there immediately.

Her heart raced as she turned around and picked up the pregnancy test. She shut her eyes, took a deep breath, and whispered, "Lord, please let it be positive."

She opened an eye and anxiously peeked at the test. Two lines.

Her heart instantly soared. I'm pregnant?

She fully opened her eyes and looked at the pregnancy test again. It truly showed she was pregnant. She screamed and began to do a silly dance. "I'm pregnant! Thank you, Lord!"

A minute later, she forced herself to calm down. I have to do this again just to be sure. She picked up the other pregnancy test, followed the instructions, and then waited for the results. Five minutes later, she picked it up and looked at it. It showed the same result as the first one. She was indeed carrying her first child.

Her eyes flooded with tears of joy, and she briefly raised her hands in worship to God. She left the bathroom and went into the living room, ecstatic. She couldn't wait for Bryan to come back so she could share the good news with him.

She sat on the couch and pictured her life in the coming years. She and Bryan would be living in Rosefield with their children. Waves of excitement washed over her as she pictured her kids growing up with their aunts and cousins. She could see her daughters playing with Ruby and Audrey's kids. They would all be so happy.

She smiled as an idea came to her. She and Bryan still had the same tradition they'd started when they got married. Whenever she came home before him, she waited in the living room until he was back, and vice versa. They had dinner together, cuddled on the couch and chatted about their day. And then they both went to bed together. These days, Bryan had taken to carrying her to their room while she giggled and pretended to protest.

She went to the bedroom, opened her drawer and brought out a tube of wrapping paper and some ribbons that were left over from Christmas. She went back to the living room, wrapped up the pregnancy tests, and tied them up with a ribbon. Her heart raced with excitement as she settled on the couch again and looked at the clock on the wall. It was almost five-thirty. Bryan would be back in about thirty minutes. She couldn't wait to give him his gift. He would be so excited. He wanted to be a father as much as she wanted to be a mother and they had been waiting for this for more than a year.

"He'll make such an awesome dad," she whispered, smiling.

She looked impatiently at the clock again, sighed and said softly, "Hurry home, Bryan, my love. I have great news for you."

*****

Bryan sighed wearily and stood up from his knees. Once again, he'd heard nothing from the Lord about what he was supposed to do with his life now that he had graduated from the Bible College. For the umpteenth time since he'd begun to seek the Lord for direction, he chided himself. He'd been so absorbed with campus life and then his relationship with Sienna that throughout the time he was in school, he hadn't bothered to seek God about the future.

I guess I always assumed I would just know what I'm meant to do once I graduated. But things had not turned out like that at all. He had no idea what he was meant to do with his life.

He began to gather his notebooks and Bible, preparing to go home. Sienna would be waiting for him in the living room now. He couldn't wait to see her. She was the one source of joy when he felt discouraged…just like today. Whenever he got home and poured out his heart to her about his lack of direction, she always had a word of encouragement for him. Best of all, she always held him and kissed him until he forgot all his worries. Next to the Lord, she was everything to him.

He sighed as he picked up his Bible. "Lord, why won't you speak to me?" he cried in frustration. He'd never really had problems hearing God's voice clearly. It was the Lord who had led him to the Bible College. But now he'd been praying for over a month, asking for God's plan for his life, and he'd heard nothing at all. He'd begun to wonder if he had offended the Lord in some way.

He walked to the door and just as he made to open it, his Bible slipped from his hand and fell on the floor. He immediately stooped to pick it up and then his eyes widened in astonishment and he backed away in fear. His Bible was open, but it was the finger pointing at the open Bible that made his heart thud wildly.

He swallowed, tentatively came closer to his Bible again, and stooped to gape at the strange sight before him. The finger was plain, but it was there; it was a see-through finger made of light pointing at a verse in his Bible. He had heard God's voice often enough, and had even heard the Lord's audible voice. But he had never seen something like this before. He bit his lip and reluctantly looked away from the finger to the verse it was pointing to. Immediately, the finger disappeared.

His pulse raced as he read the verse aloud. It was

the nineteenth verse of the book of Matthew, in the twenty-eighth chapter. "Go ye therefore, and teach all nations, baptizing them in the name of the Father, and of the Son, and of the Holy Ghost." His emotions roiled as he read the next verse. "Teaching them to observe all things whatsoever I have commanded you: and, lo, I am with you always, even unto the end of the world."

He stopped and put his hands on his head as he trembled. He felt overwhelmed as he recalled clearly the day this passage of the Bible had jumped out at him.

It was a few years before, a couple of days after he'd enrolled in the Bible College. It was the one and only time he had asked the Lord what he was meant to do after he'd finished at the college. It was so strange that he had forgotten all about it.

He had gone to his room in the college, opened the Bible, and found this scripture. The words had immediately stood out and he had read it slowly. Immediately after reading it, the Lord had whispered in his heart like he usually did: "After you graduate, you are to go and live in whatever country I lead you to, and teach them about walking closely with me and hearing my voice clearly."

Bryan had blinked rapidly. "Go and live in another country… like a missionary?" At that time, he just couldn't imagine living elsewhere. He loved his hometown and he wanted to be close to his family in Green Valley. The idea of moving out of his town scared him, not to talk of moving to another country.

He had put the instruction away, hoping the Lord would forget about it. But He apparently hadn't.

Bryan couldn't bring himself to ask the Lord what country He had in mind now. His mind went to Sienna and how she would feel if he told her they had to move. They had talked a lot about moving to Rosefield once she graduated. She was always excited at the prospect of starting a family there.

He didn't mind moving there anymore, especially as Rosefield was near to Green Valley. For her, he would move anywhere. Now, even though it would be difficult for him, he would have quickly moved to another country in obedience to God except for the fact that he had Sienna to think about. He couldn't imagine telling her they had to move to another country. She was a sweet girl and shattering her dreams of living and raising their kids in the town she loved so much felt like an abomination to him. But if the Lord wanted them to move, he really didn't have a choice.

And yet…

He covered his face with his hands and shook his head. "Lord, why now? Please help me." He knelt down on the floor and stayed there for a long time, listening for the Lord's voice. But he heard nothing. At last, he stood on his feet. He had to get home before Sienna began to worry about him. He would come back tomorrow. He still had some more praying to do. He needed to find out exactly where the Lord wanted them to go. But first of all, he needed to pray for courage before he shared the news with Sienna. Maybe the Lord would provide a miracle for him and she would take the news well.

As he got into his car and drove home, he couldn't shake the images flooding his mind; images of Sienna spiraling down a pit of anxiety and depression, the way she had before they'd gotten married. He desperately prayed again, "Please, Lord, let her take it well." Because if she didn't, how would he choose between obeying God and his wife's happiness?

*****

Sienna frowned as her mind flooded with worry. He had never been this late before. She dialed Bryan's number again, put her cellphone to her ear, and listened with growing unease as his line rang and rang. It stopped ringing and she stared at her phone in frustration.

Where are you, Bryan?

She dialed his number again and then looked up as the door handle twisted. Bryan entered the house and she gasped. She flew to him and hugged him tightly. Drawing back slightly, she kissed him on the lips and then frowned. He looked slightly worried. "What is it, honey?" she asked him.

He placed his forehead against hers and smiled. "It's nothing, Sienna. How are you?"

She searched his eyes. There was something bothering him. He had that look on his face that let her know he was troubled about something but didn't want to worry her with whatever it was. She opened her mouth to ask again what the problem was, but he brushed his nose against hers and said, "You looked really cheery when I came in, like you had something to tell me." He moved back and took her hands in his. "Now, let me know what you are hiding, sweetie." He kissed the back of her left hand and then her right.

She didn't say anything for a second, and then

she smiled widely, unable to keep her good news to herself anymore. Once he heard her news, it would hopefully chase away the cloud of worry on his face. "Okay, hold on a minute." She removed her hands from his, went to get the pregnancy test she had wrapped up, and handed it to him.

His eyes danced as he looked at her. "What is this, precious?"

"A gift for you."

"But it's not my birthday . . ." His brows lifted in alarm, "Or have I forgotten an important anniversary?"

She giggled. "Nothing like that, Bryan. Just open the gift."

She watched him closely as he untied the red ribbon and then unwrapped the package. For a second, he stared at the pregnancy tests with a look of confusion on his face. And then his eyes grew as round as saucers and his jaw dropped. He looked up at her and said, "You are pregnant? We are pregnant!"

She nodded. She gasped as he suddenly swept her off her feet and swung her around. She laughed when he whooped and he set her on her feet again. He kissed her hair, her nose, and her lips.

"I'm going to be a father!" he yelled, and then put his hand on her stomach. "When did you do the test?"

"Earlier today," she answered.

He gently drew her close and kissed her. When he drew back, she frowned in concern. The worry that had shadowed his face some minutes before was back. What can possibly be so bad that even news about our coming baby can't shake it? She took his hand and pulled him down on the sofa. She sat next to him and said, "Bryan, please tell me what's wrong."

He sighed. "I wanted to wait until I got the full leading from the Lord before telling you about it."

She raised her brows. "Full leading? The Lord has given you direction about what you are supposed to do? That's great news, isn't it?" She took his other hand and threaded her fingers through his. "Even if you haven't gotten the full plan for what you are meant to do yet, at least you have some idea."

He shook his head. "I'm not worried because I haven't gotten God's complete direction for my life." He sighed and then looked away from her. "I'm worried because of what he's already told me." He looked at her and said, "And I'm worried about what you will say when I tell you what he said to me."

She shifted closer to him, her heart drumming. "What is it, Bryan? What did the Lord tell you to do? I promise not to say anything stupid. And you know I will always support you no matter what."

He studied her face for a minute and then said, "Okay. The Lord wants me… us… to move to another country."

Her mouth fell open and then she shut it. "What? Are you sure about that?"

"Positive." He began to narrate the encounter he'd had with the Lord in his office. She listened, her stomach clenching as he talked.

She had lived in New York during her modeling years, but had never felt completely at home there. When she'd finally come back to Rosefield and then to Green Valley, she had vowed never to leave again.

She was totally happy here. Besides, the thought of not seeing Trisha or Audrey for however long felt agonizing. Even the thought of not seeing Faizan, who she'd only known for about a year, made her deeply sad. The worst part, however, was picturing her dream of raising her kids in Rosefield washing away before it ever came to pass.

She and Bryan had talked about it so many times. Now he was talking about moving, not even to another state, but out of the country. It felt like a betrayal, somehow, even though she knew it wasn't his idea to move. She tried to control her emotions as she said, "Bryan, you said the Lord hasn't told you exactly where we are supposed to move to. Maybe it's not really outside the country. Maybe it's not even outside Boise. You should definitely pray about it again. Just because that scripture said 'all nations' doesn't mean we are literally supposed to pack up and leave the country."

He gave her a small smile and said, "You are right. Even though I immediately believed the Lord meant for us to move to another country when I read that verse, it might not be so. And I hope it isn't. I'll keep praying about it until I get a more specific word from God."

She nodded and her anxiety eased some. She had started to feel a slight tremor in her hands and legs, signs of one of her panic attacks. She hadn't had one since the day Derrick had kidnapped her. She couldn't afford to ever have one again, especially carrying their baby. But the thought of moving out of Rosefield and the country was a bit too much for her. She put her hand on her belly. When Bryan put his hand on top of hers, she forced a smile.

"Remember, we now have our baby to think about," she said. "Surely, the Lord wouldn't ask us to pack up and go to a strange country to raise our child there. We have so much support here in Green Valley and in Rosefield."

He smiled sadly. "We don't get to tell the Lord what He should or shouldn't do, Sienna. You know that."

"I know. I just hope He puts into consideration what I just said." In spite of herself, she laughed at the look on his face. "I know. I know. The Lord's decisions are the best, no matter what. But I really want to raise this baby in Rosefield. I just hope the Lord feels the same way I do... even if that does sound silly."

THREE

Trisha applied a coat of lip gloss onto her lips while she asked herself what on earth she was doing. Frank was coming to visit today, and she had just taken a shower to prepare for his visit. She was supposed to wear something simple and comfortable, but here she was, dressed in a beautiful striped dress, with makeup on.

She stared at her reflection in the mirror and smiled in self-mockery. *And yet you keep telling yourself you are not interested in him.* She definitely didn't look like someone who wasn't romantically interested in the guy she was about to see. In fact, she looked like she was going on a date with him. But this was definitely not a date.

Do you want it to be a date?

She scoffed at the thought. She definitely didn't want to go on a date with him. He was just an old friend visiting her, nothing more. She needed to remember that.

But you called him up because you missed him. Because you now realize that he's a catch.

She groaned and put her hand on her forehead. Why was she so conflicted about this? Why couldn't she just make up her mind about Frank?

The doorbell rang and she jumped. Frank was here. She gathered herself together and went out of the bedroom. Heading down the stairs, she took deep breaths until she reached the bottom. She put on a smile as she got to the door, told herself to act normal, and opened up for Frank. And then she gasped.

"Stan!" She stared at her ex-husband who had all but disappeared into thin air for more than a year. "What in the world…?"

"Trish, can I come in?" He looked past her into the living room.

She shook her head. "No. No, you can't! I haven't seen or heard from you for over a year, and yet you think you can just appear out of thin air and waltz into my house? You have never even laid eyes on your own daughter!"

Stan looked down and then looked up at her. His face was clouded with shame, but that did not move her. He pleaded, "Please, Trish. I know I was wrong to just disappear… just like that. But, please, I need to see her now, Trish!"

"No, you can't see her, Stan!"

"She is my daughter too, Trish. Besides, you weren't granted full custody of her."

"Yes, but you abandoned her. That gives me full custody even if the courts didn't grant it to me."

His entire face contorted and he looked like he was about to cry. "Please, Trisha. Please let me see my daughter. I want nothing else. I was doing really badly for a long time, but I'm a changed man now.

God got a hold of me and changed me."

She tilted her head and stared. "God? You found God?"

He nodded.

She laughed incredulously. "Yeah right!"

"Is it so hard to believe?"

"I know you are a liar, dear ex-husband! You will say anything to have your way."

"It's true, Trisha. God changed me. I know without a doubt that I did wrong. I have to be in my daughter's life. There is nothing I want more than to make amends now, and start to be the father I wasn't for so long." He stared intently at her. "Our daughter needs a father, Trish. You know that."

Trisha sighed. It was true. Hadn't she been dreading the fact that Ruby might grow up without a father? Maybe this was God's answer to her prayers. After all, Stan was Ruby's biological father. She had foolishly been hoping that Frank would somehow take that role, but it belonged to no other than Stan.

"Please, Trisha," Stan pleaded again.

Her heart melted and she said, "Okay, Stan. You can see her. But you have to promise me that you will not just suddenly disappear again. Our daughter needs a stable dad, not one that is here today and then gone tomorrow. Can you promise me that?"

He nodded vigorously. "I promise."

She looked at him for a few seconds more and then stood aside to let him in.

He came into the house and looked around. "You've changed some of the furniture," he said.

She didn't reply. Instead, she studied him for a brief moment. He still looked the same as the last time she saw him. His dark hair was perfectly coifed. As usual, not a strand was out of place. He was dressed in his signature outfit: a white button up shirt, the buttons opened down to his chest and revealing a thin gold chain, a black blazer, black pants, and black dress shoes.

His appearance reminded her of why she'd found him intensely attractive before they got married and through most of their married life. He was always carefully groomed, his expensive clothes matching his aristocratic-looking features. Now, as she looked at him, she felt different, like his appearance was all too much; fake, somehow.

"Trisha?"

"Yes, Stan?"

"I don't even know my daughter's name. What is it?" He studied her face intently, as though he would find the answer to his question written on her features.

Trisha didn't speak for a few seconds and then she answered, "Her name is Ruby."

"Ruby. I like that name for our daughter."

Trisha nodded and then suddenly remembered that she was expecting Frank. Her insides twisted. She didn't want both men together in her living room. She clenched her fists nervously. If only Frank would postpone his visit.

Stan sat down on the loveseat and she said to him, "Let me go get Ruby. She's been asleep for some hours now. I think she will soon be ready to wake up."

He smiled and nodded.

As she started to leave the living room, the doorbell rang and her stomach flipped. Oh my Lord,

Frank is here.

She sighed, went to the door without looking at Stan, and opened it.

"Hi, Trisha!" Frank had a huge smile on his face. He reached out and hugged her briefly.

She gave him a small smile and then told him to come in. She thinned her lips as he entered.

He paused when he saw Stan, and a look of consternation crept into his face. She sighed wearily again, knowing she had the same look on hers.

"Please sit, Frank. Let me go and get Ruby."

Frank sat and she left the living room quickly, hoping both men would be civil with each other. She wasn't worried about Frank, as he was always a perfect gentleman. But Stan scared her. Even though they were divorced now, she knew how territorial he could be. She had been lying to herself for a while now, but without a doubt, she admitted to herself that she wanted her and Frank to be more than friends. And the last thing she needed was Stan spoiling it for her.

"Lord, please help me today," she prayed before entering Ruby's room.

*****

Frank sat on the couch facing Stan and folded his hands, feeling uncomfortable. The last person he had expected to see here was Trisha's ex-husband. He felt a tightness in his chest as troubling thoughts entered his mind. What if Trisha told you she missed you only to be polite? What if she is now back with Stan?

He sighed and then looked up at Stan. The man

was glaring at him. Frank smiled at Stan and said, "Hi, Stan. I haven't seen you in a long time."

Stan gave him a dirty look and then turned away.

Frank shrugged Stan's hostile attitude off, but the troubling thoughts about Trisha and Stan together didn't leave his mind. He'd been thinking about winning Trisha's heart when it seemed she still hadn't cut ties with her ex. But she was too special to give up on.

When she'd started dating Stan years before, he'd been heartbroken—not just because of how much he loved her, but also because he knew Stan was a no-good womanizer. He'd decided to wait for her to discover who Stan really was and leave him, but she had married him. For weeks after she'd gotten married, he had grieved almost as though he had lost a loved one. He'd asked himself what he could have done to stop the marriage. But he could not have done anything. She was madly in love with Stan.

Unfortunately, he'd been unable to move on after that. He'd dated a few times, but his heart had never been in it. Now that she was divorced and had expressed a level of interest in him, however small, his hope that he would finally be with her had been revived... until now. Stan's presence was threatening to dash it again. But this time, he would fight for her. He would not lie down and let Stan win her over again and then treat her like dirt.

He looked up as Trisha came into the living room with Ruby in her arms. Butterflies filled his stomach as it always did whenever he saw her.

Trisha glanced at him and then at Stan and pressed her lips together. She looked like she wanted to be anywhere else but here, with him and Stan. His heart went out to her. He was so worried about himself that he hadn't considered how uncomfortable she would feel. He stood up to help her with Ruby, but Stan immediately got up and blocked his path.

"Stay away!" Stan growled. "She's my daughter, not yours!"

Ruby, who'd been asleep in Trisha's arms, opened her eyes and began to cry.

"Stan!" Trisha said, glaring at him. "Why did you do that?"

Stan looked apologetic. He gave Frank a forced smile. "I'm sorry. It's just that I have never seen my daughter and I just want to hold her." He looked pleadingly at Trisha and then his eyes widened as he stared at Ruby. He gasped. "She looks like me." He held out his hand. "Please, I'm sorry, baby. Stop crying. Daddy's here."

Trisha had a look of sadness mixed with surprise as Ruby immediately went into Stan's arms, as though he'd been with her since she'd been born.

Frank was surprised as well, as Audrey had told him Stan had never seen his daughter. Still, he smiled, albeit a little sadly, knowing that Stan was Ruby's dad. Even if he finally won Trisha's heart, Stan would remain a part of their lives. He went and sat down again while Trisha sat on the other end of the couch.

Stan sat on the loveseat again, Ruby smiling in his arms. Stan looked taken with her and said, "Can you say Daddy?"

Ruby grinned at him and said, "Da!"

His face lit up and he nodded. "That's good,

Ruby. I'm your Da."

Frank felt his chest tighten. He took a deep breath, and then turned to look at Trisha again. The moment felt so awkward. He wondered how she was feeling now. She was watching Stan and Ruby with a big smile and a look of pride on her face. His heart thudded with a mix of despair and resignation and he suddenly felt like an intruder. He stood and forced a smile.

"Trisha, I've got to go."

Trisha frowned and looked up at him. "So soon? I hope you're not leaving for Boise today."

He shook his head. "No. I'm still in Rosefield." He turned toward the door and then turned to Stan. "Some other time, then."

Stan nodded curtly.

Frank opened the door and then felt Trisha's hand on his shoulder. He turned to her, his heart burning with his love for her.

"Will you come again tomorrow?" she asked him.

"I will," he said immediately.

The smile on her face widened. "Good." She looked a little uncomfortable, as though she wanted to say something but wasn't sure she should.

He looked over at Stan and sighed. He didn't want to leave her with him, but it was the right thing to do now. The man needed space and time to get to know his daughter. "I'll be here in the morning," he said loudly so Stan would hear him. He wanted the man to know that even though he was leaving now, he wasn't leaving Trisha's life... unless she told him to his face that she didn't want him.

Trisha opened the door and he walked out of the

house. Before she shut the door, he said to her, "I love you, Trisha. Remember that."

She smiled sadly. "I know."

He turned around again and walked to the black Jeep he'd rented as soon as he'd arrived in Rosefield. He got into the car, started it, and then drove out of Trisha's driveway. He looked out the car window and his heart skipped a beat. Trisha was still watching him. He smiled and waved at her, and she waved back.

All the way back to his parents' house, he couldn't wipe the smile off his face, in spite of Stan's presence at Trisha's. He kept picturing the look on her face when she'd smiled at him as he drove away. It said she couldn't wait for him to come back again.

FOUR

Zainah came into the tent that was used as the camp kitchen and put down the bucket of water she had fetched for the women who were cooking dinner for the whole camp. She smiled at the women and went out of the tent again.

The sun was setting as she walked past several brightly colored tents, glancing at some children playing a game of hide and seek on the desert grounds. She smiled at their loud, cheery laughter despite her mood. She took the long route to the tent she shared with some other women, avoiding the shortest path as she didn't want to pass by Miriam's tent today. The woman was usually weaving on her loom outside her tent. Nothing awry or amiss escaped her, including the varying moods of most of the inhabitants in this camp. As Zainah headed to her tent, she thought about what Miriam had told her after Faizan left.

"You know he isn't coming back, Zainah," Miriam had said to her after observing her mourning his departure for months. "I don't want you to keep on like this. You are a shadow of your former self." Even when Zainah had told her she believed it was God's will for her to marry Faizan because of the dreams she'd had, Miriam had stood her ground. "You can't be sure that those dreams are from God. I know how much you love him. You've been deeply in love with him for some time now." Zainah's eyes had widened in surprise, but Miriam had nodded. "You didn't know that I had noticed… but frankly, everyone who has eyes in this camp knows how you feel about him."

Miriam had put her hand on her shoulder. "Zainah, I think you had those dreams because of your desire to be married and because you miss Faizan terribly. For all you know, the Lord still expects you to keep the vow you made to him."

Zainah had frowned in confusion. She deeply respected Miriam and her opinions. The older woman was wise and godly. Still, the dreams she'd had, especially the last one, had seemed so real, and she'd been so sure it was from the Lord. Doubts had flooded her mind.

She had smiled and nodded, promising Miriam she would keep praying about it. And she had. For months, she'd prayed. The more she did, the more certain she had been that her dreams were from God and that she was meant to be with the man she loved with all her heart. The only problem was that God had still not answered her prayers. Faizan had not returned. It was over a year now since he'd left and she yearned for him with everything in her.

After another session of earnest prayers the previous night, she had finally decided that she couldn't just keep hoping and praying that Faizan would return to her. She had to do something about it. She needed to tell Leila what she had decided to do.

Entering her tent, she immediately made her way to Leila's corner. Her best friend was folding some clothes she'd washed earlier in the day. She smiled when Zainah reached her.

"You've finished fetching the water for dinner?" Leila asked, still folding her clothes.

"Yes. Umm… Leila, I need to tell you something. But you have to promise not to get riled up."

Leila looked at her with her brows raised. "What is it?"

Zainah glanced at two of their tent-mates, who were sitting and chatting at the other side of the tent. She lowered her voice and said, "I'm going to leave the camp soon, Leila. I want to go and find Faizan."

For a long moment, Leila stared at her, a look of disbelief on her face. She finally said, "Zainah, are you sure you want to do that? You don't even know where exactly he is. How are you going to find him when you have no information about his whereabouts?"

"I know he is in America. And I remember the name of his birth father. I can start with that."

Leila shook her head and said incredulously, "America is a big place. How are you going to find him with just one name?" She raised her hand. "What am I even saying? How are you going to get to America, Zainah?" She shook her head again. "It's impossible."

Zainah had already thought about these questions Leila was asking, and even though she had no answers to them yet, she believed with all her heart that God wanted her to be with Faizan. If he didn't come to her, then she was going to go to him and the Lord would help her get to wherever he was.

"The Lord will provide everything I need, Leila. I believe that."

Leila gave her a thin smile. "You know I'm a hopeless romantic. I believe in love… but I don't see how it will work, Zainah. You have nothing with which to start this search of yours except a single name. As much as I wanted you and Faizan to be together when he was here, I don't see how you will find him now. It's been over a year and he still hasn't come looking for you. I say let him go."

Zainah stared at her. "Who are you and what have you done with my friend? Last year, you were the one encouraging me to marry Faizan, even though I told you I had made a vow of chastity to the Lord. Now, you are discouraging me from trying to find him." She sighed. "I can't let him go, Leila. I love him with all my heart and I want to be his wife. I have to find him."

"But why hasn't he come looking for you if he really loves you?"

"I don't know. Maybe something happened…" Her heart twisted in fear and she brushed away that train of thought. The Lord would not have shown her that they belonged together if Faizan wasn't alive and well. "I don't know why he hasn't come to see me. But I think it was because I told him about the vow. He's an honorable man. Even though he loves me, he would not want me to break the vow I made to God." She shrugged. "It doesn't matter. I'll find out when I see him. All that matters is that I find him and let him know that I am free to be his wife."

Leila stared at her for a long moment and then sighed. "You know what, Zainah? I envy you." She smiled. "I'm coming with you."

Zainah studied her friend. "Are you sure you want to do that?"

"You want me to miss out on being part of one of the greatest love stories I have ever heard?" She looked up and sighed wistfully. "It's all so romantic, going to find Faizan. I want to be a part of that, even if we end up not finding him. Besides, you need me to keep you out of trouble."

Zainah laughed. "You mean the other way around, right, Leila? Because I don't know what you'll do without me here." She put her hands on Leila's shoulders. "Maybe you will meet someone out there just like you've always dreamed about."

Leila nodded. "I hope so. I can only pray and believe that I will meet the love of my life the way you've met yours."

Zainah nodded. "I'll pray that it happens for you."

Leila rubbed her hands together and asked excitedly, "So, when do we leave?"

"Shh, do you want everyone to know about our plans?" Zainah whispered as she looked around the tent. The women talking on the other corner had turned to stare at them. "We will leave as soon as I'm able to make all the arrangements for everything we need to get us to town. After that, we will be in God's hands. But we have to be careful so Miriam doesn't find out. I don't want her to try to stop us."

Leila nodded. "That would not be good if she finds out. Miriam can talk a hen into giving up her beloved chicks." She smiled broadly. "I am so excited."

Zainah grinned. "I am, too. I know our journey will be hard, but I believe the Lord will help us and provide everything we need." She wrapped her arm around Leila's waist. "Thank you for deciding to come with me. I feel so much better knowing you will be by my side."

Leila nodded.

Zainah left her sleeping tent again and went to the prayer tent. She knelt on the floor and thanked the Lord for the provisions he had made so far in her quest to find Faizan. She'd secretly spoken to the young women who came to the camp every month to collect the rugs some of the women here had woven for sale. The women had promised to send their driver back here the following week to take her to town. Now Leila would be coming with her. God had provided a ride to town and now the company of her best friend. The God who had provided these things would also provide everything else she needed. She was certain of that.

*****

The doorbell rang and Trisha stood up from the couch. She'd been waiting with apprehension for Frank to arrive. She had asked him if he would come back today. When he said he would, she'd been excited because she would finally be able to spend the day with him without interruption. She'd even imagined telling him that she would go out with him, at least to see where things led. But spending the evening with Stan the day before had changed her mind.

By the time Stan left the house, all the hurt she'd felt about his betrayal and their broken marriage flooded her heart. She never wanted to feel like that again. She'd made a promise to herself that she would stay off relationships for now, after all. She had to keep it. Plus, she didn't have any need for a father for Ruby anymore. Her daughter now had the father she had been yearning and praying for. She had her real father. There was no need for another.

Trisha opened the door reluctantly. She'd seen the glint of hope in Frank's eyes when he had come to the house the day before, before he'd met Stan. She had also noticed the huge smile on his face after she'd asked if he would come back the next day. Worst of all, he had declared his love for her again. She was weary of breaking his heart again and again. But there was nothing she could do about it now. She had to let him know she couldn't be with him.

Her heart skipped a beat as she took in Frank's handsome face and tall, muscular body. Lord, help me, she prayed silently. Pasting on a smile, she said, "Hi, Frank. Come in."

She sucked in her breath at the excited smile he gave her, and then shut the door as he walked into the house.

He sat down on the couch and she sat on the sofa facing his; it was the one Stan had sat on the previous day. Stan had promised to come back today. Hopefully, Frank would have left by the time he did. She just didn't want to deal with all the tension that would be in the air with both men in the same room. She didn't need that sort of tension in her life. She looked at Frank again and sighed. He would be so disappointed when she told him she couldn't date him. But she had to do that, no matter how hard it was for her.

She opened her mouth to speak, but Frank asked, "Where's Ruby?"

"Sleeping," she answered.

"Aww… I came all the way for a play date." He put on a pretend sad face.

She laughed. "You'll have to postpone your play date. That girl can sleep. She'll probably still be at it by the time you leave." Immediately, when she'd said the word "leave," she regretted it. He would think she didn't want him here, though that was partly true. She liked that he had come, but she didn't want him here by the time Stan came by.

He didn't seem to take offence. He smiled. "That's fine. I'll just enjoy her mother's company then."

Trisha sucked in her breath at the way Frank was looking at her—like she was a precious jewel he had just discovered. Are you sure you don't want to date him? She asked herself. She quickly brushed aside the thought and decided to tell him now that she wasn't interested in a relationship with him before she changed her mind.

She opened her mouth to speak, but a loud cry stopped her. She bit her lip and stood. "It's your lucky day, Frank. Ruby is awake. I guess you get to have your play date after all."

"Yay!" he said, raising his hand.

She laughed and shook her head. Leaving the

living room, she went straight to Ruby's room and found her daughter trying to climb out of her crib. Trisha smiled and quickly went to lift her out of it. She placed Ruby down on the lilac shaggy rug on the floor.

Ruby immediately stopped crying and looked up at her with huge eyes; Stan's eyes. Trisha sighed and said, "If only you didn't look so much like your Dad."

Ruby nodded as though she clearly understood what Trisha had said to her.

Trisha lifted Ruby into her arms and went out of her daughter's room. She walked back into the living room, praying that she could tell Frank what she wanted to, without fear. She also prayed that he would be able to get over her quickly. She just didn't want to keep stringing him along. It wasn't fair to him. Maybe she could help him move on by introducing him to someone. And she knew exactly who.

She entered the living room, and immediately Frank's face lit up. She sighed silently, and then went to hand Ruby over to him.

Frank sat Ruby on his lap and said to her, "So, little baby, what shall we do today?"

Ruby stared curiously at him and then went back to playing with her hands.

"Alright, we are having a hand modeling game?" He held out one of his large hands and Ruby grabbed his fingers. She studied his hands and then studied hers.

Frank laughed, lifted her up with him, and swung her around.

She screamed with laughter as he threw her

up slightly and caught her again. He kept making roaring sounds as he swayed her back and forth while Ruby laughed with delight.

Trisha's emotions roiled as she watched them. *Do I really need to tell him I don't want to date him? And why can't I date him again?*

Her stomach flipped as the doorbell rang. *Stan! That's why I don't want to date Frank or anyone else. I can't deal with a relationship right now… or ever again.* She turned to Frank and told him Stan was at the door in order to encourage him to get going.

Why did you even tell him to come? She chided herself as she went to open the door.

Stan stood there, smiling at her.

"Come in," she said to him. She heard the eagerness in her voice and cringed. *Was this why she didn't want Frank? Was she still in love with Stan?*

The thought terrified her and strengthened her decision to not date anyone now or maybe ever again. She'd had enough heartbreak to last a lifetime.

She gingerly went back to sit on the couch while Stan sat next to her. He gave Frank a look that clearly said Frank had no right playing with his daughter.

Trisha sighed. Hopefully Frank would leave now before it became too awkward for all of them.

But Frank didn't look like he was ready to leave. In fact, he settled Ruby in his lap, cheerily greeted Stan, and then continued playing with Ruby.

Trisha held her breath. How had she gotten herself into this uncomfortable situation, caught between two men? She asked the Lord again for help, and then breathed a sigh of relief when Frank got up and told her he was leaving, promising to come back soon.

It was only after he left that she remembered she still hadn't told him she wasn't interested in a relationship with him. But what was worse was that she knew she'd knowingly put off telling him. It was wrong. She was still stringing him along.

She felt guilty as she watched Stan playing with Ruby. It was time she did what she'd been planning to do for so long. She was going to set Frank up with her new friend, Lauren. Hopefully, they would hit it off. Then she could finally be free from the guilt that tormented her whenever she saw him.

*****

Faizan opened the door to let Ken into the house. He'd just arrived from Miami and he had a traveling bag with him. Ken shook Faizan's hand.

"Where is Audrey?" Ken asked as he dropped his bag on the floor and flopped down onto the couch.

"She just went inside now." He opened his mouth to call out to Audrey, but she came out. She hurried over to Ken and fell into his arms. "I've missed you so much," she said, kissing his forehead and then his lips.

Faizan watched them with a tinge of jealousy. He missed Zainah terribly, but unlike Ken, he would not get to see her soon… unless he did something about it.

Audrey said, "I don't think we've been apart for this long since we got married."

Faizan laughed. "It's only been a few days."

"It feels like longer," Ken said.

Audrey stood and looked at Faizan. "I'm so sorry, Faizan. I wasn't thinking about how you would feel, even though you just told me how much you missed your girl the other day."

Ken lifted his brows. "Faizan has a girl?""I told you about her a few months ago, Ken. Faizan left a girl he is in love with in Algeria. Or is it Morocco?"

Faizan smiled sadly. "Somewhere between the two countries. I'm not sure exactly where." He sighed. "And she isn't really my girl… even though I want her to be."

Audrey nodded. "Ah, yes. The vow!"

Ken shook his head. "What are you both talking about?"

"It's a really beautiful but heartbreaking love story," Audrey answered. "Faizan, you said you were going to ask Ken about going to see her?"

Faizan nodded. He sat down on the sofa across from Ken and Audrey, and began to tell Ken everything about Zainah, from the plane crash which had nearly claimed his life to his conversion to Christ because of her persistence. "She saved me physically and spiritually. I gradually fell in love with her and then discovered she was in love with me, too."

He told Ken about her vow and how, because of it, they were destined to never be together. And then he told Ken what was on his mind now. "I miss her so badly, it hurts," he said. "I just have to see her or go crazy."

Audrey gave a long sigh. "So romantic, but so sad. I told Faizan he might be risking his heart by going to see her, but he insists. And I understand."

Faizan looked at Ken, who had not spoken for a while, and said, "It will just be a brief visit. I was wondering if you could call Jake and find out if he would provide some of the things I need to get there. If not, I'll understand."

Ken had a thoughtful expression on his face. After a minute, he said, "I don't know, Faizan. The fed agents were pretty clear when they said you were not to leave the country at all."

Faizan's heart pounded. It would be a disaster if he wasn't allowed out of the country. "Can you just call Jake for me?"

"I could… but you can call your handler yourself, you know. You are sort of a federal agent now."

Faizan sighed. "I know that. I feel uncomfortable every time I remember that I have a double identity. It reminds me of my past life."

Ken smiled sympathetically. "Except that you are on the right side of the law now."

"I dread the day I will be called upon again for some other 'covert operation.' Right now, I feel like a suburban American high school teacher. I love the job I have now, teaching Arabic at Rosefield High. I always have to remind myself that I'm just playing a role." He shook his head. "Anyway, can you ask Jake for me, Ken? I don't want to talk or get involved with those federal agents unless I really have to. Besides, you and Jake are friends."

Ken nodded. "'Kay! I'll call Jake tomorrow."

"Thanks, Ken. I appreciate that."

Ken nodded and Audrey smiled. She wrapped her arms around Ken and he kissed her hair.

Faizan said, "Alright, let me leave you two lovebirds alone. Maybe I will go and see Trisha."

"Talking about Trisha," Audrey said and turned to Ken. "Did you know that Stan is back?"

"What? When did he come back? I hope Trisha hasn't let him back into her life."

Faizan frowned. "Who on earth is Stan?"

"The philandering jerk Trisha was married to before she thankfully got rid of him."

Ken shook his head at Audrey.

"Frank is in town now," Audrey continued. "I hope he is able to win my sister's heart before that Stan wins her over with his glib tongue and fake charm. She has a weakness for him, and I'm worried she will fall for his lies again."

"Trish is a strong woman," Ken said. "I think she's learned her lesson and will stay away from him. However, he does need to see his daughter."

Audrey looked like she was about to disagree, but she said nothing.

Faizan smiled. "Okay, I'm off." He walked to the door. "If I see the jerk, Stan, in Trisha's house, I'll make sure he knows he can't mess with my sister."

"Just don't get into a fight," Ken said, chuckling.

"It's not my way anymore," Faizan replied. He opened the door and left the house.

As he strolled to Trisha's, he prayed that Ken would be able to find out the information he needed from Jake and that, most of all, he would be allowed to go visit Zainah. Because he had to see her and hug her. He needed to tell her to her face again that he loved her. He also longed to hear her say once more that she loved him, even if they would never be able to explore their love for each other.

*****

The next day, a Saturday morning, Audrey came into Faizan's room and told him Ken wanted to speak with him in the living room. He quickly got out of bed, pulled on his robe, and went out of the bedroom with Audrey. He went into the living room and found Ken sipping a cup of coffee in his pajamas.

Faizan sat down and greeted him.

Ken returned the greeting and then got straight to the point. "I'm so sorry, Faizan," he said. "Jake and the team insist that there is no way you can leave the country. And you are not allowed to contact her by phone, either."

Faizan shot up from the sofa. He raked his fingers through his hair while his heart raced with anger and frustration.

Audrey stood and took his hand. "Please sit, Faizan. Maybe we can find another solution to this."

"What other solution is there?" he roared, and then immediately regretted his outburst. "I'm sorry, Audrey. I didn't mean to yell at you. I'm just so angry. I was looking forward to seeing Zainah after a year of missing her. Now, who knows when or if I will ever see her again."

"I'm sorry," Ken said again.

"It's not your fault," Faizan told him. He felt like weeping, but he held himself together. For now, it seemed like he wouldn't get to see Zainah. But he would not give up. There had to be a way to contact her.

"Maybe I should call Jake myself," he said.

Ken shrugged. "You could do that, but I doubt it will change anything. They were pretty adamant about you not leaving the country or contacting any of the people you knew in the past until they tell you to."

"So I'll never be able to speak to Zainah, even on the phone?"

Ken gave him a sympathetic look. "They might let you do that one day. I don't know when, though."

Faizan sat down and threaded his fingers together. He sighed sadly and then nodded. "I hope they let me talk to her soon. If not, I don't know what I will do…" He didn't finish the sentence. For now, he had to keep his yearning for Zainah to himself and continue to pray that God would make a way for him to visit her. There was nothing in this world he wanted more than to see her face.

*****

Bryan stood up from his knees and paced his small office at the Bible College chapel. Since the Lord told him he was going to move to another country as a missionary, he had prayed constantly for specific leading concerning what country he and Sienna were supposed to move to. Sienna had asked him to confirm that it was truly the Lord who had spoken to him. Even though he was fairly certain it was, he had promised he would find out again, just to make sure he'd heard correctly.

A week into his prayer, he had not only confirmed that God truly wanted them to move to another country, he had gotten the specific leading about what country they were supposed to move to. And the information he had gotten from the Lord only added to his worry. If he had been afraid to tell Sienna about God's leading before, now he was terrified, especially knowing she was pregnant. Sienna would not take what he was going to tell her very well.

He stopped pacing his office and gathered his things. He couldn't postpone telling her what the Lord had said to him. He had to go home now.

He left the Bible College and drove home. Ten minutes later, he entered the house and as usual, found Sienna in the living room waiting for him. His heart flooded with love for her and he rushed up to hug her. "How are you today?" he kissed her nose and smiled affectionately at her.

"Much, much better now that you are back." She kissed his lips, took his hand, and led him to the couch.

They sat down and she snuggled up to him. "So, did the Lord speak to you today about what you are supposed to do now?" she asked, her head resting on his chest.

He shut his eyes, dreading to confirm what he had told her days before. He opened them again as he felt her eyes on him. Without delaying any longer, he said, "The Lord spoke to me today." He paused for a few seconds and then went on. "It's God's will for us to move, Sienna. He told me I would get an open door soon; a ministry opportunity in Peru. He said I was to take it when it came my way."

His heart pounded as Sienna sat up and stared at him. She cried, "Peru! I can't move to Peru, Bryan! Especially now that I am pregnant. I want to raise our kids in Rosefield, the town I grew up in; where they can grow up near their aunts and cousins. I lost my parents in Rosefield, and I feel close to them whenever I am there. I moved here to Green Valley because of you and 'cause it's close to Rosefield. I don't want to move to another state, not to talk of another country." She broke down and began to cry.

Bryan felt his heart breaking for her. Probably, her tears were caused partly by pregnancy hormones, but a huge part was that she was really distraught. He hugged her to himself and then whispered in her ear, "I think everything will be fine, Sienna. In fact, I'm sure of it. You know the Lord wouldn't ask us to do anything he doesn't provide an abundant amount of grace for. He has us in the palm of his hand and he loves us. You know that. It will all work out for our good in the long run, you'll see."

She shook her head. "I don't want to move to another country, Bryan."

He blinked. "Do you want us to disobey God?"

She shrugged. "I don't know. Maybe we can pray and ask Him to let us stay here."

He stared incredulously at her. "What are you talking about, Sienna? The Lord doesn't make mistakes. If he wants us to move, it's because that is the best thing for us."

She stood. "Maybe you heard wrong."

"Where is all this coming from? You know I didn't hear wrong, Sienna."

"You are not infallible, Bryan. It's not completely impossible for you to make a mistake."

He tried to control his temper. "So you are saying I made it up? What would I possibly gain in wanting to move to another country? I don't particularly like the idea either. My parents are here, and I know how much you love being here and in Rosefield. Why would I just want to change that? I am pretty sure I heard God's voice."

She looked down at him, her eyes shimmering with tears. "And what about my classes? The Lord was the one who said I should go to Bible College. How can He just change His word? I'm just not sure that God was the one who spoke to you."

His mouth dropped open as he looked at her. She was insinuating that he had made everything up.

She looked away.

Resentment flooded his heart and he said, "I just can't believe we are having this fight." They had never had this kind of argument before. In fact, they'd never fought since they'd gotten married. He sighed deeply and brushed away his resentment and anger. Rising, he put his hand on her arm. "Sienna, I don't like this. I don't want us fighting."

She turned to him and fell into his arms. "I'm sorry. It's just that the idea of moving terrifies me. I don't know why, since I've lived in New York before."

He held her and nodded. "I think it's because of what you told me some time ago. When you lived in New York, you never felt at home until you moved back here. Besides, I understand why you want to raise our kids here. I do too. We have family here. If we move, we will have no support system." He put his hand on her belly. "But that is where faith comes in, Sienna. God will provide everything we need when we obey Him. I know we will be fine."

She smiled up at him and nodded.

He kissed the top of her head and then said, "Let's go have dinner. We can whip up something together."

She shook her head. "No, I made beef stroganoff. We will have that."

"'Kay then!"

They went to the kitchen together and as she dished out the food and he carried the plates to the dining table, he prayed silently that this issue would not cause a rift in their marriage. He loved her so much. Their little argument just now weighed heavily on him, especially as he knew this was not the end of it, especially as he didn't even know what part of Peru they were going to move to.

What if it's in a part without access to basic amenities? It would be terrible, particularly because she was pregnant. He kept worrying until they sat at the table to eat. He brushed away all the troubling thoughts, as he didn't want to think about it all right now. There was no use borrowing trouble from tomorrow. All he could do was focus on his beautiful wife and pray that God would keep his marriage intact.

Frank left his uncompleted restaurant building after speaking with the foreman. The front of the building was almost finished, but the back was still under construction. He got into his car while making a mental note to call his business partner, Nick, and update him on the progress the builders had made. For now, he had to attend to his number one goal—winning Trisha's heart.

He drove to the florist near the public library and bought Trisha her favorite flowers when they were kids—pink lilies. As he drove on to her house, his emotions roiled. He was excited about seeing her again, but he was also nervous. When he'd seen her the day before, she'd seemed a little more distant than the previous day. And when Stan had knocked on the door, she had all but told him to leave. Stan might be there now and he would have to compete for her attention.

He turned onto her street and sighed. He could see it in Stan's eyes. Despite what he would have told Trisha about his reasons for coming back now,

Stan still wanted Trisha. And if Stan was anything like he was in high school, he would not fight fair until he got her for himself.

"Well, two can play that game," Frank said and then shook his head. That wasn't who he was. He liked to play fair. But still. This was his one chance to win Trisha over, or lose her to her ex. He had loved her for a lifetime. He could not afford to lose her now.

He parked in front of Trisha's house and for the thousandth time since he'd come to Rosefield, asked that the Lord would help him win her heart.

But what if winning her heart isn't God's will for you... or her?

His eyes widened in alarm at the clear whisper in his ears. He had never considered that. Not even when Trisha married Stan did he think that she might not be God's will for him. He had just believed that she'd married the wrong person. And her divorce from her ex after the multiple affairs had proven him right. Or so he had thought.

His heart thudded with fear as he exited the car. The thought of trying to forget about Trisha or trying not to love her again seemed incomprehensible to him. But if she wasn't God's will for him, it was exactly what he had to do. He had never bothered to ask the Lord what He wanted for him. Instead, he had held on to his dream of marrying Trisha one day. But what if that never happened? With Stan back now, and with her weakness for her ex, a devastating heartbreak seemed inevitable. Perhaps the Lord was trying to keep that from happening to him by letting him know he needed to back off now.

Frank looked up at Trisha's house, sighed deeply, and then gathered his thoughts together. He needed to put away all these doubts in his mind. He loved Trisha with all his heart and would do anything for her. Surely, that was a sign from God that they belonged together. Plus, Stan had been a total jerk and treated her badly. He couldn't be God's will for Trisha.

He brushed away all his doubtful thoughts. He would hold on to what she had told him the day before he came to Rosefield—that she missed him and was thinking about him. He would fight for his dream and believe with all his heart that he and Trisha would be married one day, no matter what Stan's plans were.

He finally rang the doorbell and waited for her to come to the door. He had enjoyed playing with Ruby these last two days. He was eager to see the child again as well.

Trisha opened the door, looking as beautiful as ever in a simple pale green dress that hugged her curves. He sucked in his breath sharply and then smiled at her. "Hi, Trish! You look perfect as always."

She blushed vividly and then laughed. "I'm hardly perfect, Frank… but thank you." She let him in.

He sat on the couch and exhaled in relief at the fact that Stan wasn't present; at least not yet. If Stan came again while he was here, he would not leave this time; unless of course, Trish asked him to.

She sat down next to him but shifted slightly away. He chose to ignore the action.

"Where is Ruby?" he asked.

"She's asleep as always."

He pretended to be dismayed. "Shucks! I should have come before her nap time."

Trisha laughed and then her expression turned sober. "Frank, there is something I want to tell you."

He looked intently at her. "There is something I want to tell you, too… though you already can guess what it is."

"I think I can," she said. "And that is part of what I want to talk to you about."

His heart jumped at the look on her face. What she wanted to tell him wasn't going to be good, he was sure. He suddenly became desperate to speak his mind. He said quickly, "Trish, before you say what you want to, please hear me out."

She nodded. "Okay."

He searched her pretty face and his heart raced wildly. Lord, please help me. I can't afford to fail. This is my chance to win her heart before I leave Rosefield again.

"Trisha, you know that I have been deeply in love with you since we were teenagers. I don't want to pressure you or anything like that, and I want to apologize beforehand if you feel in any way like I am. But can you not just give me a chance? At least I know you don't despise me or I wouldn't be here in your house. All I am asking for is just one chance to actually show you just how much I love you." He tentatively took her hand. "Please, Trisha."

She pressed her lips together. She didn't speak for a long time, and his heart kept skipping in fear and anticipation as he waited for her to say something.

At last, she looked into his eyes and said, "Will you just give me a day or so to think about it?"

A small thread of disappointment went through him, but he nodded. Be patient, man, he chided himself. At least what she had said was better than an outright rejection. He smiled at her. "I have waited for years. What is another day or two?"

She looked away and he sighed ruefully. He was pressuring her.

"I'm sorry, Trisha. I shouldn't have brought that up."

"No need to apologize," she murmured. She stood up. "Well… let me go get Ruby. It's time for lunch." She looked down at him before she left the living room. "Will you join us, Frank?"

He nodded eagerly. "I'd love that."

She left and he exhaled. He needed to be patient, but he couldn't help the desperate thoughts running through his mind. Somehow, he knew without a doubt that her answer to his request would be final, and that no matter what he did, he would not be able to change it. That made him incredibly nervous. He was on the brink of finally getting a chance with the only girl he had ever loved, or forever losing the chance to be with her.

*****

The stars were shining brightly when Zainah got into the back of the truck and Leila got in beside her. The driver had already put their bags into the trunk of the car. She said to the driver, "Please hurry. We have to leave before Miriam comes out of her tent and sees us."

The driver nodded and started the car.

Zainah kept looking back, her heart beating in

fear, as the truck sped away. She did not relax until they were far away from the camp. She turned to Leila and said, "Thank God we are out of there."

Leila smiled and replied, "We are going to have such an adventure!"

Zainah didn't speak, but Leila chattered on. She half-listened to Leila while wondering and silently praying about what their next move would be. After a while, she fell asleep and dreamt that she was with Faizan. She woke with a start when she felt a hand on her shoulder. She turned and saw it was Leila.

Leila said in a shaky voice, "The driver wants us to get off here."

Zainah looked all around her, and her eyes widened in alarm. It was nighttime but they were in the middle of a well-lit, busy market. The place was noisy and droves of people walked by the car. She leaned forward and said to the driver, "Where are we?"

The man turned and answered abruptly, "We are in Blima. You need to get out."

Zainah's heart drummed. "I thought the agreement was to take us to a house in town."

The man frowned deeply and said, "Amira told me no such thing. All she said was to pick you up from the camp and take you to town. This market is where your leader, Miriam, stops when I pick her up, and so this is where I have brought you. You have to find your way from here."

"You can't just leave us here!" Leila exclaimed. "We don't know anyone around this place."

The man laughed harshly and then said, "What do I care? I did what I was asked to do. Please come down from my car. I need to leave now." He exited the truck and ordered them to get out.

Zainah and Leila pleaded with him to take them to the agreed location, but he refused. Finally, he became violent, pulling them out of the car forcefully. Zainah watched him speed away with a mixture of anger and dread. And then she remembered that their bags were still in the trunk of the truck. "That man drove away with our bags!" she cried out.

"Oh no!" Leila exclaimed.

"It's nighttime already," Zainah said to Leila. "Where are we going to stay?"

Leila glanced around the busy market, her eyes wide with fear. "We haven't been outside the camp for years, and the first time we leave the camp, we're abandoned in the middle of a market at night, with nowhere to go. What are we going to do, Zainah?" she asked, her voice shaking.

Zainah gathered her thoughts together and brushed away the fear that had wrapped itself around her. She said, "There's only one thing we can do. And that's to pray. We have to ask the Lord to help us now."

Leila looked uncertain as she took Zainah's hand, but she closed her eyes anyway.

Zainah lowered her voice, praying very softly so those around would not hear her. "Lord," she began, "please help us. We have very little money and nowhere to go. We're stuck in the middle of this market at night. We need a place to sleep until I can decide on the next move to find Faizan." She whispered. "In Jesus' precious name I pray."

Leila whispered a frightened sounding "amen."

Just as they opened their eyes, a woman she had never seen before touched her shoulder. The woman whispered in her ear, "I heard you praying in the name of Jesus just now. It's not safe to pray in his name around here."

Zainah's eyes widened in surprise. "How did you hear me pray? I was whispering."

The woman did not answer her question. Instead, she said, "You are a Christian, aren't you?"

Zainah nodded hesitantly.

The woman whispered, "What are you doing out here at this time?"

Zainah opened her mouth to answer, but the woman said, "Never mind. I was passing by and the Lord told me clearly to help you. You both need a place to stay, don't you?"

Zainah's mouth fell open while Leila's eyes were as round as saucers.

The woman did not wait for them to answer. She said, "Follow me." She started to walk away and Zainah quickly began to follow her. Leila walked beside him and whispered, "Are you sure we can trust her?"

"We have no choice, Leila. Besides, I think the Lord really did a miracle for us. I believe he was the one who sent this woman to help us."

They walked for a long time. Zainah kept praying quietly while Leila clutched her hand. "Lord, I've decided to believe that this woman was sent by you because we have no choice. Please help us."

At last, the woman stopped in front of a field of flowers.

Leila raised her brows and looked at Zainah. When Zainah asked the woman why they had stopped there, she did not answer. She parted the flowers with her hand and began to walk through them.

Zainah and Leila followed. Soon, Zainah's eyes widened in surprise as a small bungalow emerged as though by a miracle. The woman knocked, and a minute later a girl who looked about nineteen or twenty years old came to the door. She smiled when she saw the woman and opened the door wide. The woman stepped in and beckoned for Zainah and Leila to enter.

Zainah stepped into the house tentatively and Leila entered behind her.

Zainah looked around the room they'd entered. It was a simply furnished room with a single couch and a small TV set that sat on a wooden stand. Dark brown curtains shrouded the windows, and the cement floor was bare except for a small rug at the center of the room.

The woman said to Zainah, "Welcome to my home. You can sleep here tonight and then tell me all about your mission tomorrow morning. I think the Lord wants me to help you with your accommodation, though it's not that great," she waved her hand around the room, "as you can see."

Zainah felt tears in her eyes. "Thank you," she said to the woman. "It's perfect. We didn't know what to do when our driver left us at that market."

The woman nodded and said to Zainah and Leila, "Come and take a shower, and then I'll show you to the room where you both will stay until you are ready to leave."

As they lay in bed after the simple meal the woman had given them, Zainah said to Leila, "God is so good. See how He helped us by sending a stranger? And now, she said we can stay as long as we want to."

Before she drifted off to sleep, Zainah lifted up a prayer of thanksgiving to the Lord, and then prayed for wisdom to know what step to take next in order to find Faizan.

*****

Faizan walked into the doors of the New Day Fellowship Church. He had started going there the year before. On his first day, he had gone with Audrey and Trisha. He clearly remembered how excited they were to take him to their church. He'd been excited as well, and a little nervous as he had never attended a formal church service before. But his nervousness hadn't lasted, as the church members had made him feel right at home. Plus, he had enjoyed the service tremendously. Now, a year later, it wasn't just Audrey or Trisha's church, it was his church.

He walked through the carpeted foyer, greeted some of the ushers who were welcoming people into the church, and walked into the main sanctuary. He walked down the aisle of the church, and took a seat in the third row. Service had not fully started. Some of the instrumentalists and singers were standing at the pulpit, checking the microphones and musical instruments. Looking around him, he noticed that the church was already half-full.

He looked at the pulpit again and remembered clearly the day Pastor Mark had called him into his office and asked if he would give his testimony in front of the church the next Sunday. For the first time in his life, he'd actually been scared. What would the people in the church say when they found out he was a former jihadist? He'd asked the senior pastor for time to think and pray about it.

For the whole week before the Sunday service, he had prayed earnestly. By Sunday, he knew without a doubt that the Lord wanted him to share his testimony. So he had, with fear and trembling, as the apostle Paul had said in the Bible. When, after service, people came up to him and told him that his testimony had blessed and encouraged them, he was relieved. Nobody had looked down on him or become afraid of him as he had feared. Instead, the opposite was the case.

Since then, he had made acquaintances and friends in the church and he'd joined the welfare department. When one of the members of the department had asked if he wanted to join, he'd said he didn't. He had been sure he wasn't cut out for it. He had never cared much about other people's welfare before he became a follower of Christ. The church member had asked him to pray about it and he had said he would in order to get rid of the man. In order not to lie, he'd said a perfunctory prayer when he got home and then promptly forgotten about it.

The next day, however, he was reading his Bible when a verse from the book of James had jumped out at him: "Pure religion and undefiled before God and the Father is this, to visit the fatherless and widows in their affliction, and to keep oneself unspotted from the world."

He had been deeply touched by the words. He

knew what it meant to be fatherless. Maybe if a Christian man had visited him and been a sort of father figure to him, he would not have followed the violent path he had. Mustafa had taken the role of a father and had taught him to hate and kill. All he could do now was become to someone what he'd never had—a godly role model. A man who loved God and was willing to show other young men and women how to do that as well.

He had joined the welfare department that Sunday and had risen to become the leader now. His faith was growing stronger every day and his life would have been perfect were it not for the constant ache in his heart for Zainah.

He sighed wearily and then pushed the familiar sadness and yearning out of his mind. He bowed his head to say a brief prayer before the service began and felt someone take the seat next to his. A sweet floral fragrance filled his nostrils and he unwittingly breathed it in deeply. He focused on his prayer and asked the Lord to speak to him as the service commenced. He also asked that God would use the service to draw him closer to Jesus.

He opened his eyes and turned to smile in greeting at whoever it was that was sitting beside him. A blonde he didn't know very well except for the fact that she was an old friend of Ken's, smiled brightly at him.

"Hi... Faizan?" the blonde said.

He nodded, surprised that she knew his name. He'd seen her from afar here in church a few times. Once, he had spoken briefly to her when she came to the house to see Ken, but it was only to tell her that Ken wasn't in town. "Hi, umm... I'm sorry, I can't remember your name," he said.

"Lauren," she replied in a soft voice.

"Yes. Lauren. I should have remembered."

Lauren opened her mouth to say something just as the worship leader asked everyone to rise up to start the praise and worship session. Faizan turned away and focused his attention on the worship leader. As the singer raised one song after another, he lifted his hands with the congregation and worshipped from the depths of his heart. The presence and the love of God surrounded him, and the euphoria did not lift until the service was over two hours later.

After the closing prayers, Pastor Mark asked everyone to greet the person next to them. Faizan turned and only then fully remembered Lauren was beside him. He smiled at her and shook her hand.

He started to turn to greet the man on his left side, but Lauren said, "Sorry, but I'm a hugger." She grabbed him before he could say anything and hugged him tightly.

She drew back and he turned to greet the man briefly. He bent down to pick up his Bible from his seat. When he straightened, he was surprised to find that she was still standing there, looking at him.

"You are a member of the welfare department, aren't you?" she asked.

"Yes," he answered. "What department are you in?"

"Umm... I haven't yet joined any. Do you enjoy serving in your department? I was thinking of joining it."

He smiled widely and nodded. He was always on the lookout for new members. "I definitely enjoy serving in the welfare department. I'm the leader now, actually. I think you'll like it if you are ready to visit as many members and visitors as you are assigned to." He looked at the back of the church where he had seen his assistant moments before and then turned back to Lauren. "You can get a form from Sarah over there," he pointed at his be-spectacled assistant. "We have our meetings here in church on Thursdays at six o'clock in the evening. You are welcome to join us."

He began to walk away and pointed at Sarah again. "Remember to get a form from Sarah before you leave, Lauren."

Lauren touched his arm and stopped him. "Umm… is Ken around? I might stop by today."

"No… he and Audrey left for Miami this morn-ing."

Lauren looked disappointed. "Oh."

Faizan started to walk away again, but Lauren said, "Will you be in church when I come on Thurs-day?"

He gazed curiously at her. "Yes, I will be. I have to as the leader of the department."

She nodded while he wondered why she'd asked him that question.

"There is no need to be nervous, Lauren. We are all nice people at the welfare department. I think you will enjoy serving with all the members. I'll see you later." He left quickly before she could stop him again. He had to get home and figure out a way to at least talk to Zainah again. His sanity and future happiness depended on it.

*****

Zainah spent every day looking through Facebook profiles, trying to find anyone who was related to Phil Gardner. She'd had a severe culture shock for a few days after she and Leila had arrived at Fatima's house—the widow who had taken her and Leila in. After she confided in Fatima about her mission, the soft-spoken, middle-aged woman had told her she could start with social media.

"What is social media?" Zainah had asked.

Fatima had laughed out loud and then stared at her with a quizzical expression. "You don't know what social media is? Facebook, Instagram…?"

Zainah had stared dumbly at her and then said she had never heard of those things.

"Wow!" Fatima had exclaimed. "You have been totally isolated. How long have you been living at that camp?"

Zainah had already told her about the women's camp she and Leila came from. Zainah answered, "I've been living there since I was eighteen. This is the first time I've left the place since I was taken there eleven years ago. Well, except for when we had to change camps…"

"But how did you get your basic needs met if you never left the place?" "Miriam, the oldest woman in the camp, went to town about twice a month to get everything we all needed. We agreed to do that to keep the location of the camp secret. Since most of us came from places where we were severely persecuted for our faith, it was a necessary thing to do so we would not be found by anyone who hated

Christians or wanted to harm us in any way."

Fatima nodded. "I understand that. Around here, people know we are Christians, but we are treated with derision and not allowed to speak publicly about our faith in Christ. Once in a while, someone has threatened us, but so far, the Lord has kept us safe."

Zainah looked round the bedroom she and Leila shared and then curiously asked Fatima for the whereabouts of her friend.

"She went out with Safia, my oldest daughter. Don't worry about it. She'll be safe with Safia... Unless..." Fatima looked up with a thoughtful expression on her face.

Fear gripped Zainah. "Unless what? Is Leila in trouble?"

Fatima smiled and shook her head. "It's nothing. She will be safe."

"But where did they go?"

"Ehm, Leila told Safia she was tired of staying indoors and Safia decided some fresh air and a long walk would do her good." Fatima smiled. "Now, stop worrying and let me show you how to search for people you want to find on Facebook." She chuckled and then shook her head. "What I meant to say is that my son, Samir, will help you. I have to admit that I am quite useless with these social media platforms. My kids tend to help me if I need to do anything on them." She called out to Samir, a sprightly boy who looked about thirteen.

That had been days ago. Now, Zainah had mostly learned how to navigate Facebook after Samir helped her open an account and taught her how to use it to find whoever she wanted. But, in spite of her diligent search, she'd not found what she was looking for and frustration was already setting in. To make matters worse, Leila was never here now. She went out with Safia every single day.

Zainah tossed aside the cheap cellphone Fatima had gotten her in frustration. She got up from the bed and paced the almost empty room. She clasped her hands together and said, "Lord, how am I going to find Faizan? Please help me!"

Why did I think it was going to be easier than this to find Faizan when I was at the camp? Even without knowing there was such a resource as social media, she had believed the Lord would do a quick miracle and that she would find him almost immediately. But she'd gotten nowhere with this social media search. She had to change her methods.

The door suddenly burst open and Leila skipped into the room. She unwrapped her scarf from around her shoulders and tossed it onto the bed.

Zainah's mouth fell open with shock and then she closed it again. "What are you wearing, Leila?" Zainah asked, staring at her friend with her eyes wide. Leila was dressed in a long, very tight, striped dress with no sleeves. All her curves were on full display in the dress.

Leila shrugged. "It's Safia's. All the young people are dressed like this now."

Zainah stared at her, wondering if she had lost her mind. "Firstly, you aren't young enough to be wearing this... and nobody in their right mind should be dressed like this anyway . . . with all their curves on display."

"Calm down, Zainah. I wrapped my scarf

around my body. Besides, you are shocked because you are so used to completely covering up in our camp. Here, in the outside world, people are a bit freer with their dressing. You would know that if you left this house."

Zainah shook her head. "I know how free people can be in the outside world. I just need you to be careful. And you are never here these days."

"I'm always careful." She sighed and sat down on the bed beside Zainah. "I still haven't given up on my dream to find a husband and have children. I won't find one by sitting in the house. You are lucky because you've already found the man you love and want to spend the rest of your life with. I don't have that yet. I want that with everything in me."

Zainah smiled sympathetically at Leila. "I don't think just going out to random places will help you find a husband. I think you should keep praying about it and the Lord will bring you someone who loves you the way He brought me Faizan."

"You know things don't usually work out that way, Zainah," Leila said. "Faizan literally fell down from the sky for you."

"That's not funny!" Zainah said, and then chuckled in spite of herself.

"But he did fall down from the sky. And I wasn't trying to be funny! You are blessed, Zainah. Sometimes, I get a little jealous."

"Maybe we should change places then." Zainah sighed. "You can be the one who falls madly in love with someone you haven't seen or heard from for more than a year. When you have experienced that kind of misery, then come back and tell me about how blessed I am."

Leila put her hand on Zainah's arm and said softly, "I'm sorry. You still haven't found Faizan or anyone who might be related to him on that Facebook thing?"

"No… I haven't. I'll keep searching but I have to look for another way to find him."

Leila nodded.

Zainah wrapped her arm around Leila's waist. "Let's never argue again. But when you go out, promise me you will be careful. And ask God for a life partner instead of going out to look for one yourself. Okay?"

Leila smiled sadly. "Okay. I'll be careful… but I don't know about just sitting and waiting for God to send me a husband. It might never happen."

"If it doesn't, then it's not God's will for you to get married."

Leila glowered at her. "Easy for you to say!"

Zainah sighed wearily. "I just said now that we shouldn't fight again. But you can do whatever you want to. I'm tired."

Leila stood. "I will!" She marched out of the room.

Zainah put her hand on her forehead and shut her eyes. If only Leila understood how she felt now. Leila just thought she was the lucky one because she was in love. "I'd give anything to be in her shoes right now," Zainah whispered. Because this love she felt for Faizan, as strong as it was, felt more like a burden to her right now than a blessing.

SIX

Trisha watched with conflicting emotions as Stan played around the living room with Ruby. He'd arrived in the house that morning and had helped feed, change, and watch Ruby while she got some needed rest. Sometimes she couldn't help smiling at Ruby's joyful laughter as she crawled round the room while Stan chased after her. At other times, she wanted to yell at him and throw him out for being absent from Ruby's life for a full year and then suddenly appearing again with vague explanations.

She forced a smile when Ruby looked up at her before she continued playing with her father. With all her heart, she loved that Ruby now had her dad present in her life, but she was afraid it would not last. She was scared that Stan would disappear one day. He was flighty and untrustworthy. If she could hold him down physically so that he never disappeared from their daughter's life, she would. But she couldn't.

Her emotions continued to churn as her mind went to Frank and his request to give him a chance at a romantic relationship. She had told him to give her a day or two, but it had been almost a week now and she hadn't yet given him an answer. Thankfully, he hadn't bugged her about it, but she wasn't being fair to him. She had to give him an answer now. The problem was that her answer hadn't changed from what she'd told him before. She liked him a lot, but…

But what, Trish? she asked herself.

Her eyes unconsciously went to Stan and she groaned. Stan was the cause of it all. She'd decided to avoid relationships because of him, but something in her also yearned to keep him in her life, maybe even take him back if he asked.

She shuddered at the thought. What are you thinking, Trisha? she chided herself.

But she couldn't deny her feelings. It wasn't love she felt for him. It was a comfortable familiarity and a strong desire to be a complete family with her daughter's biological father; the kind of family she'd had growing up, before fate had snatched away her parents.

She sighed again. It almost felt like Frank was in the way of her having that. The feeling was crazy, but it was what was on her mind now. She liked Frank, but she wanted Stan.

She stood up. The earlier she told Frank about her decision and maybe found him a date, the better. She had to stop postponing the inevitable. Frank would be coming by this evening, hopefully after Stan had left. She would tell him she couldn't be with him then.

"It's time for her dinner, Stan," she said.

Stan looked up at her and then rose from his

knees. He had been crawling around the room with Ruby, making funny faces at their baby daughter. "I'll feed her," he said. "You just relax today."

"I need to bathe her first of all."

"I'll do that as well."

She smiled gratefully at him and began to tell him how to make the mashed potatoes she planned to feed Ruby this evening.

"I know what to do," he said quickly.

She shrugged and said, "Okay."

He came into the living room with Ruby twenty minutes later. He had bathed and changed her into her pajamas. As he fed her, Trisha watched him closely. He was patient, allowing Ruby to eat on her own sometimes and then feeding her again when she started to throw her food about.

Ruby looked up at him, said, "Dada," and continued to eat.

Trisha's jaw dropped as she stared at her daughter. She had just called Stan "Dad." Ruby had already started to call her "Mama," but now she had called her father "Dada." It felt like a confirmation of what Trisha had been thinking for the past hour—that she wanted her and Stan to be together to parent their daughter.

Stan was looking at her and smiling widely. "She just called me Dada. Did you hear that?"

"Yes, I did, Stan." She smiled in spite of herself.

Stan looked at her intently; it was the first time he had looked at her for that long since he'd come back from God knew where. His intentions were clear in his eyes. He wanted her too... but not just for the reasons she wanted him.

Trisha blushed and looked away. She hadn't really thought about the intimacy that would be involved if she and Stan remarried. Could she still be physically intimate with him after all the heartache he'd caused her?

Her eyes went to the clock and her heart pounded. Frank would be here any minute now, and she didn't want Stan here when he came. It would be a very awkward and tension-filled scenario. Plus, she wanted to tell Frank about her decision in private.

She looked at Stan as he fed Ruby and pressed her lips tightly together. She couldn't just ask him to leave. A knock on the door caused her to jump.

Oh no! Frank is here!

Her heart in her mouth, she stood up reluctantly, plastered on a smile, and went to open the door. She blinked in surprise at the visitor at the door. It wasn't Frank. She looked at the blond beauty and then smiled genuinely. It was her friend, Lauren.

"Lauren! What a surprise!"

"I'm sorry, Trisha, for just coming to your house like this. I've been calling your phone for a few hours now. You didn't pick up."

"Oh… I've been in the living room for hours. I must have left it in my bedroom." She stepped aside so Lauren could enter the house.

Lauren looked over at Stan, turned to her, and smiled. "You have a visitor. I can come back tomorrow."

"No… please stay."

Stan looked over at her and Trisha introduced them briefly. She motioned for Lauren to sit as her pulse raced. What were the chances of Lauren coming here today just when she was thinking about actually setting her up with Frank? At last he would get to meet her when he came and maybe they would hit it off organically.

Stan wiped Ruby's mouth, carried her out of her high chair, and then straightened. "I guess I'll be going now, Trish." He walked up to her and handed Ruby over. He went to the door, opened it, and then turned to wink at her. "I'll see you tomorrow."

He left and she turned back to Lauren.

"You are blushing, Trisha. Who was that?" Lauren asked as she reached out to caress Ruby's cheeks. "You seem to like him."

Trisha waved her hand dismissively, but her heart thudded. "I don't like him… at least not in that way. He's my ex-husband. Ruby's father."

Lauren's eyes widened in clear surprise. "Ruby's father? The guy you told me cheated on you? Wow! I didn't know he was back in your life."

Ruby looked up at Trisha and then at Lauren. She grabbed her feet and began to play with them.

"He just appeared out of nowhere about a week ago," Trisha said. She didn't want to talk to Lauren about Stan. Things were complicated right now and she wasn't ready to tell anyone what was in her heart. She quickly changed the subject before Lauren could say anything more about her ex and asked how Lauren was doing.

Since Lauren had divorced her abusive husband almost a year before, she'd been working on herself at the Gibsons', trying to piece her life back together. She had been an emotional wreck the months after she'd come back to Rosefield, but now, she was glowing. She had gotten a job as an elementary school teacher, moved into her own apartment, and had fully given her heart to God about a month before. She would be a good match for Frank. Trisha looked at the clock again. He was a little late today.

Usually, he was here by this time.

"I'm good," Lauren answered. She tilted her head toward Trisha and said, "I came to speak to you about something."

Trisha rubbed Ruby's back as her daughter lay her head on her chest. She looked quizzically at Lauren. "What is it?"

"You remember the day you were asking me if I was ready to date again… and I said I wasn't sure?"

Trisha looked up thoughtfully, wondering where the conversation was going. "Yeah!"

"Well… I am now. I met someone in church. Actually, I've seen him a couple of times, but I actually spoke to him on Sunday."

Trisha's heart sank. Here she was thinking about setting Lauren up with Frank, and the girl had found someone she liked already. Trisha forced a smile and asked, "Is it someone I know?"

Lauren shifted on her seat. "Actually, that's why I came. It's your… brother, Faizan. I really like him."

Trisha raised her brows in surprise. She hadn't expected that at all. Faizan was handsome, but she had never really thought about him dating, especially as he had mentioned that he was still in love with some girl he'd met in North Africa. Trisha didn't know what to say to Lauren.

"You are against the idea, Trisha?"

"Umm… no. It's just that I don't know if Faizan is ready to date anyone at this time."

"Oh… well, could you help me find out? I'd really appreciate that."

Trisha sighed resignedly. So much for her plans. Lauren was a beautiful woman. Maybe Faizan could fall for her and then stop moping over that girl he'd left behind in his past life. He'd been depressed for some time because of her. She smiled at Lauren. "I'll try to find out if he is open to dating right now and see what he thinks about you."

"Thank you so much, Trisha."

"You are welcome," Trisha said.

They changed topics and chatted about random things. Thirty minutes into their pleasant conversation, a knock sounded at the door and again. Trisha's pulse raced. It has to be Frank this time, she thought. Lauren took Ruby, who was now asleep, her energetic play date with her father having knocked her out, and Trisha got up. She went to the door and opened it.

"Hey, Trisha!" Frank smiled broadly and handed her a bouquet of flowers.

She smiled nervously as she recalled what she had to tell him this evening. He would probably be devastated. Did she really want to do that to him... again? "Come in," she said to him.

He entered the house and then looked at Lauren, who had Ruby in her arms.

"Frank, this is my friend, Lauren," she said. "Lauren, this is my... umm... my old friend, Frank."

They exchanged pleasantries and then Lauren said, "I have to go, Trisha." She handed Ruby over.

Trisha nodded and saw her to the door. "I'll call you as soon as I find out what Faizan thinks, okay?"

"Thanks again," Lauren said.

After she left, Trisha looked at Frank and excused herself. She went into Ruby's bedroom, carefully placed her in her crib, and came back to the living room. She sat beside Frank on the couch but shifted slightly away from him. Her heart pounded as she looked him in the eye and said, "About what you asked last week."

He sat up and nodded, the expression on his face a mixture of anxiety and anticipation.

She bit her lip, not wanting to hurt him, but knowing she was about to. She had no choice. All she could do was deliver the news to him as gently as possible. Now that she had no one to set him up with, maybe the blow would be harder on him. Or maybe it would make no difference.

"Frank, I'm so sorry. I wish things were different… I wish I felt different than I do right now. But I don't. I like you… but I can't be with you. I'm so, so sorry."

The devastated expression on his face made her heart hurt. She blinked as she saw tears shimmering in his eyes.

Did I do the right thing? she questioned herself.

*****

Frank left Trisha's house feeling despondent. He didn't know what to do. Why did I think Trisha was going to say anything other than what she has said to me? he thought to himself as he drove to his parents' house, blinking back the tears that threatened to spill down his cheeks. His heart felt like it had been smashed into tiny pieces.

He got to his parents', went into his room and flopped onto the bed. He was thankful his parents weren't around so he wouldn't have to deal with their questions. He covered his face with his hands and took a deep breath to stop himself from breaking down. He stood again and went to look out the window, as if at any minute he would see Trisha walking by. Five minutes later, he began to pace the room.

Lord, what am I going to do?

He sat on the bed again and then decided he needed to call someone. He needed to call Audrey. He took his phone from his pocket, dialed Audrey's number, and then waited as it rang.

Audrey's voice came on the line. "Hey, Frank! How are you?"

Frank shook his head as though Audrey could see him and then answered, "Not good at all. I just poured out my heart to your sister, Trisha, and she basically told me she would never be with me. I didn't know this kind of pain existed until today. I feel like my heart is being torn into tiny pieces." He put his hand on his forehead.

Audrey said in a sympathetic voice, "Frank, I'm so sorry."

"I don't know why I expected her to say any-thing different than what she did. I guess it was because she told me before I came to Rosefield that she missed me and was thinking of me. That was actually why I left Boise to come to Rosefield. She sounded like she at least wanted to give us a try, and I was so excited. I think it's time to just give up completely."

"I'm not sure, but I think Stan's presence has something to do with it," Audrey said. "But Frank, please don't give up. I know you'd be good for her."

Frank sighed and said, "But I can't force her to be with me."

Audrey replied, "You told me she was the reason you came to Rosefield and you said you were not going to leave until you won her heart. Has that changed now? Just because Trisha did what she always does? You can't give up now. I think she needs you, but she doesn't know it yet. Please fight for her, Frank. I don't want to see her go back to Stan, and I know you certainly don't want that, either."

Frank sighed again. "I don't, but she sounded pretty firm about her decision. I don't want to give up, but I've run out of ideas. I really don't know what to do now, and I can't stay in Rosefield forever."

"Frank, you love her deeply," Audrey said. "I'm sure you will figure out what to do soon."

"That is if Stan hasn't wormed his way into her heart by then," he said, his heart filled with discouragement.

"We will pray that doesn't happen."

"Audrey," Frank said.

"Yes?"

"Do you really think it's God's will for me and Trisha to be together?"

"Why do you ask?"

"Because I've been wondering about that. I have never asked the Lord if it's His will, and now that Trisha has straight up rejected me, I feel as though it might be a clear sign from God to walk away. And that scares me."

"Frank, I can't tell you that I am certain it's God's will for you and Trisha to be together, but I know that your love for her is deep and that you would give your life for her if need be. If that kind of love isn't from God, I don't know what is. I also know that she likes you too, but fear keeps her back. You can pray about it, but until you hear God's clear voice telling you to move on, I think you shouldn't give up."

"Okay… I won't give up." He laughed in self-derision. "I don't even think I know how to give up on Trisha."

"Attaboy!" Audrey said.

Frank chuckled and then asked, "When will you be coming to Rosefield again?"

"I'm not sure. Before the end of this week, maybe. Don't worry about Trisha. When I come, I'll speak with her. And if Stan is still hanging around, I might just arrest him."

Frank laughed again. "Stop it, Audrey! You can't arrest Ruby's father."

"Why not?" She sniggered. "Seriously though, I'm rooting for you to win my sister's heart. It's about time. It's just very bad timing that Stan had to come back now. Or maybe it wasn't. Knowing Stan, he probably sensed from wherever he had gone that Trisha was about to find love again. His selfish, possessive soul couldn't stand by and let that happen."

Frank smiled sadly.

"I'll be praying for you, Frank. And take care of yourself."

"Thanks for your great advice and encouragement, Audrey."

"You are welcome."

"I'll let you get back to work."

"I'll talk to you later," Audrey said.

After the call ended, Frank looked up thoughtfully. Audrey had assured him that it was God's will for him to continue to pursue Trisha… but he wasn't sure it was true. Still, he would take her advice, and unless the Lord spoke plainly to him, he would not give up. He could not give up. Even if it meant he was at risk of getting his heart irreparably shattered.

If he was going to take Audrey's advice and follow his heart, he had to do something now. He dug out his phone from his pocket and dialed Trisha's number. His stomach tightened as he listened to her phone ring. It rang and rang but she didn't pick up. At last, he was diverted to voicemail and he spoke after the beep. "Trisha, it's Frank. Listen. I know you gave your answer to my question today, but I still have one more question to ask and I can't do it over the phone. I'll come over tomorrow evening around this time. I hope you will hear me out then." He sighed. "I'll love you forever."

He put his cellphone on the bedside table, lay back on the bed, looked up at the ceiling, and prayed that the Lord would soften her heart toward him.

*****

Trisha sat on the sofa in her living room, listening to Frank's voice on her phone for the hundredth time that day. After his voice message ended, she sighed wearily. She had thought Frank would finally give up and move on. But he wasn't doing that. And, strangely, there was a part of her that was glad he hadn't given up on her. However, it left her even more confused than ever. If he had just decided to move on now, she could relax and see where things led with Stan. But, Frank's attention complicated things for her.

She sighed again. "Oh, Frank. Why won't you just let me be?"

But she couldn't say she wasn't flattered by his attention, his unfailing love for her. She bit her lip.

Yes, she was flattered, but also guilt-ridden because of it.

A knock sounded on her door and she jumped. She shook her head and told herself to be calm. It seemed like these days she was always jumping whenever someone knocked on her door or rang the doorbell. But she had good reason to. It was usually either Stan, whose presence here filled her with so many conflicting emotions, or Frank, who made her heart beat fast and yet who she couldn't give her heart to.

She looked at the door, willing the person on the other side to go away. The doorbell rang again and she groaned. She looked at the clock on the wall and saw it was about the time Frank said he would come to see her; to ask another question that was sure to leave her as confused as the first.

She reluctantly got up and went to open the door. Frank stood there, but this time, he didn't have on his signature smile, neither did he bring his usual lilies for her. His expression was grave. She gave him a small smile and he returned the same to her.

She stepped aside so he could enter the house and then sat on the sofa.

He sat on the couch facing her and leaned forward to look intently at her.

Her heart raced as she gazed at him, unable to pull her eyes away. At last, she forced herself to look away and asked, "So, Frank. How was your day?" She cringed inwardly at her stupid question. How was your day?

"Trisha, can you please look at me?"

She reluctantly turned to face him.

"I told you I have one question to ask, and here it

is. Is there any part of you that likes me at all? Any part that sees a future with me?"

She pressed her lips tightly together as her heart filled with panic.

"Is there any way you can answer me?" he asked, anguish clearly written on his face.

She shut her eyes so she wouldn't see the pain on his face. Something in her wanted to cry out, "I like you and I see a future with you!" but she held herself in check. Ruby's needs came before hers. She didn't want a relationship now, but if she had to, it might as well be with her daughter's biological father. She'd decided for Ruby's sake to take Stan back if he wanted her. And she was sure he did from the way he'd looked at her the last time he'd been here. Plus, he really seemed like a changed man now.

"Trisha, say something. Please!"

Trisha sighed and looked at him. She opened her mouth to tell him her answer was still no, but look-ing at him now, she couldn't bring herself to say the word. She put down her head and then looked up again. There was only one thing she could think of doing with all these confusing emotions she was feeling. And that was to seek counsel from some-one wise. Someone she knew would give her godly and sound advice.

"Frank," she said to him, "Can you give me one more day to think about it? Please?"

Frank looked at her for a long moment and then nodded. "You know I'll wait for you forever if I have to."

"Thank you," she said to him. "I promise to give you an answer by tomorrow evening."

He nodded. And then said, "Where is my play buddy?"

She laughed. "Ruby? Guess where?"

"Asleep?"

"Umm… no, actually, she is at her Aunt Audrey's today."

"Audrey is in Rosefield? I spoke to her on the phone yesterday evening and she didn't tell me she was coming to Rosefield today."

"She actually arrived this afternoon with Ken and immediately came to get Ruby."

"Okay… I'll pay her a visit tomorrow, then."

Trisha nodded.

The doorbell rang and she groaned inwardly. Oh, great! It's probably Stan. The last thing she needed now was the two men in the same room, and Ruby wasn't even here to act as a distraction for one of them. She would be the one caught between both men. She sighed wearily as she went to open the door.

"Hi, Trish!" Stan said, smiling. He held out a bouquet of red roses to her and then came into the house.

"Where is Ru…" he frowned when he saw Frank.

Thankfully, Frank stood up, smiled at her, and said, "I have to go. I'll see you tomorrow."

Trisha followed him with her eyes as he let himself out of the house.

After he'd left, Stan grimaced and asked with jealousy clearly written on his face, "Why does he come here every day?"

Trisha shrugged. "He's an old friend and he's in Rosefield temporarily. I think he just likes seeing a familiar face here every day."

"But his parents live here," Stan said with irritation.

She waved her hand dismissively as she didn't want to talk about Frank anymore. "Umm… Ruby isn't around today. She's at Audrey's." Trisha sat down and Stan sat beside her.

"That's fine," he said. "I actually came to see you today, Trisha."

Her pulse quickened as she looked at his face. He was staring intently at her and she knew exactly what he wanted to talk to her about. As much as she had thought about getting back with him, now that it seemed it was what he wanted to ask her, she suddenly became unsure. Was it really what she wanted?

"Trisha," he paused and then continued. "I know I treated you poorly in the past… and I deserved it when you divorced me." He shifted closer to her. "I have paid dearly for my betrayal as I have missed you terribly every single day. And I missed seeing the birth of my daughter, and all her milestones so far. But I want to correct that. I know I don't deserve a second chance, but I am asking… no, begging for it. I'm still in love with you and I want us to be a family; you, me, and Ruby. I want to love you."

She looked at him and bit her lip. "How do I know you won't do the same things you did when we were married? You cheated constantly, and I know I can't live like that."

He looked her in the eye. "I know I have told you that I am a changed man, but I don't blame you for not believing me. Words are nothing. Only actions are important. So what can I do to show you that I've truly changed? Just say it. No matter what it is, I will try to do it."

She thought about Frank and his similar request

to win her heart. How did I get here, stuck between these men? She had promised to give Frank an answer tomorrow after she'd prayed earnestly for wisdom. She smiled sadly at Stan and said, "Can you give me a day to think about it?"

He nodded. "Thank you. That is all I can ask."

He left half an hour later.

That night, as she lay on her bed, she could hear the sound of her heart beating as the house was perfectly quiet. She asked God to give her wisdom to make the right decision. As she prayed, her heart filled with anxiety and despair. Without a doubt, no matter what decision she made tomorrow, someone would be terribly hurt.

SEVEN

Sienna opened the door of her and Bryan's small apartment and went in. She immediately dropped her textbooks on the coffee table and flopped down on the couch to wait for Bryan. She put her legs up on the table and heaved a sigh of relief, glad that she was finally back from classes and could rest. These days, she was getting a bit more tired than usual, but her OBGYN had assured her that she and the baby were healthy.

She was excited about her pregnancy, but her excitement was tempered by Bryan's news about moving to another country. She looked up at the clock on the wall. It was three o'clock. Bryan would not be back from Bible College for about another two hours. Thankfully, he had not brought up any talk about moving since the day she'd asked him to pray about it again. He had chosen instead to spend time at the college continuing as an assistant chaplain. She didn't mind that at all. As long as he wasn't planning for them to move anymore, she was good. Hopefully, he'd found out that the word he'd heard wasn't from the Lord.

But she doubted that. Whenever Bryan had gotten a word from the Lord in the past, it had been pretty accurate. It was not likely to be different this time, which made her very nervous.

"Lord, I don't want to move!" she said harshly.

The phone suddenly began to ring and she jumped. Calm down, girl.

She stood up from the couch, walked to the mantel near the TV stand where the phone sat, and picked up the receiver. "Hello," she said.

"Hello, is this Sienna Larson?"

Sienna frowned and asked curiously, "Yes, it is. Who is this?"

"This is James Davis, a producer from the TV show Home Runner."

Sienna's jaw dropped. "Home Runner! The popular Home Runner show on TV? I love that show!" She frowned and then sighed. "Wait. This is a prank call, isn't it? Why would someone from Home Runner call me?"

"I assure you, Mrs. Larson, that this is not a prank call. We want to start a new spinoff of the original show. Instead of the normal show about engaged couples looking for the perfect homes to start their lives in, this time we want to have a show about new couples in small towns that are very much in love and are about to start a family. We follow them as they hunt for new homes, as they prepare to have their babies, and when they bring the new babies into the world. In short, we show the viewers what they love to see—a good-looking, successful young couple who love each other deeply and are starting out their lives together."

"But how did you find my husband and I?"

"We saw a picture of you and your husband, Bryan, in Paragon Magazine. They did a piece about their married models and you both were one of the couples they wrote about. You guys are a gorgeous young couple, let me just say! We did some snooping around, and we found out that you two have everything we want. You are perfect for this new show! And we heard you are pregnant, which fits in perfectly with the theme of the show. Congratulations on your pregnancy, by the way."

She didn't answer as her head spun at his words. The producers of Home Runner want me and Bryan in their show! She could hardly believe it. In fact, she didn't. Home Runner was the only reality show she watched, and one of her favorite shows on TV. Someone who knew her well was probably playing a prank on her.

The guy continued. "Would you and your husband be interested in participating in the show, Mrs. Larson?"

Sienna shook her head and said, "Who is this? This is a prank, I know it is!"

"It isn't a prank, Mrs. Larson!" The man sounded slightly exasperated. "What can we do to make you believe it isn't?"

Sienna thought about his question for a few seconds, chuckled, and then said, "I want to meet Amber Roland, the host of Home Runner!" She chuckled again. This would definitely reveal who this prankster was or who exactly had put this guy up to it. Maybe it was Trisha, or even…

"Okay, we can do that."

She blinked rapidly. "What?"

"I said we can do that. If you agree right now, we can send a representative to Green Valley to bring the papers you need to sign. Amber Roland will come with. She likes to check out the couples and the towns she's going to work in beforehand anyway."

For the second time since this surreal conversation had started, Sienna's jaw dropped.

"Mrs. Larson, are you there? What do you say?"

Sienna's years of experience as a model suddenly kicked in and she said in an even voice, "That will be fine. Thanks."

"That means you accept to star in the show?"

She felt a prick of guilt in her heart. She hadn't even spoken to Bryan about it. How could she accept when she hadn't consulted him first? However, she brushed the guilt aside and said, "Yes. You can send the representative over... as well as Amber Roland. Once I look over the papers and everything is all right, I think we will be good to go."

"Perfect!" the man said. "Amber will probably need a few days... but I think she'll be ready to go to Idaho by the end of the week. So, expect her and the representative in Green Valley then."

"Okay. Will do."

"It was a pleasure talking with you, Sienna... can I call you that?"

"Sure... it was a pleasure talking with you as well. Goodbye."

When the call ended, Sienna stared at the phone in her hand for a full minute and then whooped. "Home Runner wants me to star in their show!" She lifted her hands and then did a little jig. Waves of excitement washed through her and she exclaimed,

"I can't believe it! Home Runner!"

And then she suddenly sobered as reality dawned on her. She hadn't spoken to Bryan about it before she'd accepted to have Amber Roland come here. She knew very well why she had done so. Without thinking, she had partly agreed to do the show as a way to figuratively dig her feet into US soil and somehow get Bryan to see that they had no option but to stay here.

She went to sit on the sofa and took a deep breath. Bryan would be disappointed if she kept this from him. And she couldn't, anyway. The show was supposed to be about both of them, not just about her. Besides, she had never kept anything from him.

She shut her eyes, worry enveloping her. This was the first time in her marriage she felt like keeping something to herself. Without a doubt, she already knew what Bryan would say when she told him about the show. He would tell her they couldn't do it because they were soon going to move.

She opened her eyes again. But maybe there was a way to convince him to do the show. Since he hadn't yet gotten word from God concerning the specific place they were supposed to move to, they could do the show now while waiting for that word. That way, she could maybe kill two birds with one stone. First, he would finally have the sense of purpose he'd been yearning for since he'd graduated, as they would be involved in a show that millions of people around the country watched. Secondly, she hoped that they would soon be so involved in the show that he would not have the time or desire to think about moving out of the country anymore.

A small voice whispered in her heart: in your

determination to stay here, you do not care about following God's will anymore.

Guilt began to press in on her, but she quickly brushed it away before it could take proper hold. She wasn't choosing not to follow God's will. She just wanted them to stay here until they truly knew what God's specific will was.

She decided to cook Bryan one of his favorite meals before he came home. Hopefully, it would make the news she was going to break to him easier to swallow. She was thrilled by the TV offer. It was a once-in-a-lifetime opportunity. However, she didn't know if Bryan would want it or not.

"Lord, please let him agree for us to star in Home Runner," she prayed silently as she went into the kitchen.

Guilt began to smother her again, but she brushed it away once more. This was a huge open door for her and Bryan. Surely only the Lord could have brought this about. This had to be God's specific will for their lives at this time.

She gathered the ingredients she would need to cook the meatloaf and mashed potatoes and began to cook the meal for Bryan quickly so she would finish before he came home. By God's grace, Bryan would not only love the meal, but also the good news she had for him.

*****

Bryan looked up as a knock sounded on his office door. He closed his Bible and smiled when he saw Dr. Lincoln, the senior chaplain, standing in the doorway. The man came in and Bryan shook his hand.

As Dr. Lincoln sat on the chair facing him, Bryan said, "I didn't know you had returned from your trip to South America, sir."

"I came back yesterday," Dr. Lincoln said.

"And how was the evangelical tour around the region?"

"It went well." The senior chaplain leaned forward and looked intently at Bryan. "That's actually why I came to see you."

Bryan sat up straight. "Oh… I see," was all he could think to say. Something about the way the man was looking at him now told him what he was about to say was very important.

"I've been very blessed to still have you around, Bryan. Even though you've graduated, you still come here every day. I know it's because you don't know what you are supposed to do now that you're through with Bible College, but I love that you still come."

Bryan listened, wondering what the chaplain was trying to say.

As if the man was reading his mind, he said, "What I am trying to say is that I like you, Bryan. You have been a great assistant. And the other day, I was thinking about your graduation and you leaving the college for good, and I found that I would miss having you. I want to offer you a permanent job, one that I think you will like and are perfect for."

Bryan's heart began to race as he realized that the word the Lord had spoken to him, about receiving an open door for ministry, was coming to pass now. He anxiously held his breath as Dr. Lincoln continued speaking.

"During my tour of South America, I felt the Lord impressing it in my heart that I would be continuing with the revival meetings there. I feel a strong urge from God to plant various churches there and need someone on the ground to oversee and pastor them while I keep doing the evangelical tours. I immediately knew who that someone should be. Someone who is godly, passionate about the things of God, and eager to win souls for Christ. You instantly came to mind. I can't think of a better person who would be suited for the job."

Bryan felt his heart beating out of his chest. The Lord had opened a door to go to South America.

Dr. Lincoln went on. "Of course, it will be a paying job, though your salary might not be a lot now. However, you will have your basic needs provided for. I know it's a huge commitment I'm asking you to make, as you will have to move to South America… Peru, for a start. I'll give you time to think about it, but I'm hoping you accept my offer. I really believe God's hand is in it."

Bryan shut his eyes as his emotions roiled. On one hand, he was extremely excited about this open door, but on the other, he was scared. What would Sienna say when he told her? He knew she was hoping they wouldn't have to move. This news might be devastating to her unless he could convince her that God would work it all out for their good. But how would he do that when her mind was set on staying here in Green Valley and then moving later to Rosefield?

Dr. Lincoln said, "Bryan… I know this is a lot to take in, but I need to have an answer before the end of this week."

Bryan nodded his head slowly and then said, "I'm sorry, Dr. Lincoln, for not saying anything. It's a great opportunity and I feel like it's from the Lord as well. But I'll have to discuss it with my wife. I'll have an answer for you before the week is out."

"Good. I'll be eagerly expecting your answer."

After the senior chaplain left, Bryan sat back on his chair and covered his face with his hands. His pulse raced as he thought about Sienna and how she would accept the news. He had to tell her right away, but he wasn't looking forward to doing that at all. "Lord, please give me the strength I need to talk to Sienna about this. I'm worried she might start having panic attacks again once I tell her about Dr. Lincoln's ministry offer. I ask that you will touch her heart so that she takes this news well."

He sighed as he opened his eyes. His emotions were still jumbled. He glanced at his wristwatch. It was time for him to go home.

As he drove home, he kept praying that Sienna would not freak out when he told her the news—that they would be moving to Peru very soon.

He got home and opened the door. As soon as he came in, the delicious aroma of spiced meat hit his nostrils. In spite of his troubled thoughts, he smiled as Sienna came into the living room wearing an apron. She quickly removed it, tossed it aside, and came to hug him. She smelled like an assortment of spices. "I see… or rather smell that you have been cooking up a storm," he said, wrapping his arms tightly around her.

She pulled back and her eyes danced with mirth. "Are you saying I smell, Bryan Larson?" she asked, giving him a teasing smile.

"No… well, yes, but you smell really nice. Like food… umm…"

"Keep digging."

He laughed. "Okay. You smell nice. I'm just going to leave it at that. What are you cooking, anyway? It seems like you have been at it for some time now. Are we celebrating something?"

A look of fear briefly passed over her face and he frowned. She smiled brightly and then said, "Well… I have some news to share with you. It's good news. At least, I hope you will see it as good news."

He looked at her in surprise, took her hand, and sat down on the sofa with her. "I have news to share with you as well, baby," he said. He studied her face and then added tentatively, "I hope you will also take it as good news." He sighed. "But you go first."

"No. Let's eat first of all, and then we can share."

They both sat at the table eating and talking about their day. Bryan kept back the information about the offer he'd gotten from Dr. Lincoln. After the meal, they cleared and washed the dishes together and then they both sat side by side on the sofa. Sienna looked at him and gave him an anxious smile.

"You can go first, Bryan," she said.

He shook his head. "No, baby. You go first."

She shifted slightly and looked him in the eye. "I got a phone call today. A man called and told me he was one of the producers from Home Runner. You know Home Runner, don't you? That show I watch almost every day."

He nodded and gazed at her quizzically, wondering why someone from a reality TV show had called her.

She continued, "He called to let me know that they were starting a spinoff of the show. This time about young married couples starting out their lives." She paused for a few seconds and then went on. "He wants us to star in the new show, Bryan!" She whooped and grinned. "Can you believe it? I thought I was dreaming when he asked me if we were interested."

Bryan's heart raced as he listened to her speak. This "opportunity" for a reality show couldn't have come at a worse time. He could see she was all gung-ho about it, but he was about to shatter her dream. He felt like a cad, but there was nothing he could do about it.

"Bryan, aren't you going to say anything?" she asked, looking worriedly at him.

"Did you accept the offer?" he asked her wearily.

She frowned. "I kinda did... but we aren't in until we sign some legal documents. The guy said a representative would bring some papers for us to go through before the end of this week." The excited expression on her face earlier returned again and she grinned. "He said Amber Roland would be coming too." She squealed. "Can you believe it? I'm going to meet Amber Roland!"

He sighed. Oh Lord, do I have to do this to her now? Maybe I should just hold back on telling her about Dr. Lincoln's offer. But he knew he couldn't postpone telling her about it. Whatever disagreement came out of the news he was about to break to her, he had to deal with it head on.

"Umm... Sienna..."

She frowned. "What is it, Bryan? I know the reality show thing is a lot to take in, but I think it would be really exciting to do. Plus, in a way, we will be sharing our faith with the rest of the country. You have been asking the Lord what you are supposed to do specifically. Maybe this is it. I know the show is seen in other parts of the world too. That might explain the scripture the Lord gave you about preaching the gospel all over the world."

He suddenly couldn't hold it in. Even though he was anxious about telling her what he wanted to, he had to do it now. "Sienna, I got an offer from Dr. Lincoln today."

She raised her brows. "What kind of offer?"

"A job offer." He smiled sadly at her. "Remember what I told you… about the word God gave me? He said I would receive a ministry open door soon in Peru. I did. Today. Dr. Lincoln wants to plant churches in South America while he continues his evangelical tour there, and he wants someone who will live there to oversee and pastor the church-es. He offered me the job and I told him I would get back to him before the end of the week. But I already know it's God's will, Sienna. We have to move to Peru soon."

Sienna's eyes were full of horror, and Bryan shut his eyes for a brief moment. He couldn't look at her, knowing he was the one causing her so much pain.

He opened his eyes when she said, "Peru, Bryan. I can't move to Peru! I want to stay here, with my family…"

His eyes widened in pain. "But I am your family, too."

She looked away from him. "You know what I mean. Trisha, Ruby, Audrey, Faizan, they are all just an hour's drive from here." She touched her belly. "I want to raise our child near family, Bryan. Not in some distant country where we know no one."

"I understand that. But we can't just disobey the Lord." He touched her shoulder. "Besides, Audrey moved for Ken, didn't she?"

"To Miami, Bryan. That is still in the United States. And they both come to Rosefield every other weekend."

"What, then, do you suggest we do? Because I have to follow God's will."

She looked at him. "How do you know that it's God's will? Maybe the reality show is God's will."

He shook his head. "Don't be ridiculous, Sienna!"

She stood. "I am being ridiculous? Says the guy who wants to move his pregnant wife away from her family to some remote place?"

"I'm sure it's not going to be…"

"Please, don't patronize me, Bryan! It will be difficult for me, and you know it!"

He raised his brows. She looked and sounded so agitated. So angry. He had never seen her like this. She was always so sweet and soft-spoken. "What has gotten into you?"

She suddenly started to cry and he groaned. Lord, please help me, he prayed silently. He stood and drew her into his arms to comfort her, but she pushed away from him.

"Don't!" she said angrily.

He stared at her. "I can't believe this! You are the one who accepted to star in a reality show without first discussing it with me, and yet I am the one who is bearing the brunt of your anger. I should be the angry one."

"You want to take me away from my family and

yet you are supposed to be the angry one?"

"Don't forget that my family lives here, too."

"Then let's stay. Please."

"But how can I when God wants us to move?"

She glared at him for a long while and said, "God may want you to move… but I am not moving!"

"What?" He stared incredulously at her. "What do you mean you are not moving? We are supposed to be one and that means you go where I go… and vice versa."

"Then stay here with me, Bryan."

"I can't! You know that."

She narrowed her eyes and glowered at him. "Then you will be going to Peru alone!" She stormed off and left him standing there, staring bemusedly at the space in front of him. After a minute, he slowly sat on the couch and ran his fingers through his hair in frustration. "Lord, what is happening to my marriage? What will I do? I can't disobey you… but I'm afraid of losing my wife. Please help me."

He listened for an answer to his plea, but he heard nothing. He lay on the couch and looked up at the ceiling. He searched through his mind for a solution, but he couldn't come up with any. Instead, fear attached itself to him. He groaned and then turned on his side and shut his eyes. I might as well make myself comfortable on this couch, he thought in self-mockery, because this is probably where I'll be sleeping until God knows when.

EIGHT

Faizan rang the doorbell of Trisha's house and waited. It had become a habit now for him to visit Trisha almost every day. He enjoyed seeing all his sisters regularly after a lifetime of not having real siblings or people who genuinely cared for him. Unfortunately, he didn't get to see Sienna as many times as he wanted to since she lived in Green Valley with Bryan. However, he tried to visit her once a week, and also saw her every weekend when she visited. He was looking forward to her visit this evening, especially now that she'd told them she was pregnant.

He smiled when Trisha opened the door.

"Hey, Faizan!" Trisha said and gave him a small smile.

"Trish!" He frowned as he looked at her. She didn't greet him with her usual exuberance. Come to think of it, she hadn't done that for the past two weeks.

Entering the house, he sat on the sofa and watched her as she sat across from him.

"What about Audrey and Ken… and my Ruby?" she asked dully.

His frown deepened. "They're good. Audrey took Ruby to the park and Ken is at home watching a football game." He leaned forward and studied her face.

She smiled at him. "Why are you looking at me like that?"

"What's wrong, Trisha? You haven't been your lively self for more than a week now." He narrowed his eyes in anger. "Is it because of that Stan guy?"

She shook her head quickly. "No… Stan didn't do anything wrong. I'm just a little confused right now. That's all."

He leaned back on the sofa and said to her, "Do you want to talk about it?"

She stared at the wall in front of her with a thoughtful expression and then turned to him. She sighed loudly. "I feel as though I am caught between two men, Faizan. Actually, I am."

"What do you mean?" he asked.

"Frank Kessler gave me an ultimatum … to date him or never see him ever again. And then Stan, my ex, wants me to get back with…"

"What?" Faizan interrupted her. "Stan, the scoundrel who cheated on you with multiple women, wants to get back with you? He had the guts to ask you to take him back?"

Trisha bit her lip, and Faizan raised his brows. "You are actually considering his request? Trisha, you can't be serious!" Faizan shook his head. "You can't get back with him. After all he put you through."

"I remember everything, Faizan. I was the

one who went through it all." She looked away. "But… I've always dreamed of raising my kids in a two-parent home. I know how it is to have a father today and then lose him tomorrow. I want Stan permanently in my daughter's life, and if marrying him again will get me that, so be it."

Faizan shook his head slowly. "Trish, I also know what it's like to lose a father. But trust me; an absent father is better than a bad one. I have had those, two of them actually, and it wasn't pretty."

"Stan isn't a bad father. He is a good father. He was just a bad husband, but I truly believe he has changed."

"Why would you think that?" Faizan asked incredulously. "You know you can have him in Ruby's life without marrying him."

"I want a real family unit, not a broken one. Besides, Faizan, you of all people should understand what it means not to judge others for their past sins."

Faizan pressed his lips together and heaved a sigh. It was true. He had a despicable past, but God had forgiven him. His sisters embraced him wholeheartedly. Even the people of Rosefield treated him well. No one ever brought up his past in a negative way. Maybe he needed to cut Stan some slack. Still, he was worried about Trisha. He didn't want her to get her heart broken.

He folded his arms and then said, "Okay. I admit that people can change. But are you sure Stan has?"

"I believe so."

Faizan sighed. "All right… but there is Frank as well. You like Frank, don't you?"

Trisha didn't say anything for a few seconds.

She rubbed her face with her hand and then said, "I do… but I don't know if I'm considering giving him a chance because of my past guilt about how I treated him on a date we had. Plus, he has loved me for such a long time and I don't want to date him because of that."

"I understand that. But Frank still loves you even after everything, and after all these years. Maybe you should give him a chance."

"That is exactly what I mean. I want to date him because I truly like him, not because I feel it's time I reciprocated his love for me." She leaned forward slightly. "The most important thing, though, is that I have decided to put Ruby's needs before mine. My only goal now is to do what is best for her. Stan is her biological father. I think it makes more sense to be with him so we can be one big family."

Faizan nodded, now fully understanding where she was coming from. But he still didn't think she should marry Stan. Audrey had told him a lot about Frank Kessler, and from what she'd said he seemed to be a really good guy. Someone he would want to see his sister married to. However, he had to trust that she would make the right decision for herself.

She sighed again. "I have been asking the Lord for wisdom. I need to give Frank and Stan an answer by this evening, and even though I have decided on the man I want, I still have my doubts."

Faizan nodded. "I understand your need to put Ruby first… and you definitely should. But I just want you to do this." He gave her a small smile. "Please also think about yourself as well. You will have to live with the guy you choose."

She nodded and then waved her hand. "I need

to think about something else for now. This is just weighing me down." She suddenly put on a bright smile. "Talking about relationships, Faizan, I think it's about time you started dating again."

He raised his brows and then chuckled. "How did we go from worrying about your love life to talking about mine?"

She shook her finger and said, "You have no love life, dear brother. It's time you got one. I know someone who really likes you."

He frowned and leaned back. "I'm not interested, Trisha. The woman I love is still in North Africa. Even if I can't see her now, I intend to someday."

"But you told me she made a vow of chastity and therefore there is no chance for a relationship between you two, didn't you?"

He sighed exasperatedly. "Yes, but…"

"Faizan, you can't continue holding on to her. I know it's hard, but you have to let go so someone else can come into your life. You can't stay single forever."

"Why not?" he murmured as he thought about Zainah. His heart grew heavy as he pictured her beautiful face, her smile, her graceful ways, and kindness. How would he ever be able to let her go?

Trisha cried, "Faizan, you see what I mean? You look like a tormented man. You have to let this woman go even though it's hard." Trisha got up and came to sit next to him. She put her hand on his back and said softly, "I know it hurts to even think about letting go of someone you love so much, but it is for the best. Besides," she smiled at him, "I just told you there's someone who likes you. Don't you want to know who it is?"

He shrugged. "Like I said, I'm not interested in anyone except Zainah."

"Are you sure? 'Cause the girl I'm talking about is very pretty and she's a really nice person. At least let me tell you who it is, and then you can decide if you want to pursue a relationship with her or not."

He wanted to tell Trisha to let him be, but he sighed and asked her who it was so he could get her off his back.

"It's Lauren. You know her. Ken and Audrey's friend. She's also my friend."

"I know her," he said absentmindedly. "She came to the house to look for Ken once." He frowned. "She sat next to me in church on Sunday."

"Good. And what do you think?" Trisha asked.

He looked at Trisha and said, "Did she really say she liked me? She asked me if she could join the welfare department and I told her we are always looking for new members." He smiled in spite of himself. "I actually thought she was genuinely interested in joining our department so she could help the needy."

"Maybe she is." Trisha smiled. "But there is nothing wrong with her being attracted to the super cute department leader."

"Stop it!" He chuckled and then thought about something. "Isn't she Ken's ex?"

"Yes. They were actually engaged to be married, but she broke it off and married someone else. Now she's divorced."

"Okay…" He nodded.

Trisha whooped. "Okay? You'll ask her out?"

"No!" He shook his head. "I didn't say I was going to ask her out."

"Well, what are you going to do, then?"

"Nothing, Trisha! I am not interested. I just said that a minute ago."

Trisha pursed her lips and then sat back. "I guess you are just like me; caught between two people."

"No, I'm not like you. You have two men vying for your love. I have a woman who I love dearly but who I can't be with."

"And another who likes you. Don't forget that."

He groaned. "Lauren likes me as a person… but she'll hardly be heartbroken if I don't ask her out. Just like you said, she's pretty. She'll find someone else."

"Ah-ha! You agree that she's pretty!"

"So? Everyone can see that she is. That doesn't mean I want to date her."

"Okay, then," Trisha said. "But don't rule her out yet. You might miss out on an opportunity to be with someone really great. Just like I said before, you can't stay single forever and Lauren is a great girl who is ready to date you. Please consider that at least."

He smiled at Trisha and then stood up. "I'm going to be late for the welfare meeting if I don't leave for church now."

Trisha saw him to the door. "Since Lauren wants to join your department, you might see her in church today. Please keep an open mind. I think you will both be lovely together if you just gave it a chance."

He looked at her. "I can say the same for you and Frank." He touched her shoulder. "I hope you make the right decision, Trish."

She hugged him. "And you too, Faizan. Thank

you." She drew back. "I love you."

"I love you too, sis. I'll see you tomorrow."

He left the house, got into his car, and drove the short distance to the church. He entered the New Day Fellowship Church while running the welfare department's agenda through his mind. They had various places to visit and he needed to divide all the members into four groups. He passed the church hallway, climbed the stairs, and strode to the vestry where the welfare group's weekly meetings were held.

A few of the members were already present. He walked up to them and asked one of the girls there, a young woman named Susan, to lead the worship and opening prayers.

As Susan led the worship, raising one song after another, other members began to arrive and join in the worship. Faizan thought about how far God had brought him. He'd come from a life of violence and hatred for Christians; now he was a dedicated Christian who loved Jesus with all his heart. He lifted up his hands to the Lord in thanksgiving as his heart flooded with gratitude.

The worship and prayer session ended about twenty-five minutes later, by which time most of the welfare members had arrived. Faizan went to the front of the group and began to read out the list he had written earlier that day, which contained the different people and places he wanted them to visit. "I'll divide everyone into different groups," he said.

He looked down at the list in his hand and then looked up. "The first group will help out in the soup kitchen. The second group will visit people who came to our church on Sunday but aren't totally sure they want to continue to come. The third group will go to the youth center with the back-to-school donations made by our church members. The fourth group will visit the old people's home to pray with them and just let them know they are loved."

His eyes went over the members of the department. A few people weren't there. He began to count. His assistant wasn't there, but...

He stopped counting as his eyes settled on Lauren. She was sitting at the back, her eyes on him. She smiled shyly at him and he almost groaned. He looked away and continued to count. There were fourteen people there, including him. He began to divide them into groups of three. "Shelly, you'll be the leader of your group. You guys are going to visit the orphanage."

He counted out three more people and selected a leader for them. He finally came to Lauren and found out that there was no one else to pair her with. He sighed silently. He had to pair up with her. He said reluctantly, "Umm... Lauren, you'll come with me to the old people's home. Okay?"

She smiled broadly and nodded.

Hopefully, she doesn't think this is a date.

Immediately, he chided himself for thinking that way. It was kind of mean. Wondering whether she thought the visit to the old people's home was a date or not was so vain. She was here to do God's work and that was all he needed to focus on.

Fifteen minutes later, after everyone except Lauren had left for their various assignments, Faizan approached her. He sat beside her and brushed away the slight self-consciousness he felt as he vividly recalled what Trisha had said about her liking him. With all his heart, he hoped she would not bring it up. Hopefully, she would come to understand as soon as possible that he wasn't interested in a relationship with her without him having to spell it out.

She gave him the same shy smile she had given him earlier.

He returned her smile. "Hi, Lauren. I'm glad to see you actually joined the department. That shows that you are serious about the needy and helpless and want to build God's kingdom."

She nodded. "I am. I was helped by a wonderful couple when I was in trouble, and I know how important it is to give back."

He remembered Ken saying something about it. She had come out of an abusive marriage and the Gibsons had taken her in. Now, she was on her own, thriving. He was impressed that her painful experience had left her with a desire to help those in need. And he was glad she hadn't joined the department just because of him, as he had previously thought.

"That's good," he said. "So, are you ready to go now?"

"Yes."

They left the church together and then it occurred to him that Fruitful Vines, the old people's home they were supposed to visit, was not somewhere they could walk to. They needed to drive there. He looked at her, wondering what to say. She looked back at him with a quizzical but trusting expression, and he smiled. "Umm... Lauren, did you bring a car? We have to drive there."

"No. I… I don't have a car right now."

"Okay, we will go in my car," he said a little reluctantly. Somehow, he felt like having her in his car would look like they were truly on a date. He quickly brushed the thought aside and went to open his car door. She entered the passenger seat and he got into the driver's.

They sat silently in the car as he drove to Fruitful Vines.

A few minutes later they got there and entered the sprawling single-story building surrounded by a variety of flowers. They entered as many rooms as possible and tried to pray for as many of the residents as they could. Almost an hour later, they headed to the last room. Faizan had thought that the visit to the home with Lauren was going to be awkward for him, but it wasn't at all. She was quite easy to talk to and she genuinely cared for the old people. Her eyes sparkled as she talked with them, and after they'd prayed for each of them, she gave them a word of encouragement and promised to come back to see them. They all seemed to love her. She reminded him of Zainah in that regard.

Faizan held the door open as they entered the room of a very old woman. She looked like she was about a hundred. She smiled broadly at them as she lay on her bed, and Faizan smiled back.

The old woman beckoned them to come closer. When they did, she told them her name was Rita and began to tell them stories about her youth. "I was once married to a handsome man like you," she said to Faizan. "My Charlie died a long time ago, but I still love him dearly."

Faizan smiled sadly as he thought about Zainah. When he was old, would he tell people about how much they'd loved each other but were never able to be together? Or would he meet someone else who would replace his love for her? He shuddered at the thought. He could never love someone else the way he loved her.

As though the old woman could read his thoughts, she said, "You both are a lovely couple. I hope you continue to love each other until you are as old as I am."

Faizan shook his head. "We are not a couple..."

The old woman continued her story as though she hadn't heard him.

Faizan looked over at Lauren who was on the other side of the bed. She was looking at him with a shy smile on her face. He looked away and faced the old woman again.

At last, the woman stopped talking and laid her head on the pillow. She seemed exhausted by all the stories she had told them, but her eyes shone with mirth.

Faizan said to her, "It's been lovely meeting you, Rita. Can we pray for you?"

"Yes. I would love that," the woman said.

Faizan prayed for God's protection, peace, and presence in her life, while Lauren asked the Lord to keep Rita always full of joy, just as she was now. After they finished praying, Faizan asked Rita if he could come back to see her some other time. She smiled widely and nodded. "Definitely!" She touched his hand and then looked at Lauren. "I would love both of you to come together to see me again. You both are such a beautiful couple."

Faizan wanted to tell her once more that they weren't a couple, but he changed his mind. It was no use. She still wouldn't listen.

"Promise me that you will," she said.

He blinked in surprise and didn't answer.

"Promise me," the woman said again.

He nodded and then said, "I promise."

He and Lauren left the old people's home together and got into his car. As he drove her home, he wondered why he had made Rita that promise and how he was ever going to keep it without giving Lauren the wrong impression.

*****

"Zainah, I think you need to hire a private investigator since you haven't been able to find Faizan yourself," Leila said.

Zainah felt a little uneasy as her friend squeezed into a pair of jeans and then wore a ruffled red blouse. She wanted to ask Leila where she was going in that outfit, but she already knew where. She shelved her concerns and focused her attention on what Leila had just told her. "I would hire one if I had any money. You know I have none… and neither do you."

"But you've been going through all those social media profiles and haven't found him. You know you need to find another way to look for him."

"I know," Zainah said. "And you're right. I need to hire an investigator. I'll have to ask Fatima if she knows someone, but first I need money to pay whoever she finds."

"But I think Fatima can help out with the money."

"No. She has three children she is taking care of alone. And she has helped us with so much. I wouldn't dream of asking her for more."

"Then how are you going to pay the investigator?"

Zainah sighed. "I guess I'll have to get a job. Besides, it's high time I got one. I can't keep living off Fatima like this." Zainah looked at Leila. She wanted to add that her friend needed to get a job too, but she didn't want to start fighting with her again. Their friendship was fragile at this point. Leila still went out almost every day. Zainah knew she was still on her quest to find a husband in spite of the advice she'd given her some time before.

"Where are you going to get a job in this town, and as what?"

"I'm not yet sure, but I can ask Fatima if she knows anyone who wants... umm... a maid." She sighed as Leila gave her a disapproving frown. "I can do that. After all, we had lots of chores back at the camp."

"But you weren't a maid then, Zainah. How can you work as a maid?"

"Why not? If that's the job I get, then that is what I will do so I can find Faizan."

"Okay, then. But don't expect me to look for the same kind of employment," Leila said. She slipped on a pair of black heels and then grabbed a multicolored scarf from the front of the closet. She wrapped it around herself and walked to the door.

Zainah suddenly couldn't hold back her concerns anymore. She said, "Leila, that man you are going to see today... are you sure he is a Christian?"

Leila turned around slowly and looked at her.

She looked surprised as she asked, "How did you know I was going to see a man?"

"I heard you talking to Safia a few days ago about the man you met at the souk. And from the way you are dressed now, I guessed you were going to see him."

Leila looked away, a guilty expression on her face. "I'm not sure he is a Christian…"

"Leila! You are seeing someone who isn't a believer!"

"He isn't a believer yet! But I'm working on it."

"Are you serious, Leila? Tell me you aren't…"

"Stop, Zainah! You are not my mother. I told you that I am working on making him a believer. Besides, isn't that what we are supposed to do? Spread the gospel wherever we go?"

"Yes, but not in order to marry someone. That isn't right. And you have no assurances that he is going to change."

Leila glowered at her. "You fell in love with Faizan before he became a believer… while he was a terrorist, in case you have forgotten."

Zainah pursed her lips and then said, "I haven't forgotten. Yes, I did fall in love with him before he became a believer, but I didn't want to. And I didn't let him know how I felt until he became a Christian."

"It's still the same thing," Leila said. "I'm not planning on marrying Ibrahim until he becomes a Christian." Leila opened the door. "I need to go now. He is waiting for me." She left before Zainah could say anything more.

Zainah heaved an exasperated sigh and then stood up. She went to the living room to look for

Fatima. When she didn't find her, she went to the kitchen. Fatima was there, bent over the kerosene stove, stirring a pot of boiling stew. She looked up at Zainah and then straightened.

"How are you this evening, Zainah?" she asked, smiling.

"I'm fine. I see you are making Safia's favorite dish today."

Fatima nodded. "Yes. It's also her brother's."

Zainah asked, "Is there anything I can help you with?"

"No, Zainah. I've nearly finished. Thanks." She turned off the stove. "How is your search coming along?" she asked, looking at Zainah.

"That's what I came to talk to you about. I haven't found him. I think I need to hire someone who is an expert at finding people. Do you know of anyone like that?"

"Ehm … no, but there is someone in our prayer meeting who might know. I can call him now if you want."

Zainah nodded. "That would be really kind of you."

Fatima wiped her hand on the kitchen napkin, took out her phone from her dress pocket, and dialed a number. After a few seconds, she spoke into the phone, asking the person on the other line exactly what Zainah had asked her. She listened closely and then nodded. She ended the call and turned to Zainah. "He said he knows someone like that, but the man is a little expensive. He charges about three hundred thousand dinar."

Zainah's eyes widened. That was a lot of money. Even if she got a job now, it would take quite some time to save up for that. But she had no choice.

Fatima said, "I would have loaned you the money, but I don't have that kind of money right now."

"I understand. I don't expect you to," Zainah told her. "Umm… do you know where I can get a job… even if it is as a maid?"

"You want to work as a maid?"

"I could be an assistant nurse since that is what I did at the camp. I helped nurse people back to health because it was a course I started in school when I was in my hometown. But I was just in the first year when I had to flee to the women's camp. I don't think any hospital or clinic will hire me without qualifications."

Fatima nodded. "Okay, I'll ask around when I go for the prayer meeting tonight. You will come with me, won't you?"

"I wouldn't miss it for the world." Zainah sighed. "Unfortunately, Leila will not be able to come as she has gone out."

"She and Safia go out a lot now," Fatima said. "I just hope they stay out of trouble."

"I hope so too," Zainah said, worried for her friend. She sighed and brushed the worry away. Leila was an adult and a Christian. Zainah didn't have the time to babysit her friend. Her priority was to find a job now so she could pay the investigator who could find the man she loved.

Fatima said, "I hope I find someone who needs a maid but will treat you well."

"I hope so too," Zainah said.

After the prayer meeting that night at the house of a woman named Hadiza, Fatima started to ask around for anyone who needed a maid or knew someone who needed one. Zainah kept praying that Fatima would find someone.

Fatima approached Hadiza, their host, and Zainah followed her. Fatima asked her the same question she'd been asking the others and Zainah's pulse quickened as Hadiza said she did know someone. "A distant relation of mine is looking for a maid as theirs quit all of a sudden. He and his wife are very wealthy and pay their staff well… but they are Muslims."

"That's okay," Zainah said. "It's okay, I can…"

"They are strict Muslims," the young woman interrupted her. "I don't know if they will want to employ a Christian."

Zainah pulled Fatima away. "I think we should keep searching. There's no point asking her about the job any further."

Fatima sighed. "Okay… but most of the wealthy people here hardly interact directly with their household servants. I doubt they will be interested in your personal faith."

Zainah shook her head. "I think it might be safer for me to look for a job somewhere else."

"Most people are Muslims here. It will be hard to find a job working for an employer who isn't. I think you should accept that job before someone else takes it. If you find that your employers really have a problem with your faith, then you can quit."

Zainah thought about what Fatima had said for a minute and then nodded. "I guess you're right. Let's tell Hadiza that I'm interested in the job."

They both went to the woman, and Zainah told her she was interested in working for her relatives. She would keep her faith as private as she could, but if her employers found out she was a Christian and had a problem with it, she would leave.

Hadiza promised to tell her relatives about her and set up an interview.

When they got back home, Zainah went to her room and found Leila in bed, sleeping. Zainah changed into a comfortable kaftan and then went on her knees and prayed that Hadiza's relative would hire her. The earlier she got a job, the earlier she could start saving and ultimately be reunited with Faizan.

NINE

Trisha wiped Ruby's lips after she'd eaten her dinner. She glanced at the clock on the wall and her pulse raced. It was six-thirty. She had asked Frank to come by at seven o'clock and Stan at eight, so they would not be there at the same time. She needed to speak to each man separately.

She lifted Ruby from her high chair, carried her to the bathroom, and bathed her. After that, she carried her to her room, quickly changed her, read a short story to her, and then laid her in her crib. She kissed her and started to leave the room, but Ruby stood up in her crib, refusing to lie down.

"Ruby, please lie down," Trisha said exasperatedly.

Ruby stared at her and giggled. "Mama," she said.

Trisha sighed and walked back to her. She laid her back on the bed and then whispered, "Sleep, little baby. Sleep."

Ruby turned on her stomach and rubbed her eyes.

"Good. You are feeling sleepy, aren't you? Now,

please sleep."

Ruby looked up at her, her eyes wide with mirth as though she was teasing her mother, daring her to make her fall asleep.

Trisha began to sing softly to her. She smiled as Ruby shut her eyes, opened them again, and then shut them. Trisha watched her for a full minute. When she didn't open her eyes again, Trisha heaved a sigh of relief.

The doorbell rang as she left Ruby's room with the door ajar. She nervously held her breath and then exhaled. Walking to the living room, she went to open the door and then let Frank in. When he sat on the couch, she came and sat next to him, but shifted slightly away. She faced him fully as her heart drummed. The anxious look on his face only made her own anxiety worse. She took a deep breath and then said, "Frank, you have been a true friend to our family. You are great guy." She paused for a second. Frank was looking intently at her. She went on. "I can't say how touched I am… have been, because of how you still love me after all these years." She looked down for a second, wishing she didn't have to break the bad news to him, but knowing she had to. There was no postponing it. "I know how this might hurt you, but I am truly sorry, Frank. I can't be with you."

She sucked in her breath sharply at how utterly devastated he looked. She said again, "I am truly sorry. You are such a great catch; you're kind, funny, and successful. You'll meet someone in no time if you just open your heart to the possibility."

She took his hand and looked him in the eye, wanting him to understand that she was truly sorry, but she didn't want him to keep holding out hope that they would be together one day.

His eyes searched hers and he said in a tortured voice, "Are you taking Stan back?"

She knew he was going to ask that question, but still it was hard for her to admit it to him, knowing it would add to his pain. She didn't say anything for a full minute and then she answered, "Yes, I am. He asked if I would, and for Ruby's sake, I will take him back."

Tears swam in Frank's eyes and she couldn't look at him any longer. She turned away. She was surprised when he gently turned her face back to his.

"Are you sure it's what you want to do, Trish?" he asked, his voice choked with emotion. "Not just for Ruby, but for yourself?"

She pressed her lips together and nodded. "I have chosen to put Ruby's needs before mine." She couldn't resist touching his cheek. "Please forgive me, Frank, for all the pain I have caused you." She withdrew her hand. "I think it would be better and easier for both of us if you stopped coming here."

He gasped and she shut her eyes briefly. The hurt she felt for him was unexpected. But it wasn't just for him… it was for herself. She opened her eyes to find him staring at her, tears trailing down his cheeks.

"I'll always love you, Trisha. I want you to never forget that."

She nodded. "I will never forget. How can I?" She reached out and wiped away his tears with her fingers. "You'll be fine, Frank. I know you will."

"It doesn't seem like that," he said, his eyes

downcast. "My heart hurts badly, and I don't think it will ever be right again."

She swallowed the sob that rose up in her and sighed. "It will." She smiled to alleviate the sadness that filled the moment and said in a teasing voice, "You will find love very soon and then forget all about me."

"Never! I will never forget about you, Trish."

Trisha knew this moment with him had to end or she would give into her feelings and tell him she'd decided to be with him instead. She looked up at the clock on the wall and was surprised it was already a few minutes to eight. Stan would soon be there. She stood up and was grateful when Frank stood up with her.

"I guess I'll leave now," he said, looking at her, the expression on his face a mixture of misery and resignation.

She followed him to the door and then stood watching as he stepped out of the house. He turned around and said, "I'll miss you terribly."

"We can still be friends, Frank. Just because we won't be together doesn't mean we can't be in each other's lives."

"I don't know if I can be friends with you."

She nodded, understanding.

"Bye, Trisha."

"Bye, Frank. I wish you all the best."

He entered his car and drove away, and she reentered the house.

*****

Stan arrived at the house at five minutes past eight o' clock. She sat down on the couch beside him and then quickly moved to the loveseat. The couch was where she and Frank had had the heartbreaking talk minutes before. She couldn't bring herself to speak to Stan while sitting there.

Stan looked at her as she sat facing him. Unlike Frank, he looked at ease, almost as if he was confident that she would agree to his request and take him back immediately. But on the other hand, it could be that he just didn't care as much as Frank did.

She studied his face and then noticed that he did have a slightly anxious look, but, typical of him, he was hiding it well. She sighed softly and threaded her fingers together nervously. She began, "Stan, you know what happened in our marriage and how messy our divorce was."

He nodded but didn't say anything.

She continued. "I loved you and I was heartbroken when I found out about your many affairs." The memory of the last sordid affair she had found out flooded her mind and she stopped talking.

Are you sure you want to make this decision? she asked herself.

She brushed aside her doubts. Remember you are doing this for your daughter.

"Before I answer your request, I want you to promise me you will never put me through what you did when we were married. I don't think I can handle that again."

His eyes widened. "Trish, are you saying you will take me back?"

"First, I need you to promise that you will never ever cheat on me again."

He stood up and went to kneel before her. "I promise, Trish. Never again. I want to be the man you and Ruby need. I will never put you through what I did when we were married."

She looked at him and then gave him a small smile. "Then I will take you back. For our daughter's sake."

He whooped, and she gasped when he suddenly pulled her up on her feet and hugged her tightly. He lifted her off her feet and then put her down again. When he knelt before her and brought out a small box from his pocket, she wasn't surprised.

"Trisha, I love you." He opened the box and showed her the ring inside—a white gold solitaire diamond ring. "Will you marry me… again?"

Doubts assailed her as she stood staring down at him. She took a deep breath and forced the doubts out of her mind. She nodded.

"You will?"

"Yes, Stan. I will marry you again."

He swept her off her feet once more. When he put her down, he lifted her chin and gently kissed her. He drew back, took the ring out of the box, and slipped it onto her finger. He smiled and kissed her for the second time. This time, his lips lingered on hers. "I promise to be the best husband I can be for you," he said as he pulled back to look into her face. "And the best father for Ruby."

*****

Sienna turned on the bed and extended her hand. She blinked when she didn't feel Bryan beside her. He's probably in the bathroom, she thought as she turned around to go back to sleep. And then she sat up as she remembered her ongoing quarrel with her husband. Bryan wasn't in the bathroom. Her heart began to race wildly and she felt a panic attack coming on.

For the past few days, he'd been sleeping in the living room. The first day, she had been too angry to care. The second day, however, she had pretended not to care when he didn't come into the bedroom at night. But she did. He left in the morning without speaking to her. When he came home, she ignored him. By the third day, her anxiety attacks had started, but she tried to ignore them.

Her heart skipped continuously, threatening to explode out of her chest. She threw aside the duvet. She couldn't stand it anymore. She missed Bryan. She missed kissing him in the morning before he left for work. She missed coming home from lectures and then waiting for him in the living room. She missed hugging him tightly when he came home in the evening. Most of all, she missed going to bed with him and the feeling of safety and comfort she felt as he wrapped her tightly in his arms while they slept.

She stood up from the bed. Even though she would miss her sisters and brother terribly, she couldn't live without Bryan. After the Lord, he was her life. If he wanted them to move to the moon, then she would move with him.

She began to walk to the living room in her nightgown, the panic attack already beginning to subside. She had to go get her husband back now. Just as she turned the corner to walk into the living room, she bumped into someone. She looked up at Bryan.

"Sienna," he said, uncertainty written on his

face. "You're up. I was coming to the bedroom to talk to you."

She smiled sadly. "I was going to the living room to speak with you."

He took her hands and looked into her eyes. "I'm so sorry, darling. I don't know how to make it right, but can you please forgive me for not trying to work it out with you?"

She shook her head. "I'm the one who should be apologizing, Bryan. I've been stubborn and bull-headed. If you want us to move to South America right now, I'll go with you. I love you so much."

He smiled and hugged her. "I've missed you so much," he said. "I never want us to fight again."

"I've missed you, too," she said, deeply inhaling the scent of his body.

He pulled back and kissed her softly and then hugged her again.

They clung to each other for a long moment and then she said, "Will you come back to the bedroom? I've missed having you sleep beside me."

He nodded and she took his hand. They went into the room together and climbed into bed. Bryan pulled her into his arms and then whispered in her ear, "I love you."

She smiled. "I love you, too."

"What about the TV show, Sienna? What will you tell them? I know how much you wanted that. Do you think they might agree to follow us to Peru and shoot there?"

She sat up and looked at him in surprise. "You would do that?"

"Of course. For you."

She exhaled and ran her fingers through his hair. "That would be such a great idea if they would agree. But I think they said the show was supposed to star couples in small-town America. I doubt they will want to shoot outside the country."

"But you can ask them," Bryan said.

"I guess it wouldn't hurt to ask them. I'll call them tomorrow. The representative and Amber Roland are supposed to arrive in Green Valley in two days' time. I'll ask them if they can shoot outside the country. If they can't, then I guess we will have to pass on the offer."

He kissed her hair and said, "I'm so sorry, Sienna. I wish things were different."

She quickly said, "No. Just as you told me some days ago, the Lord knows what's best for us. Living in Peru at this time is His perfect will for us. I will completely submit to that."

He kissed her forehead and sighed. "You are the best wife anyone could ever ask for."

"And you are the best husband in the whole wide world."

He gave a long, contented sigh and then yawned. He said, "I'll finally be able to sleep peacefully tonight." He drew her even closer. "Goodnight, my love."

"Goodnight, Bryan." She burrowed her head in his chest.

Just before she fell asleep, the reality of what they were soon going to do—move to another country—fully dawned on her. She bit her lip and asked the Lord to help her not to descend into depression again because of it. As long as she had God and Bryan with her, she would be fine, she reminded herself. A deep sense of peace began to settle on her again and she sighed in relief. She went to sleep with a smile on her face, the first in the last three days.

*****

Zainah got out from the back of the white BMW and thanked Moussa, the Rahmani family chauffeur, who had driven her to the supermarket. She carried the bag of groceries she had bought into the mansion and went straight to the kitchen to drop the bag. She greeted the chef, who was cooking up a storm, and then went to the downstairs living room to continue her cleaning. All around her was breathtaking luxury. Her father had been rich back in their small community, but it was nowhere near the wealth of this family she worked for now.

As she dusted the furniture, she thought about how she had felt when she'd started working there two weeks before. She'd been sure she wouldn't like the job; that it would be too stressful, and that it would probably not pay enough to help her hire an investigator quickly. She'd also been afraid that her employers would be difficult people. But she had been wrong on all counts. The job was far less stressful than the chores she'd done back at the women's camp. She hardly dealt directly with her employers so she never had cause to find them difficult in any way. Best of all, the pay was much more than she'd ever expected. In just a few months, she was certain she would be able to save enough to hire the investigator. And to top it all off, she had been given a furnished room in the staff quarters at the back of the house. The room was as large as the one she'd shared with several women at the camp and definitely better furnished. Leila had moved in with her a week before.

There were no small children to clean up after, as the Rahmanis' three kids were all in their early to mid-twenties and at universities outside the country.

Zainah looked up when Rania Rahmani, the elegant, forty-something-year-old matriarch of the family, came into the living room. As usual, she was dressed in an extravagant long shimmering dress and matching turban, on her way out to one of her many functions.

"Good morning, ma'am," Zainah greeted her.

"Morning," she said without looking at Zainah. Her eyes went around the living room and she frowned. She picked up one of the embroidered tasseled throws from the sofa, looked under it, and then threw it back on the couch.

"Is there anything I can help you find?" Zainah asked politely.

"Yes, I'm looking for the invitation card for the event I am going to."

Zainah's eyebrows lifted in surprise. Since she'd started working there, the woman had never spoken to her, except to give an abrupt reply when Zainah greeted her. Usually, all the instructions for the household chores she wanted done were passed to Zainah and the other staff through Mira, the caretaker.

Rania went on, "I'm running late and I won't be able to get into the venue without it." She looked around the living room again and then sighed loudly.

"I'll search for it," Zainah said.

Rania nodded. "It's a cream card with the name 'Rania Rahmani' engraved in gold letters on it." She started to walk away from the living room and then stopped and said to Zainah, "If you find it, please bring it up to my room."

Zainah nodded and then searched diligently for it in the living room. When she didn't find it, she went to the vast dining hall to search for it. But still she didn't see it. She started to leave the dining room, and then frowned when she saw something shiny sticking out from the cream runner on the table. She went and pulled it out and saw it was the invitation card Rania had been searching for.

She quickly began to make her way up the spiraling stairs, holding the ornate banister until she got to the top. She strode to the master bedroom and then paused before she knocked. Rania might be in this room she sometimes shared with her husband, Nabil. But if she wasn't, it would be awkward for Zainah to come in and find only Nabil in the room. She hardly went in to clean up the room before noon. By then, Rania and her husband, who looked the same age as she was, were out of the house.

Zainah decided to go to Rania's room instead. It would be less awkward if Rania wasn't there. She walked down the hallway and then stopped in front of Rania's room. Knocking, she waited until the door opened for her. She entered the room, which was richly decorated in hues of gold and cream. Multiple cream and gold embroidered pillows were scattered everywhere.

She glanced at the bed and then blinked in surprise. Nabil was on the bed, looking up at her.

Zainah greeted him and then quickly turned to Rania.

Rania looked at her with gratitude. "You found it. Where did you see it?"

She handed the card to her boss. "I found it in the dining hall."

"Thank you," Rania said and then turned to her husband. "I'll see you when I get back." She left the room and Zainah hurried out behind her.

Zainah finished cleaning up the house hours later, except for Rania's room. She'd kept looking out to see if Nabil would exit the room, but for some reason, he didn't go out today, neither did he leave the room. She put away the cleaning supplies and started to leave the house to go back to her own room when Mira hurried up to her.

"Master Nabil wants you to come and clean Madam Rania's room now."

"Oh… okay. I didn't know he had left the room. I would have gone to clean it up if I had known."

"He's still there," Mira said. "Go now." She went away before Zainah could say anything more.

As Zainah climbed up the stairs with the cleaning supplies, she wondered why Nabil would call her to clean the room when he was still in it. Maybe he is preparing to go out now, she thought to herself. For some reason she didn't understand, she felt nervous.

She knocked on the door. When she heard him say, "Enter," she opened the door and entered the room. Her anxiety increased when she saw he was still on the bed. She gave him a nervous smile and then said, "Mira told me you wanted me to clean the room now. But since you are still here, I can come back later."

"No, I want you to clean the room now."

She pressed her lips together and then decided to start with the en-suite bathroom. She cleaned the bathroom slowly, hoping he would have left by the time she came into the room again. When she couldn't keep cleaning anymore, she took a deep breath and went back to the bedroom. He was still there, lounging on the bed. She turned her back to him and began to arrange the dresser.

"What is your name again?" he asked in a deep voice that had inspired awe in her when she'd first started working here, but now scared her.

"Zainah, sir," she said, without turning to look at him.

"Turn around," he ordered.

She did, her heart racing.

She squirmed as his eyes traveled the length of her. "You are beautiful," he said, in a voice laden with admiration. "I could look at you all day long."

She shut her eyes briefly as panic took hold of her. What is happening here, Lord? She opened her eyes to find him still staring intently at her. She wanted to bolt out of the room, but she decided it would not be the best course of action to take. Instead, she stood her ground and asked boldly, "May I leave now? I won't be able to clean the room properly if you are still here, sir. I can come back later."

He narrowed his eyes and stared at her for a few more seconds. And then he nodded. "You may leave and come back later."

She hurried out of the room and out of the house. When she got to her room, she finally released her breath. She sat on her bed and looked around the room. Thankfully, Leila had gone out again. She didn't want to have to explain why she was trembling. Nabil had gazed at her as though he wanted to devour her. She had been so scared that he was going to jump her... or something similar.

She took in deep breaths until she stopped trembling and her heart rate normalized. She covered her face with her hands and considered quitting the job. But she quickly put the idea out of her mind. She desperately needed this job for her and Leila's upkeep, and also, she needed this place they lived in for free. Most of all, she needed the weekly money she was paid—and good money for that matter—to find Faizan. Quitting was out of the question.

I'll just have to avoid Nabil as best as I can, she thought. She would not go back to the house today, even though he had asked her to return later to clean up Rania's room. Instead, she would spend the day praying for protection and asking God's wisdom to know how to keep avoiding Nabil. Soon, with God's help, she would save enough money to live off of for some time and find Faizan. Then, she would quit.

TEN

Faizan stood at Trisha's front door and rang the bell. Trisha had called him on the phone the previous day and asked him to come to her house in the morning. When he'd jokingly asked if she was throwing a party, he was surprised when she'd answered, "Something like that." She had then told him that she had something very important to announce to everyone. Since it was a Saturday, and Audrey and Sienna would be in Rosefield with their spouses, she had said it was the perfect time to share her news with everyone.

He'd left Audrey and Ken in the house, as Audrey had kept insisting that she didn't want to go while Ken tried to change her mind. Audrey had told him earlier that she suspected Trisha was planning to marry Stan again, and that she couldn't attend what she was guessing was their surprise engagement party.

He smiled as Trisha opened the door for him and stepped in, hoping he wouldn't find Stan in the house. With all his heart, he prayed that Audrey's suspicions were unfounded. After all, he'd heard about Stan and how he'd treated Trisha; it would be unthinkable for her to marry him again. He strongly believed in second chances, having been granted that himself, but he wasn't sure Stan had changed.

He breathed a sigh of relief when he walked into the living room and Stan was nowhere in sight. However, a delicious aroma permeated the air and there were bottles of drinks and glasses on the dining table.

He sat down on the couch and said to Trisha, "So, what are you celebrating?"

Trisha looked nervous as she sat facing him. "Umm… you will see. Where are Audrey and Ken?"

"They are in the house. I'm not sure they are coming." He leaned forward and searched her eyes. "Audrey thinks that you are planning to remarry…" His brows shot up as Stan walked into the living room holding a spatula in one hand and Ruby in the other. "…Stan!"

Faizan stared at Stan. He had obviously been in Trisha's kitchen, cooking. For almost a minute, he and Stan stared at each other, and then Stan looked away.

"Trisha, please watch Ruby," Stan said, handing off Ruby to her. "She came into the kitchen while I was cooking and I don't want her to be hurt."

Trisha avoided Faizan's eyes and lifted Ruby into her arms. Stan left the living room again and Faizan turned to Trisha.

"Tell me it's not true, Trish. Tell me you are not planning to remarry that guy!"

"I am," Trisha said, and kissed Ruby's cheeks.

She looked at Faizan and said, "Please don't try to talk me out of it. My mind is already made up."

"You can't be serious, Trisha. And you might alienate Audrey. She is really upset right now at the thought that you want to marry Stan again."

"It's my decision to make. I just want you to support me."

Ruby wriggled out of Trisha's arms and crawled to Faizan. He lifted her up, sat her on his knees, and then looked at Trisha again. He wanted to ask her why she thought this was a good idea, but the look in her eyes stopped him. She was gazing at him with a look that clearly said she was weary. He would only add to her distress if he voiced his concerns right now. Maybe he would let it be for now, and then tell her how he really felt later on. He sighed and said nothing more.

Five minutes later, the doorbell rang and he told Trisha he would get it. He handed Ruby back to her and went to open the door. He grinned at Sienna and Bryan who stood there, smiling. When they came in, he hugged Bryan and then folded Sienna into his arms.

She patted his back and then pulled away.

Bryan and Sienna hugged Trisha. Sienna carried Ruby and went to sit beside Bryan.

Trisha said, "How are you, Sienna?"

"Great. Just tired of the constant morning sickness. If I have to puke here later on, please forgive me." Bryan took her hand and squeezed it. She smiled sweetly at him and then said to Trisha, "The house smells nice. What are you cooking up and what are we celebrating?"

Faizan pressed his lips tightly together to keep

from blurting out the concerns in his heart.

Trisha answered, "I want to wait until everyone is here before sharing my news."

Sienna looked at Bryan and then faced Trisha again. "We also have news to share with everyone, but it will have to wait until another day. This is a celebration after all, and I don't want to ruin it."

Trisha frowned and Faizan's heart jumped. "What is it?" he asked Sienna. "Are you okay?"

"Is the baby fine?" Trisha asked, a worried expression on her face.

Sienna smiled. "Guys, stop worrying. I'm sorry I scared you. I'm fine, really. It's not something bad. It's just… umm… different." She waved her hand in a dismissive manner, clearly to prevent any more questions. "Where is Audrey, anyway?"

"She hasn't come yet," Trisha quickly said.

"So, Trish, won't you tell us what you are celebrating today?" Bryan asked. "I know it's not your birthday."

The doorbell rang and Sienna jumped up before Faizan could stand. "I'll answer it. It's probably Audrey." Seconds later, she came back to the living room.

Faizan lifted his brows when he saw Lauren trailing behind Sienna. He stifled a desire to groan and then smiled back when Lauren smiled sweetly at him. She hugged Trisha and greeted Bryan. When she came to sit beside him, Faizan forced himself not to shift away.

Many of Trisha's friends arrived after that, but Audrey and Ken were still absent.

The living room bustled with people. A few minutes later, when Stan came out into the living room, the place immediately fell silent. And then, a few people began to whisper amongst themselves.

Faizan sighed sadly as Trisha went to stand beside Stan. He looked at Sienna. She was staring at Trisha and Stan in disbelief. She had probably guessed by now what this surprise party was about. A few of Trisha's friends had their mouths open in obvious shock. Clearly, no one had thought that Trisha would ever take Stan back; not after what he did to her.

Trisha said, "Everyone, thanks for coming." She looked around the living room, her eyes searching for something or someone. Faizan guessed she was looking for Audrey. She sighed and then continued. "I called you all here to share my happy news." She shook her head and then took Stan's hand. "No, our happy news. Stan and I are getting married again and I would appreciate everyone's support."

The room began to buzz. Trisha's best friend, Paula, said loudly, "Trish! No. You can't be serious!"

Trisha ignored her.

Sienna walked up to Trisha and took her hand. She whispered something to her and Trisha shook her head vigorously. Sienna looked disappointed as she walked back to stand at Bryan's side.

The buzz grew louder until Trisha began to tap her glass with a spoon to get everyone's attention. When silence reigned again, she said, "Please, I know most people don't understand my decision, but at least celebrate with me as my friends. And if you've ever trusted my judgment, then please trust that my decision wasn't made lightly. All I want is everyone's support."

She went in with Stan after that and came out

minutes later with the refreshments. Everyone soon separated into pairs and groups around the living room, with drinks and snacks in their hands.

Lauren came to stand beside Faizan as he poured himself a glass of limeade. He turned to her and offered to pour her a drink. She accepted and he handed her a glassful.

Lauren said to him, "I understand the shock everyone felt just now when Trisha announced her engagement. It's almost like me announcing to my friends and family that I wanted to marry my ex-husband again." Her eyes suddenly filled with a deep fear, and Faizan blinked.

"Your ex-husband cheated on you?"

She laughed harshly. "No… he never did. He just used to physically abuse me. He got angry at almost everything I did and beat me up every chance he got."

Faizan's heart went out to her. He was surprised at the anger he felt toward her ex. He had been a violent man in his past life but he'd never hit a woman. "Ken told me you came from an abusive marriage, but I didn't know it was that serious."

She sighed wearily and then began to narrate her story to him. He listened with growing dismay and anger. When she finished, he felt like taking her in his arms and comforting her. She had tears in her eyes as she said, "I vowed I would never give my heart away to any man after the divorce." She looked at him and smiled. "At least, until I met you."

He looked away from her and raked his fingers through his hair, completely lost for words. Finally, he turned back to her and said, "Lauren, you are a really nice girl. And you are very pretty. But, my heart already belongs to someone else. I'm so sorry."

She looked away, and for a full minute she didn't respond. At last, she faced him and smiled sadly. "I understand. I think you are a great guy, and that someone, whoever she is, is a very lucky girl. I truly envy her."

He put his hand on her arm and said softly, "You'll meet a great guy soon. Someone who will love you and treat you well… not like your ex did."

She nodded.

He smiled widely to lift the tension in the air and said, "I hope you will come to our welfare meeting on Thursday."

She returned his smile. "I wouldn't miss it for all the world."

*****

Zainah looked up excitedly as Leila walked into their room. She clapped her hands. "Leila, guess what? I have almost saved enough money to pay that investigator Fatima told me about. After I'm paid for this week, I'll finally have enough money to hire the man and then soon, by God's grace, Faizan will be found and we will be reunited."

Leila gave her a small smile, not the grin she had expected.

Zainah frowned as Leila took off her clothes without saying a word and changed into her nightdress. She lay down on the bed and covered her face with the pillow.

"What's wrong, Leila?" Zainah asked, worried about her friend and feeling a little guilty. Since she'd started working for the Rahmanis, she'd become so busy and preoccupied that she'd stopped checking in on Leila. They hadn't even had a full conversation for over two weeks.

Leila lifted her head briefly and said, "Nothing. Please switch off the light as soon as you can." She lay back down and covered her head with the pillow again.

Zainah shook her head. "Something is wrong, Leila." She put her hand on Leila's shoulder. "I won't let you rest until you tell me what it is."

Leila sighed loudly and sat up. "Ibrahim and I broke up yesterday."

"Ibrahim… who is Ibrahim? Oh! The man you've been seeing for some time now." Zainah hid her relief and asked, "What happened?"

"He tried to get me to… umm… sleep with him. When I refused, he said I was useless to him and that he wasn't interested in a relationship with me anymore."

"I'm so sorry, Leila."

Leila bit her lip. "I was beginning to fall for him." Tears slipped down her cheeks and she wiped them off quickly. "I guess I have to keep looking."

Zainah took Leila's hands. "You know, you really don't. Why don't you commit your desire into the Lord's hands? Remember, He said that if we delight ourselves in Him, He would give us the desires of our hearts."

"You think I haven't?" Leila stared at her. "I'm thirty-one, Zainah. I've been a Christian since I was a teenager. You think I haven't tried to delight myself in the Lord while waiting patiently for Him to answer my prayer? I have, but it hasn't worked. Perhaps the Lord isn't particularly interested in handing out life partners, especially to people like me."

"What do you mean, to people like you? You are His child and He cares about you."

"I know all that. I just think God isn't interested in giving me a husband, and so I have to look for one myself."

"And what if the one you find is an awful person? Maybe he hides his real character until you get married and then you see his true colors. What will you do then? I think you should just leave it all to the Lord."

"It's easier said than done, Zainah. I'm running out of time. Soon, I won't be able to have children and what I want most is to be a mother."

Zainah pressed her lips together. She didn't know what to tell Leila anymore.

Leila lay back down and turned her back to Zainah. "Please turn off the light when you are ready to go to sleep."

Zainah sighed, turned off the light, lay down on the bed, and soon fell asleep.

The next day, she got ready and went to work while Leila was still sleeping. The moon was still in the sky when she stepped out of her room. She walked briskly and reached the Rahmani mansion moments later. Only two of the household staff, one being Mira, were up and about.

Since the incident with Nabil, Zainah had started coming to work very early. By the time her employers woke up, she was already through with the house, except for their rooms. She usually made herself scarce so she wouldn't run into Nabil. Once he and Rania left the house, she then went to clean their rooms.

She went into the storeroom where the household cleaning supplies and equipment were kept. Gathering the ones she needed, she took them out of the store and went to the kitchen to start working.

Four hours later, at about nine o'clock, she had cleaned the entire house except for her bosses' rooms. She carried her cleaning gear up the stairs and went into the family gym where she usually stayed to wait for her employers to leave the house. Standing behind the curtain so she would not be seen, she looked out the window, watching and waiting for when Rania and Nabil would come out of the house.

Fifteen minutes later, Rania came out dressed in a long, lilac gown and a matching turban. She got into the back of her car and her driver drove away. Nabil came out ten minutes later and was driven away in his black Mercedes.

Zainah heaved a sigh of relief and came out from behind the curtain. She carried her gear to Rania's room and cleaned the entire room and bathroom in an hour. She went to the master bedroom and started cleaning the bathroom first. Soon, she heard the bedroom door open, and assuming it was Mira, continued cleaning. Two minutes later, when Mira still hadn't come into the bathroom, she went out to see what the caretaker wanted.

Her breath caught in her throat at the sight of Nabil standing in the middle of the room, staring at her. She forced a smile and greeted him. "Good morning, sir. I thought you had left."

He gave her a sly smile. "Of course you did. You

have been avoiding me for weeks now. I've finally caught you."

Her heart began to race in fear as she looked at him. The lustful look in his eyes told her clearly what his intentions were. She looked at the door and began to mentally calculate how she was going to get past him. She decided to distract him. Turning toward the bathroom, she forced herself to be calm and said, "There is something clogging the sink. Can you take a look at it?"

He smiled smugly, clearly his way of letting her know that he knew what she was trying to do. "I'll look at it later on. I'm more interested in looking at you now," he began to walk toward her, "and touching you."

She desperately whispered under her breath, "Lord, please help me." She waited for him to reach her and then dived for the door. She twisted the handle but it did not open. He had locked it. She shook the door in frustration and then turned to glare at him.

"Open the door now or I'll scream!"

He laughed. "No one is going to hear you. I sent everyone away on errands."

She began to suck in deep breaths as terror gripped her. "Please let me go."

Like a flash of lightning, he reached her and grabbed her hands. "I'm not going to hurt you, Zainah. I just want us to enjoy..."

She kicked him as hard as she could in the stomach, and he doubled over. He groaned as he held his belly and she frantically searched his pants pocket for the key. Finding it, she unlocked the door. Quickly, before he could recover, she ran out of the room and down the stairs. She bolted out of the house, ran to the staff quarters, and entered her room. Leila was still in her nightgown, roaming the room aimlessly.

Zainah yelled, "Leila, pack your things now! We're leaving!"

"What!" Leila's face contorted with confusion.

Zainah threw open the closet, brought out a traveling bag, and began to grab the small number of clothes she had. She dumped them into the bag, along with her two pairs of shoes. She looked up at Leila, who was still staring at her, a perplexed look on her face.

"Leila, I said you should get your things. We are leaving this place right now!"

"Why?" Leila asked, unmoving.

Zainah said, "I'll explain later, but we need to leave now. Before..." She stopped talking and began to bring out Leila's clothes as well. She dumped them on the bed. "Here are your clothes, Leila. Pack them up into a bag now!"

She quickly zipped up her own traveling bag and then looked at Leila, who was slowly packing her bag while grumbling.

"I don't even know why we are packing, Zainah. Can't this wait until tomorrow?"

Zainah sighed in frustration as she watched Leila packing her things very slowly. She went out to the door, opened it, and looked out. Thankfully, Nabil was nowhere in sight. But who knew when he would decide to come after her? She went back to Leila and saw that her friend had stopped packing.

"What are you doing, Leila?" she cried. "Why are you not packing your things?"

"I don't want to leave, that's why. How can you suddenly decide…?"

"Nabil tried to rape me!" Zainah said.

Leila's eyes grew round and her mouth fell open. She shook her head and said, "He what?"

"Please, Leila. I'll tell you about it later. Pack up!"

Leila began to pack her things quickly. In just a minute, she said, "I'm through, Zainah. Let's go."

Zainah hastily left the room with Leila. She was thankful no one was around as they ran to the gate. The security men looked at them a little strangely.

One of them stopped her and Leila. Zainah's heart drummed as he looked at their bags and asked, "Are you both leaving?"

She tried to steady her voice as best as she could as she said, "Just running some errands, that's all."

He nodded to the man who manned the gates. Zainah breathed a sigh of relief when the gate opened up for them.

They walked for a long time, on their way to Fatima's house. At last, Leila sighed wearily. "I can't go on anymore with this bag. Can't we take a taxi there?"

Zainah mentally calculated how much she had. Most of her earnings from her housekeeping at the Rahmanis were in the bank account she'd opened when she'd started the job. She had a little cash with her, but she needed all the money she had now. Tears stung her eyes as she realized she wouldn't be able to hire the private investigator anytime soon, as she still didn't have enough money. There was no point keeping what little she had on her, anyway. She might as well get a taxi for both of them before they fainted on the way.

They stood by the road and waited. Soon, a taxi approached and they waved it down. They entered after telling the driver where they were going. They got to Fatima's thirty minutes later.

After Zainah narrated everything that had happened, Fatima shook her head with a mournful look on her face. "I feel so guilty. I wish I had not encouraged you to work for that beast. I should have suspected something when Hadiza told me the Rahmanis' former maid quit so suddenly. I'm so sorry."

"It's not your fault," Zainah said. "You couldn't have known."

Fatima sighed sadly. "Anyway, you are both welcome to stay as long as you like. I hope you will be able to get another job soon."

Zainah nodded. It was imperative that she did or she could kiss finding Faizan goodbye.

ELEVEN

Faizan looked up from his Bible when someone called his name. He had come to the church earlier than usual for the welfare meeting. He'd gone to Trisha's in the afternoon, and since he had stayed a bit longer than usual, he had decided to go straight to church so he wouldn't be late for the meeting.

Lauren stood in front of him, smiling.

He smiled back at her. "Hi, Lauren," he said. "You are early today."

She sat next to him and nodded. "I went to visit the Gibsons and decided to come straight to church rather than go home."

He grinned. "Same here. I went to Trish's house and then came straight here."

"How is Trisha?" Lauren asked. "I haven't seen her since her engagement party."

Faizan shrugged. "She's still with Stan, if that is what you are asking. She and Audrey are at loggerheads these days. Ken must have told you how Audrey is. She says exactly what is on her mind."

Lauren grinned. "I have actually been at the

receiving end of her brutal frankness. She once threatened to shoot me."

Faizan lifted his brows. "What?"

Lauren laughed. "She thought Ken and I were an item. That was before they got married."

Faizan shook his head, amused by the story.

"So, Audrey told Trisha exactly how she feels about her fiancé?" Lauren asked.

Faizan nodded. "Trish was angry with her for not coming to the party and confronted her about it. Audrey told her, amongst other things, that she would not step into her house until she got rid of Stan."

"I don't blame her for saying that. I would if she were my sister, and if I had the guts that Audrey has."

Faizan chuckled. "I guess Audrey says the things that are on our minds but which we are too scared or diplomatic to say." He remembered how brash and unsympathetic he'd been before he'd given his life to Christ and said, "I used to be like Audrey in my past life, but much worse. At least Audrey's brutal honesty comes from a place of love. Mine came from a place of self-aggrandizement and a total lack of empathy."

Images of his past, times when he'd been a total jerk, crossed his mind, and he shuddered. Where would he be if Christ hadn't saved him? He might be dead now and in a place of eternal suffering for all his sins.

Lauren gazed at him with curiosity clearly written on her face. "I've only heard bits and pieces of your testimony. Can you tell me about it?"

He looked up thoughtfully and said to her, "I

don't know if you'll want to hear the details of my life before I met Christ. I don't even want to remember the kind of person I was."

"I can handle it. Just like I told you, I come from a pretty violent past as well."

"I know you do," he said. "But the violence in your past was perpetrated against you. Mine is the other way around. I was terribly violent. Just what you'd expect of a…" He sighed, not wanting to say the word "terrorist."

"If it's too painful for you to tell me, you don't have to."

"It is painful, but I'll tell you. The Lord has delivered me from it all." He gave her a brief but thorough narration of his past. When he was through, he laughed harshly. "I haven't done that in a year. But it's good to remember how far the Lord has brought me."

She shook her head as she gazed at him. Finally, she said, "Wow! What a story. You have truly come a long way."

He smiled and then realized that she was the first person he'd actually told in real detail about his past. Several times, he'd been called upon to tell his testimony in church on Sunday or at mid-week services. He had always kept some of the more violent stories to himself. He blinked. He hadn't even shared his past in such detail with Zainah. He wondered at that. Why had he been so comfortable sharing so much with Lauren when he hadn't with Zainah? He searched his mind but came up with nothing.

He started when Lauren took his hand in hers, and she quickly let go. "I'm sorry," she said, looking embarrassed. "You looked so troubled that I wanted to offer some comfort."

He gave her a small smile. "It's okay. I'm not offended."

Her eyes searched his. "You told me that your heart belonged to another woman. Was she someone you met before you gave your heart to the Lord?"

His heart suddenly filled with pain as he thought of Zainah. He didn't want to talk about her with Lauren. He thinned his lips and then hid a sigh of relief when three other members of their welfare group came into the vestry. "We need to start now," he said to Lauren and stood up. He went to the front of the group just as more members walked in.

He struggled to put away the misery that had settled on him since Zainah had come to his mind a few minutes before. He raised a praise song and his group members joined in. He sang a few lines of the song, but found that nothing could distract him from his despair.

He signaled for his assistant to take over the praise and prayer session and went to sit at the back, misery encircling him.

Is this how my life will continue to go? he thought. Every time something brought Zainah to his mind, he grieved for her as though she were dead. If only he could see her again and at least get some relief from his despair.

He remembered what Audrey had said to him some time before. She'd told him that seeing Zainah now might not bring the relief he thought it would. Audrey believed it would make his pain worse since he would not be able to act on his love for her.

He thought about it for a short while and knew it was true. It would be pure torture to see her again and be reminded that they could never be together. He couldn't touch her the way he wanted, he couldn't kiss her. Most of all, he wouldn't even be able to really tell her he still loved her with all his heart, as he didn't want to interfere in any way with the vow she'd made to God.

Why do you keep torturing yourself like this? he thought. He looked up and the first person he saw was Lauren. Her golden hair swayed back and forth as she danced to the rhythm of the praise song. She lifted her hands in worship and he sighed. Here was a girl who was beautiful, loved God, and liked him. She had actually expressed her desire to date him. Like Trisha had asked him, he wondered why he couldn't just open up his heart to find love with someone else. It was over a year now since he'd seen Zainah. It wasn't like she was going to break her vow to God, nor would he encourage her to do so, and that was if he ever saw her again.

He shut his eyes. Maybe he needed to give Lauren a chance; to give himself a chance to love and be loved by someone other than Zainah.

But his heart rebelled against the thought. He loved Zainah too much, and he knew she loved him, even though they couldn't ever be in a romantic relationship.

When he got home from church, he found Ken alone in the living room.

"Where is Audrey?" he asked.

"She went to Green Valley to see Sienna. I think she'll spend the whole day with her and return tomorrow morning."

Faizan sat across from Ken and looked at him. "You have to help me, man. I'm going crazy thinking about Zainah. Please call Jake."

Ken shook his head. "I'm not calling Jake anymore. You call him yourself. You remember what he said the last time you told me to call him because of your Zainah. He flat out refused your request to see her."

"Ken, you have to try again," Faizan pleaded. "If I thought he would listen to me, I would call him myself. But I know he won't. He's your friend, so he's bound to at least hear you out. I need to see Zainah, or at least speak to her on the phone. I know he can make that happen."

Ken shrugged. "I don't know, Faizan. Okay, I'll try to call Jake, but I don't think his answer will be different from what he told me last time."

Faizan stared intently at Ken, and Ken raised his brows. "Oh… you want me to call him right now?"

"Yes," Faizan said. "Please."

Ken looked weary. He sighed loudly and then picked up his cellphone from the coffee table. Faizan watched as he dialed a number and then put the phone to his ear. A few seconds later, he said, "Hi, Jake. I'm calling because of my brother in-law." He paused and then sighed. "Yes, that one."

He told Jake about Faizan's request.

Faizan had not spoken to him for a long time, but as Ken argued with the man, Faizan decided he needed to speak to Jake himself.

"Let me talk to him," he said to Ken, as his brother in-law didn't seem to be getting anywhere with Jake.

Ken sighed again and handed Faizan the phone. Without mincing words, Faizan told Jake about his quandary concerning Zainah and that he needed to see her.

"I have already told Ken that it's not going to happen. You can't leave the country."

Faizan had fully expected the reply Jake gave him. He went to his plan B. "You have operatives all over that region. Send one of them with a phone to the women's camp so I can at least speak to Zainah and know she's okay."

Jake didn't say anything for some seconds, and then he said, "Okay. It's not my priority right now… but if I find someone we trust over there, I'll let you know. We can arrange for you to talk to your friend then."

Jake's answer seemed slightly evasive to Faizan, but he knew it was the best he was going to get for now. He exhaled and then said, "Okay then. Thanks."

When the call ended, Faizan looked at Ken and shook his head. "Well, I guess I'll just have to keep my fingers crossed and hope Jake keeps his word. But if I don't hear from him in two weeks' time, I'm going to have to contact him again."

Ken nodded. "Yeah! I guess all you can do right now is to keep your fingers crossed."

A thought flashed through Faizan's mind. *Here is what you can do right now. You can just move on!*

He shut his eyes to get rid of the thought. He wasn't going to move on.

His emotions continued to roil as the logical part of him kept telling him he needed to move on, while his heart held on tightly to the woman he loved dearly. He knew holding on meant continued misery, but he couldn't help it. He decided as he went to his room that he would find a way to see Zainah, or at least speak to her, with or without Jake's help. Even if that later left his heart in tatters.

TWELVE

Sienna opened the door and grinned when she saw her sister there, a duffel bag in her hand. Audrey had already told her on the phone that she was coming to spend the day with her. Since then, she'd been waiting excitedly for Audrey to arrive.

Sienna hugged her sister and then chuckled as Audrey bent down and rubbed her belly. "You haven't added any weight, Sienna," she said. "But you are super slim anyway, so I guess you might not even add much until you are almost ready to give birth to your baby."

"I probably will way before then," Sienna said. She sat down on the couch and Audrey sat beside her.

"Where is Bryan?" Audrey asked.

"He's taking a nap. We went to see his parents this morning. His brother was there with his wife and four kids. Bryan played with those boisterous kids throughout our visit. I think they tired him out."

Audrey laughed. "He better get used to spending

time with kids. I know you want lots of children."

"I do… and so does he." Sienna's smile widened. "I'm so happy that you came to spend the day with me, Audrey. But I feel a little sorry for Ken. He'll miss you."

Audrey chuckled. "He'll survive. Besides, we sometimes have to spend a full day apart when I come to Rosefield before he does or vice versa."

Sienna sighed sadly. "You both are so lucky to be able to move back and forth between Rosefield and Miami."

Audrey's eyes pierced hers. "You look sad suddenly, Sienna. What's wrong?"

Sienna looked away from Audrey's gaze and wondered whether to tell her about the move or wait until she and Bryan could tell everyone at the same time. Audrey wasn't on very good terms with Trisha now and Sienna knew it was killing her. Telling her that she was moving from the country would only add to Audrey's distress. Still, she couldn't keep hiding it. She and Bryan would be moving in about a month.

She finally opened her mouth to tell her and then changed her mind again. It was better to tell her, Ken, Trish, and Faizan at the same time. What was most important now was mending the rift between her sisters before she left for South America. She said, "It's just that I'm worried about this fight between you and Trisha. You guys need to end it."

Audrey frowned. "I'm not fighting with her. I'm just not willing to pretend that everything is all right when she's decided to marry Stan again. Stan the professional adulterer, Sienna! Why would she ever get back with him?" She looked at Sienna with an incredulous expression on her face.

"I know," Sienna sighed wearily. "I hate that she's back with him, but what can we do? We can only support her even if we don't agree with her decision. The solution is not to stop talking to her, Audrey. She needs us more than ever now. And will you cut off Ruby as well because of Stan?"

"I don't plan to permanently cut off Trish or Ruby. I just want her to come to her senses and leave Stan. I think every day of how heartbroken Frank Kessler is."

"Frank. He's back in Boise, isn't he?"

Audrey nodded. "He was supposed to stay in Rosefield for a month to try to win Trish's heart while also overseeing the building of his restaurant, but Trisha's rejection made him cut his stay abruptly. He left the day after Trish told him she wasn't interested in him. He knew Trish was planning to get back with Stan. The last time I called him, he didn't sound like his usual self. I think Trish has finally broken him."

Sienna shook her head. "Stop it, Audrey! That can't be true. He was probably just stressed out or something the day you talked to him."

"No, I don't think so. His heart is irreparably broken."

"Audrey… that is so not true! Besides, you can't blame Trish for that. It's not like you can force her to develop feelings for Frank when she doesn't have them. She loves Stan. You can't choose who you love."

"Yes, you can!"

"Umm… no, you can't! Did you choose to love Ken or did you fall in love with him?"

"I did fall in love with him… but only because I chose to. I got to know Ken and found out he was a great guy. I knew my heart would be safe with him. And love is not just a feeling. It's a choice. You can choose to fall in love or not to fall in love with someone. Trish knows that Stan is a terrible guy. She could have chosen not to fall for him again."

Sienna gazed at her sister, knowing she was right. "I guess I was really lucky with Bryan, then. I didn't really know that it was my choice to fall in love or not fall in love with him when I met him. Thankfully, he is a great guy and easy to fall in love with."

Audrey nodded. "That's what I'm saying. Why would Trisha fall for someone who has proven to her over and over again that her heart isn't safe with him?"

"You know what, Audrey? I think the reason Trish wants to remarry Stan now has little to do with her falling in love with him as her having a father for Ruby. She's told me on several occasions that the most important thing to her is for Ruby to be raised with a father and mother. I think she chose to get back with Stan because he is Ruby's biological dad."

"Just because he's Ruby's biological father doesn't mean he is fit to be a dad. He's not been in the child's life for over a year, for goodness' sake! He wasn't even there when she was born." Audrey looked up with a thoughtful expression. "Frank is a great guy and he loves kids. I think he would have made a great father for Ruby."

"Will you stop with the 'Frank is this' and 'Frank will do that'? She isn't interested in Frank and we all need to accept that."

Audrey put her hand on her forehead. "Fine! I won't talk about Frank anymore."

"And will you try to reconcile with Trish?"

"If you are asking me to visit her when Stan is almost living in the house now, then no, I won't!"

"Audrey!"

"Okay, I guess I can invite her out to lunch or something."

"Promise you will do that. For my sake…" she clamped her mouth shut as she realized she'd almost given away her secret.

Audrey shifted closer to her and looked her in the eye. "What are you hiding, little sister?"

Sienna huffed. No one could get anything past Audrey. She pressed her lips together and didn't say anything.

"Tell me, Sienna. What is it?"

"Okay," Sienna said wearily. "Bryan and I are moving… to Peru."

Audrey's eyes grew wide with shock. She shook her head slowly and then said, "Tell me you are joking, Sienna. Please."

"I'm not. He was offered a ministry position in South America and we are moving there by month's end."

"No… no… no! You aren't going anywhere. Where is that Bryan?" Audrey stood up. "Let me ask him why he wants to take my sister away to another country."

Sienna looked up at Audrey in alarm. "Please leave my husband alone. He's not taking me away. I agreed wholeheartedly to follow him."

Audrey looked down at her as though she had

lost her mind.

"Sit down, Audrey. You're making me nervous."

Audrey slowly sat. She frowned at Sienna and said, "Why would Bryan even think of accepting such a position?"

"He's sure it's God's will for us, and you know Bryan hears the Lord's voice clearly. I didn't want to go at first, but I have decided to submit to God's will for us and go without any fuss."

"But you are pregnant!"

"They have good medical facilities there, too."

Audrey shook her head as though she hadn't heard anything Sienna had said.

"What will I do without you?" she suddenly cried out.

Sienna's heart began to break again. This was why she'd been so devastated when Bryan had told her about the move. She would miss her siblings so much, and they would miss her, too. She felt bad for being the one to cause Audrey so much misery. "I'll call every day, Audrey. It will be fine."

"It won't be the same!"

"I know." Sienna put her arms around her sister and listened as Audrey moaned and grumbled. At last, after she was spent, she gave a long sigh and settled her head on Sienna's shoulder. "I just won't think about it right now," she said. "I'll just pretend that you will always be here until you leave."

Sienna rubbed Audrey's back comfortingly but didn't say anything.

One down, two to go, she thought grimly. If this was the reaction she was going to get when she told Trish about her move, she wasn't looking forward to it. Neither was she looking forward to the move, but her heart was still made up. She would go to the ends of the Earth with her husband, because he was totally worth it.

*****

Zainah flopped down on Fatima's sofa, tired after another day of combing the town for any kind of available work. She sighed and then shut her eyes and prayed for the umpteenth time since the day began. "Lord, please help me find a job." She felt hopeless as she prayed. She'd been searching for work for a long time now, and still hadn't found any.

Fatima came into the living room and smiled sympathetically at her. "Nothing, still?"

"Nothing. I'm losing hope, Fatima."

"Don't lose hope. You'll find something soon." Fatima touched her shoulder and then went back into the kitchen.

Zainah sighed again and went into the bedroom she and Leila shared. She raised her brows in surprise when she saw Leila sitting on the bed. Usually, Leila left the house in the mornings to God knew where and came back in the evenings. She had stopped asking where her friend went, even though she had her suspicions, because every time she'd questioned her in the past, it had always resulted in a fight.

Leila looked up at her. "No luck today again?"

Zainah sat on the bed and shook her head. A sudden resentment rose up in her. Why was she the only one trying to get a job? The amount she had saved up to hire an investigator when she'd worked for the Rahmanis was depleting fast because she had to take care of not just her needs but Leila's as well. She'd helped Fatima, who was a single mother, with part of the rent and food. Leila had also gotten money from her for "very important expenses."

She tried to push down her resentment but it refused to budge. Finally, she said to Leila, "Where do you go every day? You could also be looking for a job like I am."

Leila looked away and said, "I have no skills. What kind of job could I get? And if you haven't found one, what makes you think I'll have better luck finding a job?"

"You don't need any skills, really, to find a job as a…"

"Don't say maid!" Leila exclaimed. "I'm not like you. I can't work as someone's personal servant."

Anger boiled in Zainah's stomach and threatened to spill out of her mouth. She pushed it down and said to Leila, "Well, we don't have a choice. The money I saved up to find Faizan has almost run out because I used it to help Fatima with rent and food. You also took some of it, if you need me to remind you. I need to get a job fast and so do you."

Leila turned to her with guilt clearly written on her face. "You told me at the camp that your father is wealthy. Why don't you go to your family and ask your father for the money you need?"

Zainah's jaw dropped as Leila spoke. She could say nothing but stare at her friend. After a long moment, she finally found her voice. "Are you out of your mind, Leila? You want me to return to the family who ostracized me and actually chased me out of my town because of my faith?"

Leila shrugged. "I think by now your family would regret chasing you out from your community. They haven't seen you in, like, what… ten or eleven years? By now, they will miss you terribly. When you go back, they will be so happy that they'll give you anything you want." She stood up from the bed and began to shed her clothes.

Zainah bit her lip. She felt slightly tempted to do what Leila was telling her to do, but she knew it was madness. There was no way she was going back to her old community and her family.

Why not, though? a voice in her head asked. After all, you miss them very much.

She thought about it some more. Maybe Leila is right. Maybe I should go back, especially if I want to get the money to hire the investigator and ultimately find Faizan.

But she gradually rejected the idea. Her small town was a very strict Islamic community and her family was the same. That was why they had ostracized her and ultimately driven her out. She doubted they'd changed. Who knew what they would do to her now if she returned?

She went out of the room into the kitchen to help Fatima with the cooking.

As she tidied up after Fatima had finished cooking the evening meal, she thought about what Leila had said. She needed money desperately and Leila's idea, dangerous as it was, was starting to take root in her heart.

She continued to think about going back to her family, not just because of the money she needed, but because she missed them and wanted to see them again.

By the time she sat at the table to eat dinner with Fatima and both her children hours later, she had uprooted the thought of going back to her community from her mind. In spite of how badly she wanted the money in order to find Faizan, and how much she missed her family, it was too dangerous. It would threaten her faith. She had to keep searching for a job and pray earnestly that the Lord would help her find one soon. That was her only option now.

THIRTEEN

Faizan drove out of the soup kitchen parking lot after hours of volunteer work at the place. He was with three other members of the welfare department, including Lauren.

Lauren sat beside him in the passenger seat while the other two sat in the back of his car. From time to time, he listened in on their conversation, which revolved round a rumor about a TV crew planning to shoot a reality show in Rosefield. However, his mind mostly stayed on Zainah and the request he'd made to his handler. Jake had yet to get back to him.

"What do you think about that, Faizan?"

He lifted his brows and turned to Lauren, who had asked the question. "Umm... sorry, what do I think about what?"

She gave him a half-smile. "You weren't listening, Faizan? Jenny asked if any of us would ever agree to star in a reality show. I said it depends on what the show was about and I asked what you thought about it."

He shrugged. "I guess my answer will be the

same as yours… though I'd probably not."

They continued to chat while his mind strayed again. What's Zainah doing right now? He wondered. Life in the women's camp was somewhat regimented, at least from what he'd observed when he was there. It was noon where she was. That meant she would either be preparing lunch for the whole camp if it was her turn to do so, or getting water for the women whose turn it was to cook.

Or she could be tending to some other poor hurt guy who has strayed into the camp, like she tended to you.

His heart suddenly twisted with jealousy at the thought, and then he tried to brush away the irrational feeling. It was unlikely that another hurt guy would come or be found near the camp like he had been. And even if that was the case, and as the camp nurse she had to take care of the guy, she wouldn't fall in love with him.

She had told him that she loved him before he'd left the camp. She wasn't the type of woman to throw that word around or fall out of love so quickly. And there was also her vow of chastity. She'd fallen for him even though she hadn't wanted to. Surely, she still loved him just as he loved her.

Still, the worrying thought that she might have fallen out of love with him didn't leave his mind. He got to the church parking lot and everyone got out and headed to their various cars. Everyone except for Lauren.

He sat waiting for her to exit the car so he could go home. When she didn't, he turned curiously to her and found that she was looking at him.

"You were quiet throughout the drive back

here," she said to him. "I guess you have a lot on your mind."

"I do," he said to her.

"Do you want to share? Talking about it can help."

"It's not something I really want to talk about right now," he said apologetically.

She gave him a sad smile. "That's okay. I think I can guess what it is, though."

He raised his brows quizzically as he looked at her. "You can?"

"Yes. You are thinking about that woman you're in love with. I can see it in your eyes." She sighed. "That is one lucky woman."

Faizan chuckled. "I don't know about that. I'm sure if she could choose right now, she would shed her love for me. Unfortunately, even though we both love each other very much, we can't be together."

Lauren nodded. "Because of the distance."

"Umm… not just that. It's really more complicated than just the fact that we live thousands of miles apart."

"Oh," Lauren gazed at him. "I understand how complicated matters of the heart can be. I was in love with a man who abused me for years and I refused to leave him until he almost killed me."

Faizan blinked at this new revelation from her. He hadn't known her ex-husband's abuse had been as serious as almost taking her life. He shook his head as he looked at her. "That had to be so tough for you."

She nodded. "Many people I knew didn't understand why I stayed with him. I don't think I fully understood why either. At least, not until now. I just thought it was because I loved him. But I now realize it was because I was afraid no one would love me the way he had supposedly loved me. I strangely believed his jealous fits of anger were due to how much he cared for me and that he couldn't control himself because of that."

"We sometimes make excuses for the inexcusable," he said, as he remembered his past life and how he'd justified the things he had done; how he'd also justified Mustafa and looked up to him as his hero. In that way, he could totally relate to what Lauren was saying.

She nodded. "For a while after Richie, my ex-husband, went to jail, I blamed myself. If I hadn't called Ken the night he was arrested, he would not be locked up in prison. I had to learn as the months went by that he deserved what he got."

He sighed. "I deserved the same thing your ex got and even worse, but the Lord delivered me. I am forever grateful for that, but once in a while I feel guilty for not getting the punishment I was supposed to. Many times, though, I feel this separation between the woman I love and me is the punishment I deserve."

She looked intently at him. "I was holding on to so much pain because I felt like I deserved it, but I learned to let it all go. I think you should as well."

He shook his head. "But that's the thing. You didn't deserve the pain. I did. I do."

She asked softly, "And are you sure that isn't the reason why you're still holding on to that woman even though you know you'll never be able to be together?"

He blinked. "I am holding on because I love her with all my heart."

"I understand that. But you are also living the life of a martyr now. If you never open your heart to love again, you might spend the rest of your life holding on to a love that will never be."

He looked away from her, knowing she was talking about him opening up his heart to her. She was still interested in him even though she knew his heart belonged to another woman. He turned to her again and said as softly as he could, "Lauren, I'll ask you a question of my own. You know I love someone else. Even if I decide to date you, are you sure you want to be in a relationship with a man whose heart belongs to another woman?"

She answered, "Yes. Because I know you are worth it. I know that when you love, it's intense, true, and strong. And I want that. Since you've told me that you and the woman you love now will never be able to be together for whatever reason, I will gladly stick around and show you just how much I care about you, until you start to feel the same way about me. I'll pray every day that you will come to love me as much as you love Zainah now."

He gaped at her as he absorbed the intensity of her words and the look in her eyes.

She smiled sadly at him and said, "I'll see you tomorrow, Faizan." She opened the door and stepped out of the car. Shutting it, she walked away.

His eyes followed her until she disappeared out of sight, and then he realized he'd been holding his breath as she spoke. He exhaled and started his car. He drove home thinking about what she'd said. Was he holding on to his love for Zainah, even though he knew there was no future for them, because he wanted to punish himself for his many sins? Maybe it was truly time to let her go and focus on what, or rather, who he had right now. Lauren was a great girl and she wasn't afraid to tell him how she felt about him.

Lord, please show me what to do, he prayed silently.

He got home and went straight to his room to change into something more comfortable. As he put on a white T-shirt, his cellphone vibrated in his pocket. He brought it out and clicked on the message icon on the screen. And then his heart sank. The message was from Jake and it read: Faizan, someone was sent to check that women's camp you talked about. Your Zainah wasn't there. The man we sent was told that she left the camp weeks ago for an unknown destination. She hasn't been seen since then.

He slowly sat on the bed as his insides twisted. Lord, where can she be?

An intense fear gripped him as his mind flooded with images of her dead somewhere, her body bloating under the desert sun. He shook his head to try to clear his mind of the gruesome image, but it remained.

He cried out, "Lord, please protect her. I love her so much!"

Get a hold of yourself, man! He took a deep breath. Maybe she had finally decided to leave the camp because she missed the outside world or her family. But his mind wouldn't agree. She'd told him once that she would never leave the camp.

But then again, she could have changed her

mind. And if she had changed her mind, where exactly had she gone? Again, the fear that she was hurt returned, and he shut his eyes. All he could do now was pray that she was safe and that she would go back to the camp; because if she didn't, he might never have the chance to see or speak to her again.

*****

Zainah entered the small, unpainted house with her heart beating fast. She looked around her surroundings as the woman of the house, a strict-looking young woman, told her to take a seat. Compared to the Rahmanis, this house looked like an empty cubicle. She hadn't expected the house to be this small, or the surroundings so bare.

She'd heard about a woman who was searching for a nanny and housekeeper from one of the members of the prayer group she attended with Fatima. The lady from the prayer group had told her she didn't know the woman looking for a nanny personally, but had heard about her from a relative. She had given Zainah the relative's number and the girl she'd spoken to over the phone had, in turn, given her this woman's number. When Zainah had called, the woman had given her an address and invited her over for an informal interview.

The young woman, shrouded in a hijab, said to her, "So, Rekia told me you have no experience working as a nanny. How are you going to know how to take care of three children?"

"I have never worked as a nanny officially, but I have taken care of children regularly. For years, I lived in a place where there were a number of children whose mothers sometimes left them with me while they went to attend to their chores. I also have some experience with nursing and tending to sick children. I think I can be an asset in that regard."

The woman looked slightly impressed by that, but her stern countenance remained. "And I was told you worked for a well-known family in this town but left after only a few weeks. May I ask why?"

Zainah cringed inwardly. There was no way she was going to tell this woman what had really led to her fleeing her former job. She feared that she would not be believed, so she said simply, "My employer requested of me something I could never give."

The woman narrowed her eyes and stared at Zainah for a full minute. Zainah held her breath, hoping she wouldn't continue to probe. At last, the woman asked if she could start immediately, and Zainah heaved a sigh of relief.

"Yes, definitely!" Zainah answered.

The woman nodded and then told her how much she would pay Zainah monthly.

Zainah blinked in surprise as it was a really small amount. She had earned more than three times that amount in her last job. Even though this house was much smaller and therefore would be easier to clean than the Rahmanis', she was also supposed to be a nanny.

The woman looked at her expectantly.

Zainah thought about it for a few seconds and then nodded in agreement. It wasn't like she had a choice. The money she had saved from her last job was all but gone. And, she was desperate to start saving money to hire the investigator so he could search for Faizan.

"Good," the woman said. "Before you start, you will want to know the house rules." She began to list out a number of rules, from how to relate with her children to the exact way she wanted her house to look at all times. Zainah listened politely, taking note of all the rules.

"Everyone goes to the mosque together on Fridays. No exceptions," the woman said.

Zainah's heart jumped and she bit her lip. The woman did not know she was a Christian and Zainah had not intended to make it known. She wasn't going to stay in the house and so she had thought that the issue of their different faiths would never come up.

Her heart raced as the woman finally stopped reeling out her rules and asked Zainah if she had any questions. If she said that she was a Christian and therefore could not go to the mosque, this woman would probably reject her on the spot. She'd been searching for weeks without success. Where would she find an opportunity for another job? However, there was no way she was going to the mosque. And she intended to attend church as usual every Sunday and on weekdays, too. Would this woman stand for that or would she want her working on Sundays? Probably the latter.

She finally spoke up. "I'm so sorry for wasting your time," she said to the woman. "I don't think this will work for me."

The woman's eyes widened in obvious surprise. "Why not?"

Zainah stood up. "It would violate my faith," she said. "I have to go. Thanks for your time." She fled the house before the woman could say anything more. All the way home, she felt like crying. She'd held out so much hope for this job. Where would she find another?

She kept praying as she walked the long distance to Fatima's. When she finally entered the house, she flopped down on the sofa and sighed wearily.

Fatima came out of the kitchen and looked at her. "Oh no, Zainah. You didn't get it? I'm so sorry."

Zainah shook her head. "I did." She sighed again.

"Then what happened?" Fatima asked with a curious expression on her face.

"The woman of the house wanted me to go to the mosque with her and her family every Friday. I told her the job wouldn't work for me."

Fatima sat down beside Zainah and put her hand on her shoulder. "That's too bad. I'm really sorry. What will you do now? You know you can stay here as long as you like, though. For now, I'll manage with the rent."

Zainah shook her head. "I won't be able to live with myself if I don't help you out somehow. You have the children's needs to think about. I also need to get a job as soon as possible so I can hire that investigator."

Fatima nodded. "I know. I'll keep searching for you, Zainah. Don't worry about it. The Lord will make a way." She stood up and went back into the kitchen.

Fatima's youngest kids, eight-year-old Yasmine and seven-year-old Youcef, ran into the living room. They began to head to the door, jumping and laughing. Fatima came out of the kitchen and called to them. "Where are you both going?"

"To play outside," they chorused.

"No, you are not! Lunch is ready. Wait until you finish eating before going out to play."

Without grumbling, they went to their rooms, and Zainah marveled, as she'd done so many times, at how well behaved they were.

She went into the kitchen to help Fatima with lunch and said to her, "When I have children, I want them to be as well behaved as yours are." Her mind went to Faizan again and she pictured what their children would look like. "I need to find him, Fatima."

Fatima looked at her and smiled. "You will, and from what you have told me about him, you both will make beautiful babies together."

Zainah felt her face grow hot from embarrassment. If she was as fair as Faizan, she would be blushing now.

Fatima laughed. "You look like a child who has just been caught stealing meat from her mother's pot. You don't have to look so embarrassed. Making children with one's husband is a very natural thing."

Zainah smiled, still feeling self-conscious. She said, "I hope Faizan still feels the same way about me as I do him. I really want to be his wife."

"Of course he does. From what you've said about him, I believe he is a loyal person and someone who loves passionately. He will propose to you immediately when you tell him you are free to be with him. I promise."

Zainah's heart soared and then it crashed again

as she remembered her dilemma. "It won't happen if I don't find him. This outside world is so unpredictable. He might fall in love with someone else soon."

"Stop it!" Fatima said as she stirred her soup on the stove. "That won't happen."

Zainah forced herself to smile. "I guess I'm just worrying about so many things."

"You need to stop and concentrate on finding a job now. I wish I could help make that happen, but unfortunately, I can't. Still, I'll keep asking around."

Zainah said nothing more and they continued to cook together in silence. But her emotions roiled as she helped cook the meal. What if her concerns were not just silly fears? What if Faizan met some other girl and fell in love with her?

She continued to worry as she put the food on the table with Fatima. She was quiet throughout the meal with the family, and she went to her room after the meal, still troubled. When Leila came back to the house, she told her about her worries even though they hardly talked these days.

"I told you to go to your family and ask for the money you need, but you refused. By now, you would have paid the investigator to find Faizan if you had listened to me. I'll go with you if you want."

Zainah thought about what Leila had said as she lay down to sleep. She'd dismissed Leila's suggestion the last time she'd brought it up, but this time, she had to admit that there really might be little else left to do. It was probably time to start planning on going to visit her family in her little community.

Leila was probably right. She'd been gone for years now. Her family loved her. Surely, they would be so grateful to have her back home that they would not trouble her about her Christian faith anymore. Besides, she would not stay there for long. Once she got the money from her father, she would leave so she could start her search for Faizan.

FOURTEEN

Trisha forced a smile as Stan kissed her on the cheek.

"I love you. I'll see you tomorrow," he said.

She nodded and then pressed her lips together as he stared at her. After a minute, he gave a long sigh, frustration etched on his face, and then left the house. She heaved a sigh of relief and then put a hand on her forehead. Without a doubt, he had been expecting her to tell him she loved him too. He had asked her why she hadn't said it a week before and had been bugging her about it ever since.

"I always say 'I love you,'" he'd said to her two days before, "but you never say it. I know I hurt you terribly in the past, but I've apologized and I'm trying to make up for all I did. We are getting married soon. Isn't it time you left everything behind and confessed your love for me?"

He'd stared at her expectantly, just as he had done now, but she had been unable to bring herself to say the words because it wasn't how she felt. She didn't love him; not anymore. But he thought she still did. The worst part of it all was that she'd started to miss Frank. She asked herself every day why she had let go of a man like Frank for Stan.

She suddenly couldn't breathe as she thought about the decision she was planning to make. How could she marry someone she didn't love or even trust? The painful memories of Stan's many affairs came flooding back to her mind. The last betrayal where she'd caught him with another woman in their matrimonial bed suddenly began to play in her mind like a movie. She felt like throwing up, just as she had that day.

"What am I doing, planning to remarry Stan?" she asked herself. She stood up and went into Ruby's bedroom, just so she could remind herself why she wanted to marry him again. She was doing it because of her daughter.

She stood watching Ruby sleep peacefully in her crib. Ruby had to grow up with her father. That was why she was going to marry Stan even if she didn't love him anymore. Somehow, she knew Stan would not stay around if she didn't marry him.

And you still want to marry that kind of man? she silently chided herself. A man who you know will not stay for his own daughter unless he has you, and probably for his ego's sake?

She felt sick as she thought about it. Because of him, she was at loggerheads with her sister. She missed Audrey terribly. An overwhelming desire to talk to Audrey suddenly swept over her and she quickly went back to the living room. Audrey would be in Miami now, but she would call her.

Trisha picked up her phone from the coffee table to dial Audrey's number, but she lifted her head when the doorbell rang. She looked at the clock and immediately knew it was Faizan at the door. Right now, she desperately needed someone she could trust to talk to. He wasn't Audrey, but she enjoyed talking to him. Most of all, he had grown in his faith by leaps and bounds since he'd come to Rosefield. Perhaps he could give her wise counsel concerning her dilemma now.

She opened the door and smiled at Faizan.

"Hey, Faizan!" she said as he walked into the house.

He smiled brightly at her and sat on the couch. "Do you have anything that I could eat? I'm hungry and there is no food in my house."

She chuckled. "When is there ever food? You only eat home-cooked meals when you are here or Audrey and Ken are in town."

"True," he said.

"There's a chicken sandwich in the fridge. You can warm that up. Or you can eat the leftover lasagna I had for dinner yesterday."

"I'll just have the chicken sandwich," he said, getting up from the couch. Five minutes later, he came back to the living room with his sandwich.

As he ate, she watched him. Finally, she couldn't keep her problems to herself anymore. She took a deep breath and said to him, "Faizan, I need your advice."

He looked at her, dropped his half-eaten sandwich onto the plate, and asked, "What about?"

"It's about Stan," she sighed, "and Frank. I know I refused your advice before, but I was wrong. It's just that I felt attacked by you and Audrey. I felt you guys didn't understand why I wanted to marry Stan."

Faizan leaned forward and looked her in the eye. "Then make me understand, Trish."

Her gaze remained steady on him as she told him her reasons for taking Stan back. How losing her parents had caused her to vow that she would not take lightly a household where a mother and father were present.

He leaned back against the chair when she finished and said, "I understand your wanting Ruby's biological father to be in her life, but as I told you some time ago, you have to consider the fact that you'll have to live with him. You should consider your own happiness, too, because if you are not happy, I doubt that Ruby truly will be."

"But Stan has changed. I see that every day he comes here. I think he has the potential to make me happy as well. It's just that I can't get Frank out of my mind." She exhaled after she said that. She'd been keeping her feelings for Frank under wraps for a long time, especially since she'd agreed to marry Stan, but now, she felt relieved to let it out.

"You are confused about which man to choose?" Faizan asked.

Trisha answered, "Very."

*****

Faizan quietly asked the Lord for wisdom and then focused on Trisha. "I'm going to ask the Lord to give you clear direction right now about what to do," Faizan said, leaning forward again. He prayed a brief prayer. "Lord, Trish needs your help right now. She needs your wisdom to know the right man to choose for her future. Please give her wisdom. In Jesus' name, I pray."

He smiled and said to her, "Keep your eyes closed, Trish."

She raised her brows and stared inquisitively at him. "Why?"

"Please, just do it."

She closed her eyes.

"Now, imagine a future with Stan. Imagine both of you together, with Ruby, as one family, living right here in this house. And then going on trips… maybe visiting Audrey…"

Trisha grunted. "Audrey will tear him apart, Faizan. I don't think we will be visiting her together."

"Shh… just imagine it. Audrey is your sister and he has to deal with her if he wants to be in your life. He also has to deal with me."

"Okay," she said reluctantly.

"I want you to put that thought away for now, and then replace Stan with Frank."

She groaned.

"Finally, place both men side by side and compare a future between both of them. What comes to your mind when you think about being married to Stan ten years from now? What about Frank? What emotions do you feel when you think about being married to him ten years from now? Peace, unease, joy…?"

He watched as various emotions crossed her face. When he asked her to open her eyes, he saw tears shimmering in them.

"Trisha, the Bible says that the peace of God will act as an umpire. Now, what do you think the Lord wants you to do? Which man do you feel most at peace with when you think of a future with them?" Faizan asked.

Tears spilled down her face. "When I thought about my life with Stan ten years from now, I felt turmoil within me. I just knew that it would be the same as when we were married. He would cheat on me again. Plus, there was something else about him that I felt in my heart; something that wasn't right, but I couldn't put my finger on it."

Faizan nodded grimly. "And what about Frank, Trish? What did you sense in your heart about him?"

"A deep sense of peace washed over me. I knew my heart would be safe if I married him." She pressed her lips together and shook her head. "I'm just not sure that Frank would want me after rejecting him so many times."

"You'll never know until you try, Trish."

"Do you think I should call him now?"

"You definitely should," Faizan said. He felt like breathing a huge sigh of relief. At last, Trisha was finally going to get rid of that Stan. He'd been so worried about her, but because he didn't want to add to her distress, he had hidden his concerns. Thank you, Lord.

Trisha put her phone to her ear and then looked at him, a nervous expression on her face. "It's ringing," she whispered. Trisha's eyes widened and she said, "Hello, Frank!" She blinked rapidly and didn't say anything for a few seconds.

Faizan grew concerned at the despair on her face. "What is the matter?" he whispered as he looked at her.

She didn't answer. She nodded, sighed loudly and

then said, "Where did he go?" She didn't speak for another minute, and finally said, "Thank you." She ended the call and stared at her phone as though it had just bitten her.

"What is it, Trisha?" Faizan asked again.

"That was Frank's business partner. He said Frank just upped and left the country last week. The guy is blaming me for Frank's sudden decision to leave the United States. And I don't blame him for doing so. I knew he was heartbroken when I rejected him, but I didn't know it would lead to his leaving everything behind and moving away to another country."

Faizan winced at the devastated look on her face. "It's not your fault, Trisha. You can't blame yourself for Frank's decision, no matter what that guy on the phone said. People get rejected every day..." He suddenly couldn't complete his sentence as he thought about Lauren. He'd rejected her too, but that was because he was in love with someone else.

Someone you can never be with, his mind taunted him.

"What is it?" Trisha asked.

He shook his head. This wasn't about him now. It was about Trisha. "Nothing. Did you find out what country Frank moved to?"

Trisha shook her head, her eyes swimming with tears. "His business partner wouldn't tell me."

Faizan looked up, thinking. Finally, he said, "What about Audrey? She might know since she's pretty close to Frank. And don't tell me you are not speaking with her. You both need to put away this childish fight and…"

"Shhh! I'm calling her now," Trisha said, quickly dialing Audrey's number and then putting the phone to her ear.

"Hello, Audrey." Trisha put the phone on speaker. "Faizan is here."

"Well… if it isn't the stubborn middle sister!"

Faizan shook his head and chuckled. "Audrey, you are so troublesome!"

Trisha didn't appear to have heard Audrey's jibe. Without wasting any time, she said, "Audrey, do you know where Frank moved to? His partner told me he has moved to another country."

"What?" Audrey exclaimed. "Frank moved to another country? What is it with everyone moving these days, anyway?"

Faizan frowned and curiously asked, "Who else moved?"

"Never mind," Audrey said. "Frank didn't tell me he was moving. Oh Lord. You broke him, Trisha!"

Trisha sighed, guilt clearly written on her face.

"Stop, Audrey!" Faizan said. "That's not fair."

"It's the truth. The last time I spoke to him, he didn't sound like himself. I told Sienna that." Audrey sighed. "Anyway, I'll call his mom and see if she knows anything. Hopefully, she'll be able to tell me where her son is."

Trisha nodded. "Please get back to me after you speak with her."

"Why do you even care?" Audrey asked in an angry tone.

"I care more than you'll ever know," Trisha answered.

After the call ended, Trisha looked at Faizan and

sighed. "All I can do now is wait."

Faizan nodded as he thought about Zainah and how he didn't know where she was, either. All he and Trish could do now was wait and pray. But most of all, pray.

*****

After classes, Sienna walked to the Bible College chapel with her hand on her belly. She entered the chapel, which was empty as most students were either still in their classes or at the hostels. The college had already appointed another student chaplain to replace Bryan, but he still went to his old office almost every day and sometimes led the general evening prayers. She usually left him in school so she could go home, get dinner ready, and then rest up while she waited for him. Today, however, he was not leading the evening prayers and he didn't have any meetings scheduled with Dr. Lincoln or any of the school administrators. She wanted them to go home together, as she missed doing that with him.

She made her way to his office, knocked once, and opened the door. She smiled as Bryan looked up from his Bible. She plopped down on the chair facing him.

His entire face lit up as he beamed. "Hey, babe! You're here today!"

"Yes. I want us to go home together today." She leaned forward and he kissed her on the lips.

"That would be really nice," he smiled at her. "It's been a while since we went home together."

"It has," she said. "I also want you to drive with me to Rosefield so I can tell everyone that we will be moving to South America in two weeks. As you know, I have already told Audrey, but I've decided it's time to tell Trisha and Faizan."

"It was 'time' a while ago, honey," Bryan said, looking slightly amused.

"I know. I've been putting it off for so long. I called Faizan and Trish this morning to let them know that I have something to tell them. We are going to meet at our family house. I know Trish will kill me when she finds out there's just two weeks left before the move. And it will be worse when she discovers that I have already told Audrey about it." She sighed. "Without a doubt, Faizan will be disappointed that I didn't inform him already."

"Stop worrying about what your siblings will say," Bryan said. "As long as you tell them now, it's fine. I know they will be heartbroken, though."

"They will," Sienna said sadly.

Bryan smiled sympathetically at her. "I think we should leave now since we are first going to Rosefield."

She nodded. "That would be a good idea."

Bryan packed up his things and they left immediately. Sienna felt a heavy weight on her shoulders as they drove to Rosefield. She chatted with Bryan so she wouldn't have to think about Trisha and Faizan's reactions when she told them about her and Bryan's imminent move.

They reached Rosefield way too quickly. Sienna exited the car after Bryan had parked in the driveway of her parents' old house. She'd not been there since the year before. After Audrey and Ken had bought their new house and Faizan had also moved in there, there was no reason to come here.

But she'd asked Trisha and Faizan to meet her here because she somehow wanted to feel close to her parents when she told her siblings about her news. She knew they were in heaven and not in the house, but somehow, it felt like she would also be sharing the news with them at the same time she shared it with her siblings. Audrey had given her the key to the house the last time she'd visited Green Valley.

Sienna unlocked the door and Bryan took her hand. They entered the house together, and she was immediately struck by how old and musty it smelled. She immediately drew the curtains and opened the windows.

She went around the house opening all the windows and then finally came back to the living room. Bryan was sitting on the couch with his eyes closed and his head tilted back. She came and sat next to him and he opened his eyes.

She took his hand and squeezed it. "I'm nervous, Bryan. Trisha and Faizan won't like the news I'm going to share with them at all."

Bryan nodded. "I feel so guilty, being the one to uproot you out of your hometown and away from your family."

He looked so remorseful that she immediately wanted to take away his guilt. She shook her head and cupped his cheeks. "You are not the one uprooting me from my family," she said. "The Lord is… and He has His reasons. No matter how much I don't like it, I know that His plans for me and you are always good."

He smiled at her. She wanted to reassure him again that she didn't blame him, but she held back for some reason. Her heart suddenly jumped as the door opened. Trisha came in with Faizan, and Sienna smiled at them even though her heart was thumping and her hands were clammy with anxiety.

Calm down, she told herself.

She stood up and hugged Trisha and then Faizan. After that, she sat next to Bryan again while Trisha and Faizan sat facing her.

Sienna leaned forward and decided not to beat around the bush. Since she had to tell them about her and Bryan's move, she might as well tell them right now. Before she could speak, however, Faizan asked, "I thought you would wait for the weekend when Audrey and Ken are around to let us know what it is you want to tell us."

Sienna glanced nervously at Trisha and then hesitantly said, "I have already told Audrey what I want to tell you guys."

Trisha frowned but didn't say anything.

Sienna began again, "So, guys, I asked you both here in order to tell you that..." she paused for a few seconds and sighed. She took Bryan's hand and he whispered, "Do you want me to tell them?"

She quickly shook her head. "No, I'll do it."

"What is it, Sienna?" Trisha asked, her frown deepening. "You're scaring me."

Sienna smiled. "I'm sorry. I just wanted to let you guys know that Bryan and I will be moving."

Faizan's eyes grew wide.

Trisha's face clouded with worry. She leaned forward and asked, "To where?"

Sienna took a deep breath and said, "To Peru."

Trisha's forehead furrowed as she said, "Peru... Peru, where is that?" Her eyes suddenly bulged and she shook her head. "No, no! You can't be talking about Peru in South America!"

Faizan sat back in his seat and stared at her and Bryan with an inscrutable expression on his face.

Sienna nodded. "Yes, Trisha. That Peru."

Trisha looked at her as though she had just said she was going to live on the moon. "Why in the world do you want to move to Peru?" She turned to Bryan. "What have you done? Was this your idea or my sister's?"

Sienna placed a hand on Bryan's arm so he wouldn't say anything to Trisha. She said, "It's my decision, Trish. Yes, Bryan got a ministry opportunity in South America, but I agreed to go because I know it's God's will for both of us."

Trisha stood up and paced the living room. She looked down at Sienna after a minute and said, "You can't go, Sienna! You told me you and Bryan were going to raise your kids here, and that they would grow up with me," she pointed at Faizan, "and Faizan, and Audrey. What about Ruby? She won't know her cousin." She pointed at Sienna's belly. "She probably won't even know you."

Sienna felt her anxiety increasing. These very reasons and more were why she'd been so against moving at first. Now that Trisha brought them back to her mind, moving away felt like a terrible thing to do. She turned to look at Faizan and the despair on his face pierced her heart. If only he would say something instead of just staring at me with that look on his face.

Trisha stopped pacing and stood in front of her. She asked in a small voice, "When will you both leave?"

Sienna shut her eyes, knowing what would come when she answered Trisha's question. She opened her eyes and answered, "In two weeks."

Faizan finally spoke. "What? Two weeks!"

Trisha slowly sat down on the coffee table and stared at Sienna.

Sienna looked away from her siblings, but still, she could feel their pain. Bryan squeezed her hand and she turned back to them. "I know this is hard. If either of you told me you were moving to another country, I know how I would feel. But, Trisha, remember how we felt when you told us you wanted to remarry Stan? In spite of our misgivings, at least, Faizan and I, we decided to support you. Can't you do the same for me?"

"My decision to remarry Stan was a bad idea, Sienna. I just admitted that to myself recently."

Sienna's eyes widened in surprise. She took Trisha's hand. "You've called off the wedding?"

Trisha sighed loudly. "I haven't called it off. I realized Frank was the one I wanted to be with and wanted as a father for Ruby, but he has left the country. Not even Audrey knows where he is. She asked his parents where he'd moved to, but they wouldn't tell her."

"I'm sorry, Trish."

Trish bit her lip and said, "I feel like I have to marry Stan now because I can't leave Ruby without a father."

"You don't have to marry Stan for him to be a father to Ruby!" Sienna exclaimed.

"We've talked about this before. He won't stick around if I don't marry him." Trisha shook her head. "But we are not talking about me right now.

This is about you. Frank left the country, now you? Please, Sienna, say it isn't so."

"It is," Sienna said.

"In two weeks!" Faizan said, his brows knit together.

Sienna slowly nodded. "Yes."

Faizan turned to Bryan. "I know you can hear God's voice clearly, my man, but are you really sure this is God's will?"

Bryan nodded, the look on his face a mixture of sadness and conviction. "I am sure."

Faizan sighed with a look of resignation on his face. "Then we can't change their minds, Trisha. We need to accept it."

Sienna felt heartbroken for Faizan. He'd told her about the woman he loved and the vow she'd made to God which now kept them from being together. He probably would feel like the Lord was out to separate him from everyone dear to him. At least, that was how she would feel if she were him.

Trisha suddenly grabbed her and hugged her tight. "I'll miss you," she cried.

Sienna put her arm around her sister and then couldn't hold back her tears. "I'll miss you too."

Faizan put his arms around both of them and they wept together. Sienna suddenly remembered Bryan and gasped. He would feel left out. She turned to him and beckoned for him to come close. She pulled him into their hug and they all stayed that way for a long time.

At last, they separated and they talked about the preparations Sienna and Bryan had made for their move. Two hours later, Faizan and Trisha left, but not before promising to come to Green Valley to visit Sienna daily until she and Bryan were ready to leave.

That night, as they lay in bed, Bryan said to Sienna, "I was afraid that Faizan and Trisha would attack me from the way they looked at me when you told them about the move."

Sienna wrapped her arms around him. "They were just really upset. I don't think they blame you."

"I'm not so sure about that. If looks could kill, I would definitely be dead now. I think they do blame me. I know you feel really bad as well, but I love you for being such a supportive wife."

Sienna drew him even closer and kissed him passionately. If she couldn't reassure him that she didn't hold their imminent move against him with her words, then she would with her kisses. He clung to her as they kissed. When they pulled up for air, he said, "Wow! That was some kiss!"

She smiled and ran her fingers through his hair. "I hope you know now that I don't hold anything against you."

He nodded and kissed her hair. "I love you with all my heart."

"I love you too." She shut her eyes and sighed in contentment. "I love being in your arms."

Half an hour later, as he slept soundly and she gazed at him, she wondered if it was really true that she didn't blame him for the move. There was a small part of her that she had been trying to suppress that resented him for even bringing up the move to Peru. It was unreasonable to blame him when it was clearly the Lord who wanted them to go to South America, but it didn't change the fact that a tiny part of her did. And not just him, but the

Lord. She didn't understand why He had to tear her away from her family.

"Please help me to trust You," she prayed silently. She looked at Bryan's face and added, "And please help me not to hold anything against my husband." She sighed, worriedly, knowing what suppressed resentment could cause. If she kept the resentment, no matter how small, one day she would wake up in Peru and despise Bryan for taking her away from everything she knew. She didn't want that.

She looked at Bryan again and whispered, "If only we could stay here." She shut her eyes as she remembered Trisha and Faizan's reaction to her news. She felt her resentment grow and she prayed desperately again, "Lord, please help me."

But the resentment didn't leave. Instead, as she tossed and turned throughout the night, unable to sleep, the resentment grew. The next morning, she got up before Bryan did and hurriedly got dressed. Without waking him up, she left a note that read: Gone to Rosefield to spend the day with my siblings.

She left the house quickly.

As she drove to Rosefield, she realized that for the first time in a long while, she had not kissed her husband in the morning, neither had she told him she loved him in the note she'd left. She thought about turning back to do so, but it was too late now. Besides, she didn't feel like kissing him or telling him that she loved him. Once she got home that night, though, she would do that.

She pushed away all her worries about Bryan and focused on the road.

FIFTEEN

Zainah hugged Fatima tightly as tears ran down her cheeks. "I'll miss you, Fatima. Thank you so much for everything you have done for me and Leila."

Fatima patted her on the back and said with a voice choked with emotion, "I'll miss you too, Zainah. Remember that you can come back here anytime you wish. You don't have to spend money to find a place of your own."

Zainah shook her head. "It's time I did. I can't keep taking advantage of your kindness. Once I return from visiting my family, I'll get my own place."

Fatima gave her a resigned smile. "You're like a younger sister to me now. I'll be waiting with open arms whenever you decide to visit."

Zainah drew back from Fatima, and Fatima wiped the tears running down her cheeks with her fingers.

"Come here, all of you," Zainah said to Fatima's kids, Yasmine, Youcef, and Samir. They were looking at her with sad expressions on their faces. They went to her and she hugged them tightly. Safia was talking with Leila near the taxi Zainah had hired to take them to the bus station. Their suitcases were already in the taxi.

Zainah kissed the children's cheeks and then let them go. She hugged Safia last of all and then entered the taxi next to Leila. She put her hand out of the window and waved to Fatima and her children as the taxi began to drive away. She didn't stop waving until they had disappeared out of sight. She sighed sadly and turned to Leila. "I'll really miss them all, especially Fatima."

Leila smiled, tears shimmering in her eyes. "I'll miss Safia. That girl is so funny."

Zainah pressed her lips together as she thought about their time in Fatima's house. She'd enjoyed the unique combination they'd had there—a mixture of regular Christian fellowship, and interesting experiences and opportunities.

The driver reached the bus station fifteen minutes later, and Zainah and Leila exited the taxi with their suitcases. After Zainah had purchased their tickets with almost all the money she had, she and Leila entered the backseat of the bus going to Kazi, a small city an hour away from her community. When the bus finally filled up and was about to start the long, tedious journey, Zainah held Leila's hand and squeezed it out of nervousness. "We've spent almost all the money we have. If my family doesn't welcome me, we will be in serious trouble."

"You've always told me to trust God, now let me return your advice. Trust in the Lord. He'll work all out for our good."

Zainah nodded and exhaled.

All through the first day of the journey, Zainah silently and incessantly prayed that God would grant her favor before her family, especially her father. She was taking a huge risk. If they refused to take her back, not only would she not be able to find Faizan, but she and Leila would probably end up on the streets.

Hours later, the driver stopped briefly at an old motel. A lot of the passengers changed their clothes and bought food there. Zainah and Leila did, too.

On the second day, when she wasn't praying or talking with Leila, Zainah slept on and off. A few times, she stared out the window and marveled at how some of the landmarks she remembered had remained unchanged after more than a decade, while others were totally different.

Nighttime soon fell and she stopped looking out the window. She sat back on the bus and shut her eyes.

She felt someone shaking her shoulders. Looking out of the window, she saw it was morning again.

"We're here, Zainah," Leila said in a soft voice. "We are in Kazi."

Zainah rubbed her eyes and looked out the window again. They were parked close to another similar bus in a busy station. Some of the passengers were already getting off the bus.

"Let's get out," Leila said and stood up from her seat.

Zainah followed her.

They collected their suitcases from the trunk of the bus and walked to the road. They soon found another taxi to take them to Nira, Zainah's tiny community.

Throughout the hour-long trip, Zainah said nothing to Leila, too anxious to speak. She clenched and unclenched her fists and took constant deep breaths.

"Zainah," Leila said thirty minutes into the journey. "Relax. I'm sure your family will be overjoyed to see you."

Zainah nodded and tried to relax, but she couldn't.

As they neared Nira, Zainah felt like she was having a mini panic attack. She began to pray for tranquility, and then felt a supernatural peace descend on her. She took a final deep breath and silently gave thanks to God. She looked out the window as they entered her community and shook her head. "It looks basically the same as when I left," she said to Leila.

Leila smiled encouragingly at her.

She gave the driver specific directions to her family's house and sat at the edge of her seat as the driver turned onto the road leading to her father's house. Her heart drummed as she saw the house, a plain, single-story building with a red roof. Somehow, the house looked smaller than she remembered, but it wore a fresh coat of white paint. There were other mud huts around it that hadn't been there when she lived here.

The driver stopped in front of the house, and she and Leila got out of the taxi. Her stomach suddenly jerked as someone screamed and rushed out of the house.

"It can't be!" the tall woman who had come out of the house said.

Zainah's mouth hung open as she stared at her

mother, who had grown noticeably older, much older. There was more than a sprinkling of grey hair on her hairline, and there were lines on her forehead and cheeks. Zainah cried, "Mama!"

"Zainah!" her mother rushed up to her and enfolded her in her arms.

They both wept together and held each other tightly. Soon, other people began to gather around them. When her mother told them who she was, they yelled and gathered around her, touching and hugging her.

Another loud scream pierced the air as two adolescents, Zainah's sister, Khadija, and her younger brother, Sekou, came out of the house. Zainah gasped. She couldn't believe how big they were now. They hugged her and wept loudly. Soon, they were all laughing and talking at the same time. After a while, Zainah's mother shooed everyone away, except for her siblings. The three of them led Zainah into the house and Leila followed. The living room, which had seemed large when she was younger, now also looked small and a little empty.

Zainah smiled as she sat on the sofa and her mother and siblings sat next to her. After she had introduced Leila as her best friend, she asked where her father was.

"Your father is at his farm," Mama said, touching her cheeks with a look on her face that said she didn't quite believe her long lost daughter was sitting right next to her. Mama broke down again and began to weep, causing her siblings to do the same.

"Mama, Khadija, Sekou, stop it! Why are you all

still crying?"

"Because we've missed you so much," Mama answered. "And for me, because I am ashamed in the part I played in your leaving this community. I am so sorry, my dear daughter."

Tears poured down Zainah's cheeks as she hugged them again and told them she didn't hold anything against them. At last, they all stopped weeping.

"I guess I'll have to wait till evening to see Papa," she said.

Her mother shook her head. "Someone from around here would have gone to call him. Mark my words; he will be here anytime now."

Just as Mama finished speaking, a tall, strapping man rushed into the house and then stopped a few feet away from where Zainah sat. His eyes were as round as saucers.

"Malik," she cried and rushed to her half-brother. He was five years older than her, but they had been quite close when they were children.

He hugged her and then pulled away. "When they told me you had come back, I thought it was a lie, but I had to come see for myself." He gazed at her. "Is it really you, Zainah?"

"Yes," she laughed, and he hugged her again. She took his hand as they walked back to Mama and their siblings. Zainah sat down and then blinked when Malik stood staring with his mouth agape. She turned to look at what he was staring at, and found that his eyes were on Leila. Leila's eyes were also firmly planted on his, and her face had turned slightly red.

Zainah sighed wearily. Great! Now Leila is

smitten with my brother, and he with her. Leila had just come out of a relationship that hadn't worked partly because the guy was not a Christian. As far as she knew, neither was Malik. She grabbed his hand, pulled him down onto the chair beside her, and said reluctantly, "This is my best friend, Leila."

Malik and Leila didn't say a word to each other; they only kept staring. Zainah ignored them and turned back to her mother and other siblings.

"Where is she?" A loud voice called from outside the house. "Where is my daughter?"

Zainah stood up. "Papa!" she called out.

Her father came into the house and immediately went to her with tears in his eyes. "It is true. My daughter has returned to us." He hugged her and she wept, not just because she had missed him, but also because she clearly remembered his role in the events that had led to her being chased out of the house and their community. She'd forgiven him and her entire family, but she had suffered so much being separated from them for so many years. Now she realized that they had suffered just as much as she had.

Her father held her away briefly so he could look at her. "You have become such a beauty," he said proudly.

She thanked him, slightly embarrassed.

He hugged her again. After a while, they all sat together on the couch asking her a lot of questions about where she'd been. She evaded most of them, partly because she did not want to say anything specific about the women's camp in order to protect their location, and partly because she wasn't ready to tell them she'd been in a sort of Christian refugee camp.

She asked Malik where his mother, her father's other wife, and the younger siblings, were.

"They went to see her old dying mother in their village," her father answered for Malik. Zainah studied her older brother. He wasn't really paying attention to what they were all saying. His eyes were constantly straying to Leila. In turn, Leila couldn't take her eyes off him.

Zainah pursed her lips and then turned away from them. She focused her attention on her parents and siblings and continued to chat with them. Two hours later, after the novelty of her appearance had begun to wear off, her mother stood. "Let me go and prepare something special for you and your friend to eat, Zainah. You must be starving." She left quickly.

Her siblings, Sekou and Khadija, went to their rooms.

Malik also stood, albeit reluctantly. The look on his face reflected his reluctance to leave as he said, "I have to go and get Fanta from her maternal grandmother's."

"Who is Fanta?" Zainah asked.

"My daughter," he said, glancing at Leila.

Zainah heard Leila gasp and then Malik quickly added, "I'm a widower. My wife, Aminata, died giving birth to our daughter three years ago."

"I'm so sorry," Zainah said. She lifted her brows in surprise when Leila, who hadn't spoken for hours, said in a soft voice, "I'm sorry too."

He smiled at Leila, nodded, and left. Zainah noticed that he had only acknowledged Leila's words of commiseration. She would have found it all funny if not for the fact that she was afraid Leila was setting herself up for more heartbreak.

Her father looked at her and said, "I'm so happy you are back, Zainah." He held out his hand and she took it. He looked so happy, she didn't want to tell him she wasn't planning to stay forever. He squeezed her hand and said, "I have to get back to work, but if you need anything at all, just let me know."

She smiled as her raced with uncertainty and anxiety. Should I tell him about the money I need right now, or is it too early? She decided to tell him now. She needed to find Faizan as soon as possible. "Papa?"

"Yes?"

"I do have something to ask you, and it's very urgent."

"I'm listening."

She hesitated for a few seconds and then began, "I... I need some money now for a project I am embarking on. I promise to pay you back as soon as I can." She held her breath while praying he would not ask her what the project was and that he would agree to loan her the money.

He laughed. "You look so scared. And why would I loan you money? I just told you now to ask me if you need anything. Tell me, how much do you need?"

She told him.

"I'll give it to you. Don't bother paying me back."

Her heart soared and she hugged him. "Thank you," she said, pulling back.

He patted her shoulder and stood up. "I'll see you in about three hours," he said, beaming at her.

She smiled back. "Okay." She waved to him as he walked out the door and then turned to Leila and whooped. "God is so wonderful, Leila! Everything went better than I imagined it would go."

"I told you it would," Leila said, smiling.

"I'm just afraid of what they will say when I tell them I'm not staying for long."

Leila looked disappointed and said nothing.

"You want to stay here because of Malik," Zainah said, slightly irritated.

"Do you disapprove of us being together?" She looked away with a dreamy expression on her face. "It's not as if he has said that he's interested in me…"

Zainah cut in. "Yes, I disapprove. Malik is not a Christian as far as I know."

"You think I don't know that?" Leila scowled at her.

"Well, you should keep that in mind when he next appears." Zainah sighed, knowing she was being too harsh. "I'm sorry. I just don't want to see you get hurt the way you were in your last relationship. I know you really want to get married… and I want that for you. But Malik is a Muslim. I doubt that he would want to marry a Christian woman. Besides, you shouldn't even be thinking about being with someone who doesn't share your faith."

"I know, but…" She stopped talking as Zainah's mother came into the living room holding a large casserole dish in her hand. She placed the dish on the dining table at a corner of the living room and said, "Food is ready."

Zainah whispered to Leila, "We will continue this discussion later." She stood up and went to the dining table. After she'd thanked her mother,

Zainah sat at the table with Leila to eat, while praying that Leila would put away this infatuation with her brother. If not, knowing her best friend, Leila would put up a fuss when it was time to leave; or worse, she would refuse to go.

As they ate, Zainah noticed Leila pouting, but ignored her. She turned her thoughts to her father and his promise to give her the money she needed. Hopefully, he would give it to her soon.

*****

Sienna looked around the empty living room and sighed sadly. This had been her home for the past year, and even though it was tiny, she'd grown to love it.

Someone tapped her on the shoulder and she turned. "It's time for us to go, Sienna," Bryan said. He put his hand on her shoulder and said sympathetically, "I'll miss this house too."

She smiled sadly. "It's not just the house itself. It's the memories we made here. We moved in when we got married. Remember how excited we were to get this tiny house? Even after I got Dad's inheritance and we could move out, we decided we would stay here because we had come to love it so much."

He nodded. "Yes. We will always remember it because it's where we started our married life."

They held hands and walked out of the house together, and Sienna realized it was the most intimate thing they had done in two weeks. They both got into the back of the cab that would take them to the airport. Most of their furniture had already been donated and their heavy luggage sent to Peru ahead of them. Only their suitcases containing their clothes and other smaller items were in the trunk of the cab.

"What time is everyone arriving at the airport?" Bryan asked as the taxi backed out of their driveway.

They had spent most of the previous day with Bryan's family. Today, they would spend it with hers at the airport before they left the country.

"Umm… at about seven o'clock." She glanced at her watch and saw it was a quarter past six. "That means in forty-five minutes' time."

Silence reigned as they continued the drive to the airport. Sienna stared out the window as they sped past several cars. This was how it was with her and Bryan these days. They hardly had anything to say to each other. Or, rather, she hardly had anything to say to him. For two weeks, he'd tried to get her out of the shell she'd crawled into, but it was useless. She always felt resentment bubbling up in her whenever he spoke to her. Because of that, she'd decided to limit the amount of time she talked to him in order to prevent herself from verbally vomiting all her pain and resentment on him. He'd given up trying to get her to open up to him just a few days before.

She couldn't wait to see Audrey, Trisha, and Faizan at the airport. Audrey and Ken had arrived in Rosefield only the previous evening, just to see them off today. She was glad Trisha and Audrey had mended their relationship. It had hurt her heart when they weren't talking to each other.

The same way you and Bryan aren't now, a voice in her mind whispered.

She brushed away the voice. It wasn't true. She and Bryan were speaking to each other. Just not as much as before. But it was only temporary. She would begin to talk to him as much as she did before once she got over her resentment. She hoped that would be soon, before it began to cause a rift in their marriage.

They finally arrived at the airport and stepped out of the cab.

After they had checked in for their flight, they walked to the food court and ordered some snacks and then went to sit at one of the booths while they waited for everyone to arrive. Sienna glanced at her watch again just as Bryan said, "There they are!"

She looked up and her heart soared as Audrey, Trish, Faizan, and Ken approached them. She stood and rushed up to them. They all took turns hugging her, and then they all went back to where Bryan was sitting. Sienna planted herself in between Trisha and Audrey while the men sat facing them.

After everybody had ordered food and drinks, they all sat, chatting and eating.

Trisha suddenly said, "I just realized we won't be there when you have your baby, Sienna!" Her eyes were huge as she spoke.

Sienna winced. It was one of the most troubling thoughts that had continuously run through her mind since Bryan had brought up the move. It was also a little frightening for her to think about. She had never imagined a scenario where her sisters would not be there when she gave birth to her baby.

"Trisha!" Audrey exclaimed. "Why did you bring

that up? You remember that we decided not to bring up anything that would add to Sienna's anxiety about her move, don't you? Now see how sad she is."

Trisha covered her mouth with her hand. She removed her hand and said, "I'm really sorry, Sienna."

"Why would you be sorry?" Sienna looked at her and then couldn't help but turn to look at Bryan. Resentment rose up in her and she said, "You're not the one making this move."

Bryan clenched his jaw and looked straight ahead without saying anything.

An uncomfortable silence hung in the air and Sienna felt guilty for being the cause of it. She searched her mind for something to say that would break the silence, but for some reason, she couldn't come up with anything.

Finally, Trisha said, "At least you will have Bryan there with you. He loves you with all his heart. I only have Stan… and…" She covered her mouth again.

"What is it?" Sienna asked, concerned in spite of herself.

"I just realized something. Actually, it's something that I should have admitted to myself a long time ago, but your leaving now has forced me to do it."

"Out with it!" Audrey ordered impatiently.

"Audrey, calm down," Ken told her.

"I told you guys that I've admitted to myself finally that I do want to be with Frank, but he has apparently given up on me and I don't blame him. However, I thought I needed to stay engaged to Stan since I want a father for my daughter and Frank isn't available to fill that role."

Sienna nodded.

"I just realized that not only would I not trust Stan to take care of Ruby if we were alone in a strange country, I wouldn't trust him to care of her alone now. And I certainly don't trust him with my heart. I can't marry him," Trisha said, looking up thoughtfully. "Not even for Ruby's sake."

Audrey sighed. "What's new? I've been trying to tell you this all along."

"Audrey, let her have her moment," Ken said.

Sienna's heart pounded as she thought about what Trisha had said. Would she trust Bryan to look after their child if she wasn't there with him? She immediately knew the answer. She trusted him with everything in her. She knew he would be the best father in the whole world.

She stretched her hand and took his on the table. Without caring what the others thought, she said to him, "I'm sorry, Bryan, for being so difficult. I love you and I trust you fully, even now when we are moving away."

His eyes lit up and he beamed. "I love you too."

Her heart overflowed with love for him as they gazed at each other.

"Guys, get a room!" Ken said, breaking the moment.

Everyone laughed.

Audrey chuckled and playfully hit Ken on the shoulder. "Who is not letting people have their moment now?"

"'Kay! I was wrong for that," he answered, smiling sheepishly.

Audrey kissed his cheek.

Faizan sighed deeply and said, "All this talk about love and relationships is getting me down." He shook his head. "I'm sorry for being such a party pooper."

"No need to be," Trisha took his hand. "I know how you feel."

He said, "You know, Trisha, you aren't the only one with an epiphany now. With Bryan and Sienna leaving the country, I just realized that life is too short not to take the opportunity I have right now to find love and share my life with someone who cares for me."

Everyone stared at him for a few seconds and then Trisha said, "Frank loves me and he wants to be in a relationship with me, so I am going to look for him, no matter where he is."

Faizan simply said, "I'm going to ask Lauren out. I can't keep yearning for a woman who I can't be with and might never even see again."

Sienna looked at both of them. She was glad her leaving had given them these epiphanies, but seeing the pain in their eyes and knowing she wouldn't get to be there for them as they went on their emotional journeys hurt her heart.

Audrey's voice broke into the silence. "Okay, who wants dessert?"

Everyone turned to stare at her for interrupting such a serious moment with her flippant question, and then they all burst out laughing.

Audrey ordered desserts for everyone, and their conversation turned to less serious matters as they devoured the treats.

A female voice announcing the flight to Lima pierced the air and Sienna's heart sank. Bryan stood up with a gloomy expression on his face. "It's time for us to go, guys," he said.

Sienna covered her mouth as she held back a sob. Audrey stood up with Ken and hugged her. Faizan hugged her next while Audrey hugged Bryan.

Faizan rubbed Sienna's back. "Call immediately when you get there."

"I will," she said, tears trailing down her cheeks.

Trisha stood and sighed. "Stop crying, Sienna. I'm already a mess. I don't want to fall apart here."

Sienna grabbed her and they wept. Audrey put her hands around them both and they stayed that way for a long moment. The announcement came again and they drew back from Sienna.

They waved as she and Bryan backed away. Sienna turned around and took Bryan's hand.

Two hours later, as they boarded the plane, her heart still hurt. Bryan squeezed her hand and didn't let go as the plane took off. Finally, he turned to her when she sniffed and wiped her eyes.

"We will be fine, Sienna. I'll always be by your side, remember that. You won't be alone in Peru."

She smiled through her tears. "I know. I'll still miss my sisters and brother, though; but I have you and the Lord, and that's enough for me."

SIXTEEN

Trisha sighed nervously as Stan came into the house. "Thank you for coming, Stan," she said as she sat beside him on the couch. She'd called him immediately after she'd come back from the airport and asked if he could come to the house as soon as possible as she had something important to tell him. Ruby was still at Paula's. Trisha had purposely left her there so she wouldn't be around when Stan came.

Stan leaned forward and gazed at Trisha. "What do you want to tell me, Trisha? You sounded pretty upset when you called earlier."

Trisha twisted the engagement ring on her finger. "Sienna just left the country," she told him.

"Oh," he said. "I'm so sorry, Trish. You guys are super close. I can understand how you feel right—"

"That's not why I asked you to come," Trisha said, interrupting him.

"What is it, then?"

She took a deep breath and then decided to get straight to the point. "Stan, I really appreciate all your efforts to reconcile with me and build a relationship with Ruby. With everything in me, I want Ruby to have a relationship with her father. I'm glad you are in her life now, but..." she paused for a few seconds and then went on, "but I don't think it's important to marry you for that to be the case." She looked at him as he raised his brows in obvious surprise. "What I'm trying to say is that I cannot marry you. I'm sorry. I do hope you remain in your daughter's life even though we won't be a couple."

She pressed her lips together anxiously as he stared at her, his expression full of disbelief.

"You're breaking off our engagement?"

She nodded and took off the diamond ring he'd given her. "Here, Stan." She handed the ring to him.

He looked dazed as he took the ring from her.

"Again, I'm so sorry," she said.

"It's because of that Frank guy, isn't it?"

She shrugged. "It's much more than that. I don't think it's appropriate or important to bring up the reasons why I can't marry you."

He stood and looked down at her. "You know what, Trish, I've done everything I can to seek and gain your trust, but still..."

"Stan!" She looked up at him, her emotions in turmoil. "Please don't bring up trust right now. A few months of coming here almost every day and playing with Ruby does not make up for what you did or omitted to do."

"But I love you!" Stan cried.

She shook her head. "I don't know about that. I think you love something about me... but not me."

A strange look she couldn't quite place passed over his features and she blinked rapidly. Almost immediately, his features changed and clouded once more with guilt and a woe-is-me look. "You can't be serious!" he exclaimed. "I love you, Trish. You should know that."

She shrugged again. "It's over, Stan. You can continue to come here to see Ruby whenever you want, but we are through."

He shook his head. "You want to marry that Frank. Soon, my daughter will be calling him Dad instead of me. I'm not going to let that happen. I'm going to fight for full custody."

She stared at him in astonishment. She had thought he would leave her and Ruby's life immediately when she broke up with him. But now, he wanted to sue for full custody. She knew he wasn't as committed to Ruby as he was trying to make her believe he was. Something wasn't quite right. There was something wrong about Stan that had been bothering her for a while, something she still couldn't place her finger on.

She stood up and faced off with him. "If you want to do that, then I will be ready to fight you with all I have." She laughed humorlessly. "And as you know, with my inheritance, I have a lot."

He blinked rapidly and she narrowed her eyes. The strange look had returned again as she'd mentioned her inheritance.

He sighed loudly and then his combative demeanor disappeared. He said softly, "Trish, please rethink this. I'm Ruby's biological father. What's best for our daughter is to have her father and mother living under the same roof as husband and wife."

Trisha didn't say anything for a long moment as

her heart raced. Frank's face appeared in her mind and she took a deep breath. She smiled sadly and said to Stan, "I thought that, too. But just because you're someone's father it doesn't automatically make you a good one."

He opened his mouth to speak again, but she waved her hand dismissively. "I'm sorry, Stan, but I am not going to marry you!"

Stan's eyes blazed as he stared at her.

She held her breath and kept her eyes on his. Finally, he huffed, turned around, and stormed out of the house.

She exhaled and sat down. Hopefully, this was the last time she saw him. She'd wanted him to remain in Ruby's life, but his talk about suing for full custody had removed that desire from her mind.

She stood up again and went to get her purse to leave the house. It was time for the second phase of her plan.

*****

Faizan forced himself to calm down as he took his phone out of his pocket. He left Audrey and Ken in the living room and went into his room to keep the conversation he was about to have private.

He dialed Lauren's number and anxiously held his breath as the phone rang. When her voice came on the other end of the line, he exhaled and then injected a smile into his voice. "Hello, Lauren," he said cheerily.

"Hi, Faizan," she said in an eager voice.

He paused for a second. He hadn't spoken to her since the day she'd told him she would wait for him to get over Zainah. He certainly hadn't gotten over Zainah, but he definitely had to move on. He couldn't think of anyone better he could move on with than Lauren. She was fun to talk to, smart, and beautiful. Best of all, she liked him… a lot. It was certainly a good place to start a relationship.

"Umm… how are you, Lauren?" He shut his eyes as embarrassment swept through him. Why had he asked such a generic question?

"I'm good," she answered in her feathery voice.

Go straight to why you called, he silently chided himself. He already knew she would say yes, so why was he so anxious? He ran his fingers through his hair and then said, "I just called to ask if you would like to go… on a date with me."

"Really?"

"Yes. Anytime you are…"

She cut into his words and squealed. "I would love that!"

He nodded as though she could see him. He would have chuckled at her eagerness if it wasn't for how anxious and uncertain he felt. "Okay, how about this evening?"

"Certainly!" she said. "Can you pick me up at my house at around seven o'clock?"

"Yeah. We have a date this evening, then."

"Yes, we do!"

"Alright, Lauren. I'll see you at around seven o'clock."

"Faizan?"

"Yes?"

"What should I wear for our date?" She added quickly, "I'm assuming we are going to a restaurant?"

He frowned. He hadn't thought about the details of the date. He narrowed his eyes as he thought briefly about it and then said, "I think it will definitely be dinner at a restaurant. As for what you will wear, I'm not sure about that. A dinner dress?"

She chuckled. "Okay, then. A dinner dress it is."

He wanted to tell her not to take his word for it and then quickly realized she was teasing him. He smiled and said, "Okay, Lauren. I know you'll figure your outfit out yourself. I'll see you later."

When the call ended, he sat on his bed and then he put his hand on his forehead and shut his eyes. His emotions churned as he thought about his conversation with Lauren. He felt as though he'd just cheated on Zainah.

What have I done?

He immediately countered his doubts. I did the right thing. I'm moving on, as I have no choice. It's not like Zainah is going to appear in Rosefield anytime soon and declare that she is now free to be in a relationship with me.

She would never break her vow to God, and rightly so. Plus, who knew where she was now?

Fear immediately gripped him as he thought about Zainah being missing. He stood and brushed away the fear. As far as he knew, from what Miriam had told Jake's messenger, Zainah had left the camp with Leila of her own free will. She was probably safe somewhere, even though nobody knew where she was for now. Besides, he'd asked Jake to get men around the area who would keep searching for her. He wanted to make sure she was really safe.

He picked up a book he'd started the day before and began to read it so he could get his mind off

Zainah and his imminent date with Lauren. He'd gotten through a few chapters before he realized that he actually didn't remember much of what he'd read. His mind had refused to give up his worries and doubts. He sighed and shut the book.

Rising up from the bed, he went out of his room and headed for the living room to find Audrey and Ken. Conversing with them right now would be the best way to distract himself from his doubts and anxiety.

He found them still in the living room talking about Sienna's move and Bryan's ministry opportunity in Peru. He joined in, and even though the conversation left him a little morose because of Sienna's departure, it was better than the absolute confusion raging in his mind after he'd called Lauren.

Their conversation went from one topic to another. Finally, at about six o'clock, he stood up.

Audrey and Ken looked at the clock on the wall at the same time, and Audrey gasped. "Wow! It's already six o'clock. We haven't even had lunch and it's almost time for dinner."

"We should go out to eat today," Ken said. He looked at Faizan and said to him, "You'll come with us, won't you?"

Faizan shook his head. "No. I'm having dinner with someone else."

Audrey whooped happily. "You have a date, Faizan! Tell me, who is it?"

"Did I say I had a date?"

"Stop it, Faizan!" Audrey giggled. "Tell me who you're going on a date with."

Faizan glanced at Ken and wondered if it would

be weird to mention he was going on a date with his ex. He looked at Audrey again and decided there was no point hiding it. They would find out eventually. "It's Lauren."

"Lauren?" Audrey's eyes widened in surprise. "I didn't know you liked her."

Faizan turned to look at Ken. He didn't seem to mind. He just looked a little surprised. "I hope you don't mind, Ken. I know she's your ex."

Ken shook his head. "That was such a long time ago. I don't mind at all."

Faizan smiled.

Audrey said, "I think you'd be great together."

Faizan chuckled. "Calm down, girl. It's just a date. I don't know yet where it will lead."

Audrey put her hand on his shoulder. "Well, I hope it ultimately leads to marriage. I've hated seeing you so miserable because of that Zainah lady. I'm just glad you are beginning to open up your heart to finding love elsewhere. And I hope it's with Lauren. She's a great girl."

"She is," Faizan agreed. "So, I have to go prepare for my date. I'm picking Lauren up at her place around seven o'clock."

"Where are you guys going?" Ken asked.

Faizan shrugged. "To tell you the truth, I don't know yet. Can you recommend a great restaurant that I can take her for our date?"

"There aren't many restaurants in Rosefield," Ken said. "I only know of one that I love and have taken Audrey to a couple of times."

"Sophie's Place!" Audrey answered before Ken could say anything. "You know Sophie's, Faizan."

He nodded. "Everyone does, I guess. So, Sophie's

Place it is." He smiled and then left the living room to prepare for his date with Lauren. But he didn't immediately start to. He dallied until he knew he would be late if he didn't dress up and leave the house immediately. Fifteen minutes later, he was in his car, driving towards Lauren's, his heart drumming.

*****

Trisha exited her car and walked to the front door of the small stone house on the outskirts of town. She exhaled, rang the bell, and waited. A minute later, a woman in her late fifties opened the door.

Trisha smiled. "Hello, Mrs. Kessler."

Dorothy Kessler looked at her oddly, as though trying to decide if she wanted to return her greeting or not. At last, she gave Trisha a small smile and said, "Hi, Trisha. How are you?"

"I'm good." Trisha winced inwardly at the woman's cold behavior toward her. When her parents were alive, they had been regular visitors at their family house. Trisha and her sisters also visited the Kesslers' regularly. She didn't blame Dorothy, though. If a man played with Ruby's heart and emotions the way she'd done with Frank's, she would be angry and resentful too. She looked past the woman into the living room, wondering if she would be allowed in.

Dorothy eyed her briefly and then opened the door wide to let her in.

Trisha thanked her and entered the house. She wasn't surprised that it looked exactly the same as the last time she was there, which was about eight years before. The living room was furnished simply, with polished wooden floors, brown leather sofas, and a big TV stand where a 50-inch TV sat.

Dorothy sat down on the sofa facing Trisha and said, "It's been a really long time, Trish. How are your siblings? Is Audrey in town?"

"They're fine, and no, she's in Miami now."

Dorothy nodded. "She visited Steve and I two weeks ago." Dorothy stared accusingly at Trisha. "She's the only one who visits us… or cares about our Frank."

Trisha's heart raced. She'd come to ask Frank's parents if they could tell her what country Frank had moved to and if she could get a number to reach him. But with his mother's cold behavior, she doubted the woman would give away any information about her son. Still, she needed to try. First, though, she asked about Frank's dad, Steve.

"He is good. He's not back from work right now, but I'll tell him you visited."

Trisha winced again. Was this Dorothy's way of telling her to leave?

Well, she wouldn't leave now. Not until she got the information she wanted. Trisha said, "I was wondering if you could tell me what country Frank moved to or give me his new phone number. I have been trying to reach him, but I haven't been able to. Audrey hasn't been able to reach him either."

Trisha bit her lip. The woman was looking at her as though Trisha had asked her to jump off a cliff.

"I can't give you his number or tell you where he is," Dorothy Kessler said. "Frankly, I only let you into the house because your late parents were our good friends."

"I didn't mean—"

"Let me finish," Dorothy interrupted Trisha. "I know it's your prerogative who you love or don't love, but you played with his heart, Trisha. He has loved you for years and you know that. You made him leave everything in Boise to come here because you made him believe you missed him and wanted him here. And then, as you've always done, you broke his heart by choosing someone else."

Trisha bowed her head. She deserved the woman's anger. "I didn't mean to hurt him."

"You've been hurting him for a long time, so what do you mean by that?"

Tears flooded Trisha's eyes, but she blinked them back. "I was wrong," Trisha said, in a voice choked with emotion. "I just want to speak to him now and tell him that I do love him. I didn't realize it until a few days ago."

Dorothy shook her head. "I'm sorry. I can't help you. Please understand. I'm just a mother wanting to protect her son. You've caused him so much pain, and as much as I like you, Trisha, I don't want Frank involved with you. You will eventually break his heart… as always."

"But I have never told Frank how I feel about him, really. I need to tell him now, and I think he needs to know. Please, Mrs. Kessler. Please give me his number."

Dorothy shook her head. "I can't. Besides, Frank told us not to give his number to anyone. He just wants to clear his head and try to find some peace now. I don't want anything to distract him from finding the peace of mind he needs."

Trisha looked at Dorothy's set jaw and knew she

wasn't going to budge. She stood and smiled sadly. "I understand. I'll give him some time, but I won't give up until I find him."

Dorothy stared at her and then followed her as she walked to the door.

Trisha opened the door with her heart aching. Everyone blamed her for Frank's sudden move out of the United States. She blamed herself, too. If she hadn't foolishly chosen Stan over him, he would be in Rosefield now, and she would have declared her love for him. She knew now without a doubt that she did love him.

She stepped out of the house and then turned when Dorothy Kessler called her name.

"I'm sorry for not being able to help you," Dorothy said. "But I have to protect Frank."

Trisha nodded sadly and then went to her car. Tears fell down her cheeks as she drove home. They were tears of overwhelming sadness because she knew she would probably never get another chance to be with the guy who had loved her for all these years.

*****

Dressed in a blue blazer and a white button-down shirt, Faizan knocked on Lauren's apartment door and waited. He exhaled to try to let go of his nervousness and then stood with his hands behind his back, waiting for her to open the door.

The door opened a minute later and Faizan smiled at Lauren. She was dressed in a fitted short black dress, and she looked very pretty. "You look beautiful," he said to her.

Her smile widened. "Thank you. You look great yourself."

"I see you are ready to go," he said.

She nodded.

He opened the passenger door of his car for her, and she thanked him and got in. He got into the driver's seat and drove away. All through the drive to the restaurant, he made small talk with her while trying to push away all the doubts and guilt in his mind.

They entered Sophie's Place with its calming ambience and dim lights, and the host immediately led them to an empty table by the window. Even though it was a weekend, the restaurant was half empty today, but Faizan wasn't surprised. People in Rosefield hardly ever came to the posh restaurant, choosing other, less formal places, even for dates. It reminded him of the new restaurant that Frank Kessler was building some distance from there. Frank had been AWOL for a while, and the construction seemed to have stopped.

Lauren leaned forward with her fingers threaded together and looked him in the eye. "A penny for your thoughts."

He shrugged. "Umm…I was only thinking about this restaurant and Frank Kessler's."

Lauren nodded. "Trisha told me he moved to another country. And talking about moving to another country, Sienna and her husband have finally moved, haven't they?"

"Yes." Faizan sighed. "I already miss her even though she left just yesterday."

She smiled sympathetically at him. "I wish I knew what it was like to have siblings you love so much. I was such a lonely child because my parents split up when I was seven and my mom never re-married."

He raised his brows in surprise and said, "I was adopted and raised as an only child too." He began to tell her about his childhood but skipped the part about Mustafa. He'd already told her a little about the man who'd raised him to be a terrorist, but he didn't want to talk about any of that this evening. She, in turn, told him about growing up without siblings and an absent father.

"We have quite a lot in common," she said to him.

Just as he opened his mouth to answer, a waiter came to their table. After they had both looked through the menu and ordered, she continued to talk about her childhood right up till she'd gone to college.

"I met Ken when I was a freshman," she said. She talked animatedly about her adventures in college until she reached the part where she'd met her ex-husband. She sighed and paused for a second. "I don't think I'll ever fully get over all I went through at the hands of my ex."

This time, he was the one who smiled sympathetically. "He was a fool to hurt someone as sweet as you, Lauren. You need to try to let go of all that so you can focus on your future and all that the Lord has for you." He blinked in surprise when she took his hand on the table.

"Thanks, Faizan, for being such a good friend… and I hope more soon."

For a few seconds, they gazed at each other, and then he pulled his eyes away from hers. She let go of his hand and he realized he'd been holding his breath. He breathed a sigh of relief when the waiter came with their food.

As they tucked into their seafood platters, they chatted about random stuff. From time to time, Faizan's mind went back to Zainah. Every time, he pressed her image from his mind, only for her face to reappear minutes later. He was thankful that Lauren didn't say anything more about wanting to be more than friends. He wanted them to take things slow. The thought of immediately entering into a relationship with someone other than Zainah was starting to freak him out.

But you told everyone at the airport that you were ready to move on, he chided himself.

It was true. He'd told his siblings and their spouses he was going to stop holding on to Zainah and ask Lauren out with the purpose of dating her. He couldn't just change his mind. Besides, he'd given Lauren hope of a relationship in the future by asking her out. He wasn't the type of person to lead a woman on. If he wanted to truly open his heart to find someone to spend the rest of his life with, he needed to try to forget about Zainah and completely focus on Lauren. Zainah was his past, but Lauren was his future… at least, he needed to see it that way from now on.

"Faizan, are you listening to what I'm saying?" Lauren said to him. "You aren't even eating your food."

He winced inwardly and said, "I'm sorry, Lauren." He looked down at his food and took a bite of his salad. He smiled at her. "Please go on. I'm listening."

She sighed. "I asked if you are thinking of Zainah."

He frowned and leaned forward. She'd guessed what was on his mind, but then, maybe it wasn't difficult for her. She knew how deeply in love he was with Zainah. His frown deepened. How could she put up with him when she knew he was still in love with someone else? He decided to tell her the truth. "I was, but I was also making up my mind to forget about her and focus completely on you."

She smiled and the expression on her face was a mixture of pleasure and uncertainty. To take her doubts about his seriousness away, he gently took her hand on the table, even though it was hard for him to do.

Her smile deepened and the uncertain look disappeared from her face.

She continued telling him about her life while they ate.

Half an hour later, they left the restaurant still chatting and laughing.

As they drove away from the restaurant, Lauren said, "So I ask my friend's three-year-old daughter what she wants to be when she grows up, and she says she wants to be Peppa Pig."

Faizan laughed and Lauren laughed along. "Kids are hilarious," he said.

"They are," Lauren replied, still giggling. Suddenly, she stopped laughing and said, "Richie, my ex, wanted kids badly. I did want kids as well, but because of his constant abuse, I just decided to put off having them until he changed. Of course, he never did, but I hope I can have children one day… soon."

Faizan didn't turn to look at her, as he could feel her eyes on him. He kept his eyes on the road while his emotions roiled. For the remainder of the journey to her house, neither of them said anything. He finally got to her house and parked in front of it. Her front porch was brightly lit. He walked her to her door and then stood waiting while she dug in her purse for her keys. When she unlocked her door, he stepped back.

"I had a great time," he said, smiling at her. "I'll see you in church tomorrow." He began to turn away but she called his name and he stopped. She stepped forward and stood in front of him.

"I had a great time too," she said to him.

He sucked in his breath at the sultry expression on her face. When she took his face in her hands and drew near, he knew she was going to kiss him. He tried to force himself to stand still, but Zainah's face appeared in his mind and he immediately drew back.

She winced.

He looked at her and said softly, "I'm so sorry, Lauren. But I can't. I thought I could do this, but I just can't seem to forget about Zainah. I'm still deeply in love with her, and I don't think it's fair to keep stringing you along."

Lauren sighed and looked down for a few seconds. She looked up again and said, "I'm sorry, too." She bit her lip and then smiled sadly. "I guess it's not meant to be."

He could feel her disappointment and pain, but there was nothing he could do about it. It was better this way… before she got in too deep with him only to get her heart badly broken.

She stepped into her house and then turned around. "Goodnight, Faizan."

"I hope we can still be friends," he said guiltily.

She didn't answer. She shut the door slowly.

He took a deep breath and then went to his car. Grabbing the steering wheel, he shut his eyes and asked himself what he thought he was doing. He'd made a decision to move on and had told his family he would. Now he'd reneged on that promise. He was still holding on to his love for Zainah, fully knowing it would only lead to a lifetime of loneliness.

Lord, what am I doing? I should go and knock on Lauren's door, tell her I am sorry and that I want a relationship with her.

But he knew he couldn't do that. He didn't want to. He started the car and drove out of Lauren's driveway. As he sped back home, he held the image of the only woman he'd ever loved close to his heart. Despite the consequences, he was certain he would love her forever.

SEVENTEEN

Zainah had already spent a couple of days in her family home and still her father hadn't given her the money he'd promised. She'd also been too embarrassed to ask him again since she had figured he would give it to her when he was ready. Now, though, she was getting impatient. She had to leave soon so she could start the search for Faizan again. She needed to swallow her embarrassment and pride and ask her father for the money.

She woke up very early in the morning, said a brief prayer, and then stood up from the bed. She glanced over at the other end of her old bedroom where Leila's bed was and then frowned. Leila wasn't in bed. She usually slept until about ten o'clock. Zainah had teased her about it and Leila had smiled. "After years of waking up at five o'clock every morning, I'm very grateful for this opportunity to wake up whenever I want, even if it's just temporary."

After a quick bath, Zainah opened her closet. As she'd done the first day she'd come home, she went through her old clothes with a feeling of painful nostalgia. Most of her things had been left exactly as they were when she'd left home years before. It left her feeling sad about the years she'd missed spending with her parents and siblings. Most of the dresses in the closet still fit her, even though they weren't exactly the kinds of clothes she would normally wear now.

She chose a long, cream, casual dress and a scarf, left the room, and sat in the living room waiting for her dad to come out so she could speak to him before he left for work. She heard someone who sounded like Leila giggling just outside the front door and stood. She opened the door and her jaw dropped. Leila was enfolded in Malik's arms. They were kissing and laughing at the same time.

Leila was the first to notice Zainah. She pulled away from Malik and looked down sheepishly.

Malik pulled her into his arms again and glared at Zainah. "Why are you looking at us like that?" he chided her. "Haven't you seen a couple kissing before?"

Zainah scowled at them. "I have, but I don't really want to see my brother and my best friend at it, especially when…" She didn't finish her sentence. She just glared at Leila. Malik didn't know Leila was a Christian, but Leila knew he wasn't one. "You should know better than to do this," she said to Leila.

"I should know better than what? Is it wrong to kiss the guy I like just because he's your brother?" Leila stared defiantly at her.

"Stop being like that, Leila. You know exactly what I mean."

"You mean that I am a Christian and he isn't?"

Zainah's eyes widened in surprise and panic.

"Stop staring at me like that, Zainah!" Leila said. "Malik already knows that I am a Christian. I told him. Besides, it's not exactly hard to guess seeing that was the reason why you were chased out of this community."

Zainah turned to Malik, still surprised, and asked, "So, you know she's a Christian and you're still interested?"

He shrugged. "It doesn't matter to me."

Zainah shook her head and turned back to Leila. "First of all, it should matter to you, Leila, that he doesn't share your faith." She held up her hand when Leila opened her mouth to say something. "And don't tell me you are working on making him a Christian. As much as I want that, too, it might never happen." She looked back to make sure no one was coming before turning to Malik and saying, "Secondly, you know that Papa will be angry if he finds out you are involved with a Christian woman. He hasn't asked me about my faith yet, but I think he's hoping that I've finally come back to Islam again and that is why I came back home. I intend to leave this house before he asks me about that and it becomes an issue."

She was surprised when Malik nodded. "You are right. Papa does think you both are Muslims. He actually told me he was glad that you had finally come back to your senses." He looked at Leila. "Zainah is right. We need to be careful. If our father finds out that you both are Christians, it could get a little dangerous…"

"So I see you haven't actually come to your senses after all!"

Zainah gasped and her heart jumped as she turned around. Papa was standing at the door and staring at her with blazing eyes.

Malik shook his head. "Umm... Papa, I didn't mean..."

"Shut up and keep out of this!" Papa said, holding out his hand in Malik's direction. He said in a cold voice, "Tell me the truth, Zainah. Have you returned to Islam or are you still a Christian?"

Zainah's heart raced wildly as she looked at her father. His face was red with rage and he was looking at her with disgust. She pressed her lips tightly together, knowing her answer would not just ensure that she didn't get the resources she needed to find Faizan, but that Leila would be part of whatever punishment her father decided to mete out. Lord, help me, she prayed. She exhaled and then told him the truth.

"I am a follower of Christ," she said simply.

He laughed harshly. "So you didn't come back here because you had finally come to your senses. You simply came to get money from me and then go back to wherever you've been for all these years."

She said nothing.

He looked at Malik and narrowed his eyes. "You knew they were Christians and you said nothing."

Malik shook his head. "I didn't think it mattered so..."

"Shut up!" Papa nodded and turned back to Zainah. "Now, you are going to tell me if you are ready to convert back to Islam of your own will," he turned to Leila briefly and then turned back to her, "or forcefully. You both get to choose either option."

Zainah's jaw dropped. She'd thought her father would, at best, shame her for her faith, or at worst, send her and Leila away. But never had she considered him forcing her to convert to Islam. Her heart thudded as she looked at Leila. Her best friend looked terrified. Would she be able to stand or would she convert under pressure? And if they even stood on their faith, what was the point if they would somehow be forced to convert?

She prayed for strength again and then looked her father in the eye. She would not convert willingly. Still, she wondered how her father was going to force her and Leila to convert. "I will not convert," she said as boldly as she could. "I will not turn my back on my savior."

Papa smiled coldly. He looked at Leila, and Zainah bit her lip in fear as he asked the same question he'd asked her.

Leila looked at Malik, her eyes full of dread. She looked at Zainah and then turned to Papa.

Lord, please help her to stand strong, Zainah prayed.

Leila looked down and whispered, "I choose to stand for Christ."

Papa laughed bitterly. "Okay, then. You are both going to convert whether you like it or not."

"You can't force us to," Zainah said, her stomach clenching.

"Yes, I can!" Papa said. A few young men Zainah hadn't noticed before gathered around them. "Since you both are unmarried, you'll be given away as brides to two men in this town. Men who are dedicated Muslims and will not tolerate any act of rebellion from their wives. They will not be as lenient as I am," he said to Zainah. "You will live with them and their other wives as good Muslim brides or suffer the ultimate consequence for your disobedience."

Zainah stared at her father as though he was a stranger and then she shut her eyes. She prayed desperately, Lord, this cannot be happening. Please deliver us.

Leila cried out and Malik stood in front of their father, rage written clearly on his face. "You can't do this to them!"

Papa looked at the young men standing around them and nodded. "Take them away."

Four of the men grabbed Zainah and Leila, and the others held Malik back while he kicked and threatened them.

Zainah felt a sense of detachment as the men led her and Leila to the back of their house. There was a shack a short distance away from the house that hadn't been there years before. Leila cried as the men led them to the shack and pushed them inside.

Leila cried out as she fell, and Zainah went to help her up.

"You will both stay here until you either convert or are given away in marriage," one of the young men said.

Zainah gave him an evil look, but he had already turned around. They left and Zainah went to the door to try to open it. It was locked. She looked around for any way of escape, but found none. There was only a small window big enough for a cat to crawl through with iron bars.

Zainah finally couldn't keep it together anymore.

She sat on the dirty floor and wept. Leila wrapped her arms around her and they sobbed together.

"I'm so sorry, Leila. It's all my fault. I should never have brought you here with me."

Leila shook her head and sniffled. "No, it's my fault. I was the one who suggested you come back here."

"What are we going to do now?" Zainah said, feeling hopeless.

"Pray. That is all we can do for now."

Zainah nodded. Even though her heart was full of fear, she held hands with Leila and prayed. She reiterated her trust in the Lord and asked Him to do only what He could do—deliver them out of their prison.

They continued to pray until the shack began to get dark. Soon they became exhausted and fell asleep.

Zainah jerked up, awoken by a clanging sound. Her ears perked up as she listened. The sound wasn't loud, but it was constant. She stood up and followed the sound until she figured out where exactly it was coming from. Someone outside was hitting the bars on the small window.

Zainah pressed the switch on the wall and breathed a sigh of relief when the lightbulb over them lit up. She looked down at the corner of the shack and found that Leila was still sleeping. Tiptoeing to the window, she stood on her toes and peered out. And then she gasped. Malik was standing there, hitting the iron bars with a short stick.

"Malik!" she called out.

"Shh… not so loud," he cautioned. He held the bars and peered at her. "Where is Leila?" he asked.

"She's asleep."

"Listen, Zainah," he whispered, "Papa is already planning your wedding. Leila's, too. The men he wants to marry you off to are both cruel." Malik frowned deeply. "I won't let him marry Leila off."

Zainah's mouth fell open. "Thanks for your care, brother!"

"And you too, obviously," he added.

Zainah's heart felt like it was about to explode with dread. She put her hand on her forehead and asked, "What are we going to do? Can you help us get out of here, Malik?"

"I don't know where Papa kept the keys to this shack and trying to force the door open might attract the wrong attention. I'll try to find the keys as soon as possible. But I promise, I'll find a way to get you both out of this place."

Leila moaned and Zainah looked in her direction. She stood and said to Zainah, "Who are you talking to?"

"Malik."

Leila hurried over and nudged her away. "Malik!" she said and stuck her fingers out of the bars. She touched his cheeks and he brushed back the hair from her face.

"How are you?" he asked her worriedly.

"Not so good," she answered.

He told her what he'd said to Zainah and then added, "I'll not rest until you are free. We will be together somehow."

Zainah watched them, her emotions roiling. Pain shot through Zainah's heart as Faizan's face appeared clearly in her mind. She exhaled to try to get rid of it, but couldn't. Malik and Leila did look like they loved each other, but just like her and Faizan, though for different reasons, they could not be together. Even if they somehow found a way to escape this place, they had to leave this town as soon as possible. Plus, in spite of Leila's stubbornness, she would not marry a non-Christian. Her alliance lay first with the Lord.

Tears stung Zainah's eyes as she thought of Faizan. If her father succeeded in marrying her off to some other man, apart from the fact that her faith or her life would be in jeopardy, she would never see Faizan again. She began to hyperventilate as the pain felt too heavy to bear.

"Zainah!" Malik called to her again.

She came near.

"As soon as I find that key, I'll let you both out. You have to be ready to leave then. Okay?"

Zainah nodded as a shiver ran through her.

Malik waved goodbye and walked away quickly. As she watched him, Zainah prayed earnestly that he would find the key quickly, before her father married her and her best friend away and all hope was lost.

*****

Sienna sat on the couch and looked up at the clock on the wall. It was almost eleven p.m. and still Bryan wasn't back. She took a deep breath and shook her head. Frustration and anger boiled inside of her. Since they'd come to Peru, he'd begun to come home late, his constant excuse being that his meetings and evangelistic outreaches ran longer than he thought they would. She stood up and went into the large bedroom she shared with him. She'd tried at first to continue their Green Valley tradition of waiting in the living room till he came back home, but she'd gotten tired of doing that now.

She changed into her nightgown and stretched out on the bed. The anger and frustration she felt grew as she tossed and turned. He'd promised he would always be there for her, but now he left her alone almost every day. He knew she didn't know anyone here yet. She took her classes online, so she didn't really have an opportunity to meet other people who she could make friends with. Yet, he didn't care. His excuses meant little to her. If he really wanted to come home early, she was certain he could find a way to do that.

She sat up as she heard the door open and then sighed in relief when she heard his footsteps approaching. Even though she was relieved he was back, she was still angry with him. She lay back down and pretended to be asleep. She didn't want to say anything to him that she would regret later.

She heard him enter the room. Ten minutes later, she felt the blanket move and then his arms went around her. She opened her eyes as he planted a gentle kiss on her forehead. This was now their new everyday routine. Most times, she kept her eyes shut when he kissed her, but today, she couldn't keep back her ire.

He lifted his brows and stared into her eyes. "You are awake today. I'm sorry if I woke you up."

"If you were paying better attention, you would know I'm always awake when you come home. I just pretend to sleep so I don't pour out my anger on you."

He blinked rapidly. "Sienna? What is it?"

"How can you even ask me that?" she spat out. "You leave the house very early in the morning and you don't come back until eleven or twelve o'clock at night. You know I don't know anyone here and therefore will be lonely, yet you see nothing wrong with leaving me all alone every single day."

He sat up and looked at her. "I didn't know you felt so lonely."

She stared at him and blurted out, "Are you serious? I'm alone every day and you didn't know that I would feel lonely?"

He sighed loudly. "I have explained why I come home late, Sienna. Please try to understand and bear with me." He reached out to touch her, but she shifted away from him. He looked at her and pleaded, "What can I do to make it up to you?"

With her back to him, she said, "You can start by coming home early from now on."

He placed his hand on her back as he said, "I'll try. It's not easy to get away from meetings and the outreaches, especially the outreaches. I wish you could come along, but many of the places we go aren't safe for you and our baby. Plus, you are taking classes all day long."

She instinctively touched her growing belly and her resentment doubled. "What if something happens to our baby when you're not around?"

"Sienna, come on. Nothing is going to happen. Besides, you have my number for emergencies."

She laughed without humor as she turned to face him. "And I called you twice on it on the days you came back after midnight, but you didn't answer on either occasion."

Bryan sighed again. "I'm sorry, Sienna. I'll try to do better from now on."

She shook her head. "You've said that before… but here we are, having the same argument."

Bryan put his hands around her, drew her close, and kissed her. At first, she didn't respond to his kiss, but he kept kissing her until she melted in his arms.

An hour later, she lay wrapped in his arms, listening to his light breathing. She stared at him for a full minute and then slowly extricated herself from him. She went into the living room, sat on the couch, and looked at the clock on the wall. It was past midnight. She thought about Audrey and Trisha and Faizan. What had they done during the day? What were their plans for the weekend? An overwhelming feeling of loss settled on her. Back in Green Valley, whenever she'd started thinking about her siblings this way, she would make plans to visit them the next day or during the weekend. Not so here.

She pressed her lips tightly together. She'd thought she had forgiven Bryan, but she had only buried the hurt within her. Now that her mind had returned to her family in the United States, all the hurt resurfaced again. She realized she still blamed him for keeping her apart from them.

She stretched out on the couch and decided she would call Audrey tomorrow and ask her for advice. She couldn't keep holding this resentment against her husband in her heart, but it was getting more and more difficult not to. Not only had he separated her from her family and everyone she knew, he'd not kept his promise to always be there for her. She was married, and yet she felt lonelier than when she was single.

She prayed, "Lord, please forgive me. I know he's doing Your work, but it's so hard. I feel so alone."

Gradually, she drifted off to sleep. When she woke up the next morning, she found that Bryan had already left for work. She sat on the bed, closed her eyes, and prayed he would keep his promise today and come back early. Because if he continued to leave her all alone, every day, she wasn't sure what her next step would be. All she knew was that she couldn't go on living like this.

*****

Trisha handed Ruby to Paula and then kissed her daughter's cheeks. When Ruby cried out for her, she put her hand on Ruby's cheek and said, "I'll be back tomorrow, Ruby. I promise."

Paula rubbed Ruby's back comfortingly and said to Trisha, "So, you are really going to Boise. I didn't know you were this crazy about Frank."

Trisha shrugged. "I've always liked him, but it took some time to get to this place where I am now. I can say I am in love with him now. Unfortunately, I still don't know where he is."

"Frank's business partner… are you sure he's going to tell you where Frank is? Why can't you just call him instead of going all the way to Boise?"

"I told you before, Paula," Trisha said. "Audrey has asked him a few times to tell her where Frank is, and he's refused every time. I doubt that he would agree to tell me on the phone. Face to face, though, I think, or at least I hope, I can convince him to." Trisha sighed. "If not, I at least hope he'll let me have Frank's phone number so I can call him."

Paula smiled at her. "I'll pray that everything works out. I'm rooting for you and Frank. I'm so glad that Stan is out of the picture. I actually regret encouraging you to date him when we were teenagers."

"Well, what's important now is that we all learn from our past mistakes, and I have been an expert at making mistakes." She picked up her purse from Paula's sofa. "It's time to go." She hugged Paula and kissed Ruby's cheeks again.

"Mama," Ruby cried.

"Mama will be back in no time," Paula said.

Trisha waved to her best friend and her daughter and then left the house quickly. She got in her car and began the drive to the airport. All the way there, she struggled to stay positive, while a voice in her head kept insisting that her trip would be in vain.

She read a novel throughout her flight to Boise in order to keep her mind from dwelling on negative thoughts about the outcome of her trip. When she arrived at the airport in Boise, she immediately took a taxi to the address Frank had given her months before.

She exited the taxi when it stopped in front of Frank's restaurant. She looked up at the building and smiled. "Frankly Eating," she said quietly, reading the name engraved on the roof of the restaurant.

She stepped into the restaurant and wasn't surprised to find it was very busy even though it wasn't a weekend. She sat at the table the hostess led her to and then asked the young woman if the co-owner of the restaurant, Nick Carrington, was in today. When she was told he was, she asked if she could speak with him and told the hostess to tell him her name was Trisha Coleman. The lady started to walk away and she quickly called her back. "I'm sorry. Tell him it's Trisha Gardner."

The hostess nodded and went away.

Trisha sighed. She hadn't changed her surname back to her maiden name after she'd divorced Stan because she couldn't be bothered. She'd decided not to ever be in a relationship again after the way Stan had treated her. Now that she was sure that she wanted to be with Frank, she needed to change it as soon as possible.

A waitress came and Trisha ordered a mocktail. She looked around the busy restaurant as she waited so as to distract herself from worrying. When her drink arrived five minutes later, she took sips while she continued to wait.

Ten minutes later, a young man she guessed was Nick strode toward her, an impatient expression on his face. When he reached her table, he gave her a tight smile. "I was told you wanted to speak with me," he said.

She smiled widely. "Yes. I'm Trisha Gardner—"

"I know who you are," he cut in. His smile had dropped off his face. "What do you want?"

She refused to let the antagonism in his voice scare her. With her smile firmly in place, she said, "I've been trying to reach Frank Kessler but haven't been able to. My sister, who is a close friend of his, told me you said Frank had moved to another country, but you wouldn't tell her what country it is."

He smiled, but a smile of mockery rather than pleasure. "Yes, I didn't tell her because I didn't want her to tell you where Frank is."

"But I have—"

He cut her off again. "You've done enough harm, Mrs. Coleman, or whatever you are called now. Please just leave Frank alone."

Trisha sighed sadly. "I know I deserve your anger. But please, even if you can't tell me where he is, just let me have a phone number to reach him. I need to talk to him."Nick shook his head. "No. I'm not even going to give you a phone number to reach him. The last time you talked to him on the phone, he packed up his things and went to Rosefield to win your heart. I told him it was a bad idea, but he wouldn't listen. I was right. You broke his heart and now he's gone… again." He narrowed his eyes as he stared at her. "So, do not ask me to give you his number; because I won't."

Trisha bit her bottom lip until it hurt. "I know I'm to blame, but I really need your help. Please. I have realized that I love him and I need to tell him that. I need to repair what I have broken. Please."

"I'm sorry," he said coldly. "I can't help you. I have work to do now." He waved his hand around the restaurant. "As you can see, I am a very busy man." He stared at her accusingly. "I would be less busy, though, if my partner were here."

She stood up and studied Nick's face. His jaw was set, his features rigid. She knew he wasn't going to tell her where Frank was or give her Frank's number. She sighed again and said, "Thank you anyway."

Striding out of the restaurant, she fought the

disappointment and despair that flooded her heart. She would go straight to the airport and fly home to Rosefield, but she wouldn't stop looking for a way to reach Frank. It was her fault that he'd fallen off the grid. She would do whatever it took to get him back, even if it meant camping in front of his parents' house until they told her exactly where he was.

EIGHTEEN

Bryan hurriedly entered his car and raced home. His heart drummed as he drove. He'd promised Sienna that he would begin to come home early, but a day after he'd made her that promise, Dr. Lincoln had announced that there would be a series of revival meetings in a town far away from where they lived. He'd tried his best to come home early on the first day of the revival meeting, but he'd still arrived at ten o'clock. Apologizing profusely to Sienna, he'd promised to do better the next day, but he had not. He had come home even later. He gave her the real reason for his lateness—that God's presence had been so strong in the meeting that he couldn't get away. But she had seemed uninterested in his explanation.

Today, it was almost midnight. She would be angry. If she spoke to him at all today, he would be lucky. He had to find a way to start coming home early. He couldn't keep disappointing her.

Thankfully, because it was late, there was no traffic. He got home forty-five minutes later and opened the door with his pulse racing. Lord, help me, he prayed silently as he shut the door behind him and walked to the bedroom.

His heart hurt. Gone were the days when she waited for him eagerly in the living room every day. He missed those days so much. He took a deep breath as he stood in front of the bedroom door and prayed for wisdom to know what to say to calm her down if she blew up on him.

I don't like that I have turned her into this constantly angry person, he thought. She'd been so sweet and soft-spoken when they'd gotten married. She hardly ever raised her voice. He knew part of it was her pregnancy hormones acting up, but a large part was his fault. "Lord, please let her forgive me… again," he whispered.

Entering the bedroom, he took another deep breath and then walked up to the bed. He breathed a sigh of relief when he saw the light was off and she was already asleep. Hopefully, she wouldn't awaken when he got into bed. He would have some reprieve tonight before he faced her the next morning.

Using his phone as a flashlight, he changed into his pajamas, slowly and quietly got into the bed, and got under the covers. And then he blinked in surprise. He turned on the light and saw she wasn't under the covers as he had thought. The duvet was just bunched up and the pillow was under it, but she wasn't there.

He sat up, wondering where she was. Beginning to worry, he climbed out of the bed and went to the bathroom to see if she was there. She wasn't. He raked his fingers through his hair as a sense of dread came over him. Lord, where is she?

He searched their tiny apartment but didn't find her. He became frantic as he went back into the bedroom and picked up his phone from the bedside table. He dialed her number and listened as her phone rang. But she didn't answer. He called again, but still she didn't pick up.

He shook his head and paced the room, fear threatening to suffocate him. As he walked to the end of the room, a thought suddenly entered his mind and he went to the closet. He threw it open and then sharply sucked in his breath. Her clothes and shoes were gone. He looked down and noticed that the big suitcase she'd packed her clothes in when they'd come to Peru was also missing.

"Lord, she has left me," he cried and tossed his phone on the bed. He sat on the bed as all his strength drained away from his body. *What am I going to do now?*

He felt like crying and ran his fingers through his hair. He exhaled and tried to gather himself together. Picking up his phone, he dialed Trisha's number and waited impatiently as it rang.

Trisha's voice came on the line, sounding groggy. "Hello… Bryan, is everything okay?"

"Do you know where Sienna is? I came home to find her gone. All her clothes are also gone."

"What?" Trisha exclaimed. "I don't know where she is. Oh, Bryan, what happened? Did you two have a fight?"

"It's a long story," he said, tapping his feet in frustration. "Let me call Audrey and Faizan. Maybe she told one of them where she went."

Trisha said in a shaky voice, "Okay. I'll try calling her number and see if she answers."

Bryan ended the call and dialed Audrey's number. She didn't answer. He tried Faizan's and waited as it rang. When Faizan answered, Bryan told him that Sienna was missing and asked if she had told him where she was going.

"She didn't say anything about leaving when I spoke with her yesterday," Faizan said, his voice ringing with alarm.

After they both promised to call each other if they heard anything, Bryan ended the call and sat looking at the ceiling. He slid to his knees and prayed earnestly that the Lord would keep her safe and keep the baby safe as well. He asked the Lord for wisdom as he didn't know what to do. There was nothing more he wanted than to make her happy, but he also had to fulfill the ministry God had called him to.

He got up once more, changed back to his day clothes, grabbed his car keys from the dresser, and went out. He knew exactly where she'd gone. He just hoped he wasn't too late by the time he got there.

*****

Zainah awoke with a start as she heard her name and Leila's being called by someone outside. They'd been locked up in this smelly shack for days. "Zainah, Leila!" the voice called again. It sounded like Malik's and it seemed he'd been calling them for some time now. The shack was dark except for a stream of light coming through the small window with iron bars. She slowly stood at the same time Leila did and went to the window. Sure enough,

Malik's face peered at them through the bars, illuminated by the flashlight he was holding.

Zainah smiled in relief as she looked at him. His eyes were on Leila beside her.

"I've been calling both of you for some time now. Come to the door," he whispered. "I have the key."

Leila let out a sob.

Zainah shut her eyes and briefly whispered a prayer of thanksgiving to God. As she walked to the door she kept touching the wall, looking for the light switch. At last she found it and switched the light on. The overhead bulb lit up the room. She held Leila tightly as they stood in front of the door and waited for Malik to open up for them.

The door flew open, and Malik and Leila immediately fell into each other's arms. Zainah briefly hugged him in gratitude as he pulled away from Leila. "Thank you, Malik," she said to him.

He nodded and said, "You both have to leave right now. I hired a taxi to take you to Kazi. There, you can take a bus back to wherever you want."

Leila looked somberly at him. "Will you come with us?" she asked in a soft voice.

He took her hands in his and gazed at her, the look on his face sad. "You know I can't leave now because of my daughter."

She nodded and smiled sadly at him.

He reached out and touched her cheeks as tears fell down them. "I'll miss you," he said to her. "But I have your number and you have mine. Call me as soon as you get far away from this place."

"I will."

He tucked a strand of her hair behind her ear and wiped her tears away with his thumb. "I told you we will be together one day, and I promise it will happen no matter what. I'll find a way to come to you, but it might take a while." He leaned in and kissed her, and she returned his kiss.

As they kissed, Zainah watched them with a tinge of envy and an overwhelming sadness. And then she coughed to get their attention. "We have to go now."

Malik stepped back from Leila. "You do have to go now." He took Leila's hand and beckoned for Zainah to follow him.

They walked quickly, stopping intermittently to look around and make sure no one was following. Except for the light from Malik's flashlight and dim shafts of light coming from kerosene lamps in a few houses, Nira was dark. They walked between two small houses some distance from Zainah's family house, and came out to an open field. Nostalgia filled Zainah's mind as she remembered playing with her friends in this field. On the other side was a small car waiting with its engine running. They hurried to the car.

The driver, whose features Zainah could barely make out, spoke to Malik while she and Leila got into the backseat of the car. Zainah's heart kept beating fast as she looked around her continuously, praying that no one would discover them. Her father was well respected in their small town. Most people would probably have heard about her impending forced marriage. If they saw her trying to get away, they would not hesitate to inform her father.

Leila stuck her head out of the car window as Malik finished speaking with the man. He kissed her again and then smiled at Zainah. "God be with you both," he said.

She nodded and waved as the car drove away. When she finally turned around and settled down on her seat, she found that Leila was weeping softly, her hands covering her face. Zainah hugged her tightly.

"Just as he said, he'll call soon," was all she could say to Leila. She didn't want to repeat what Malik had said about being reunited with Leila soon. As much as she loved them both, Malik didn't share their faith. Besides, she didn't want to give Leila false hope, as Malik's promise might not come to pass. In time, he might, or most likely, would come to forget Leila.

The driver continued to drive until they got to the outskirts of Nira. He suddenly stopped and Zainah frowned. Her frown deepened when he opened the door and came out of the car.

"What is it?" she asked him. "Do we have a flat tire or something?"

Leila, who had begun to doze off, awakened and stared out the window at the driver. She turned to Zainah. "What's happening?"

"I don't know," Zainah answered. "I think something is wrong with the car." They stared curiously at the driver and asked him what was wrong again. When he didn't answer or even check any part of the car, Zainah became worried. The man stood with his back to them, as though he were waiting for someone, or something.

The hair on the back of Zainah's neck stood up and she whispered to Leila, "I don't like this. It's like he's waiting for someone. I don't think we can trust him. Maybe we should get out of the car and make a run for it."

Leila said, "I don't think Malik would find us a driver who isn't trustworthy, Zainah. Let's stay calm and ask him what's wrong again."

Zainah shook her head. "How many times are we supposed to do that?" She took Leila's hand. "Let's leave now. It's not safe for…" She gasped and widened her eyes as two men with flashlights suddenly appeared from nowhere, shining the lights in their faces.

Zainah instinctively covered her eyes with her hands, her heart drumming.

The men yelled and wrenched open the car door. Leila screamed as one of them grabbed her. Another man grabbed Zainah's wrist. She tried to wrench it away, without success.

Leila screamed as the men pulled her out of the car, while Zainah fought them with all her heart. They yanked her out roughly and then began to drag her away with them. She fought and screamed but they didn't stop, neither did anyone come to her rescue. Leila was sobbing and yelling at them beside her.

They bundled her and Leila into the back of a truck not far away. They all got in, squeezing Leila and Zainah between them. One covered Zainah's mouth before she could scream again and another clamped his hand over Leila's.

Zainah began to hyperventilate as they approached the shack behind her father's house. Her father was standing near the shack with two other men. The truck stopped in front of him, and he stared at her with derision written on his face. She and Leila were carried out of the car.

The men set her down before her father, and Zainah stared at him with a mixture of loathing and surprise. "How can you treat your own daughter like this?" she screamed at him.

He blinked and then slapped her hard. "I should be the one asking you that question."

Zainah staggered back and moaned in pain. She held her cheek and said to him, "At least let Leila go. Your anger is directed toward me and not her."

Her father shook his head and sneered. "No. I am not letting anyone go. You both are marrying Ahmed and Bakari. Your joint wedding was supposed to be in two weeks' time, but because you chose to run away, the wedding will be in two days."

Zainah gasped in fear and pleaded with her father to reconsider. But he didn't listen.

He looked at Leila, who looked too shocked to speak, and then glared at Zainah. "Prepare yourselves. In two days, you will both be married to good Muslim men."

Zainah kept pleading, but her father didn't even look at her again. He ordered the men to lock her and Leila in the shack again. Before they did, he said to her, "Tomorrow morning, your sister and some other women will come and get you and your friend to start the wedding preparations." He shook his head as he stared at her. "One day, you will thank me for what I'm doing for you now." He turned around and walked out of the shack.

The other men walked out after him and the door was firmly locked. Leila went to the door and began to bang on it while she screamed and begged to be let out. She turned to Zainah after a while and said in a fear-filled voice, "That driver sold us out. But how did he contact your father's men so quickly when we didn't even see him make a phone call?"

Zainah forced down the sob threatening to burst out of her mouth. "There is no other explanation I can think of. It must have been Malik. Maybe Father forced him to tell him where we were or maybe he did it of his own volition."

Leila shook her head slowly, her eyes wide with fear. "I don't believe that!"

"Then where is he now? My father didn't even ask how we escaped." She couldn't hold back her sobs anymore. Kneeling on the floor, she wept.

NINETEEN

The stars were shining bright in the sky when Miriam came out of her tent. The whole camp was completely silent. She headed toward the prayer tent, her heart deeply troubled. For the past week, she'd been worried about Zainah and Leila. When they'd left the camp several weeks before, she'd been worried about them, but somehow she'd known they were fine, wherever they were. She'd waited for the driver who took her to town every month to come to the camp so she could ask him where Zainah and Leila had gone to. She figured they had arranged with her regular driver to come pick them up without anyone's knowledge. But for some reason, that driver did not come when it was time for her to go to town. Instead, another driver had picked her up.

Miriam had been disappointed and had kept Zainah and Leila constantly in her prayers since then. But the week before, she'd felt a tug in her heart urging her to pray more specifically for their protection. The day before, the urgency to pray for them had increased. She'd prayed till late into the night. Throughout today, she had intermittently prayed for them as well. Now, she felt even more burdened to intercede on their behalf.

She entered the prayer tent and knelt down on the floor. Just as she started to pray, she heard the familiar voice of the Spirit say in her heart, Go now to the community you rescued Zainah from eleven years ago. My daughters are in trouble.

She frowned and whispered, "Lord, it's the middle of the night and her community is very far from here. How am I supposed to get there… and at this time?"

"Go outside."

Miriam's frown deepened, but she obeyed. She stepped out of the tent, wondering why the Lord had asked her to come out. And then her ears perked up as she heard the sound of a vehicle approaching. She blinked rapidly. Vehicles didn't appear at the camp in the middle of the night. In fact, no vehicle came here except for the agreed truck once a month.

She watched the truck approaching with her mouth open. When it stopped in front of her and her old driver came out, her eyes widened in astonishment. "How come you are here… at this time?" she asked him.

The bearded driver said to her, "I'm sorry for stopping by so late. My boss sent me on an errand to the border this morning, and I'm only just returning now. I was passing through here and decided to stop as the roads leading to town have become very dangerous at night." He pleaded, "Please, I know this is a women's camp, but can I spend the night here? I promise to leave as soon as it is dawn."

For a full minute, she stared, in awe of God, and then she laughed out loud. He put his palms together in a pleading gesture but she shook her head. "No… I mean, yes. Of course you can stay. But I'll need you to do me a huge favor." She asked him if he could take her to a small town in Mali.

He nodded eagerly. "My boss will not need me or the truck until Saturday. I can take you, but I will have to return immediately after we get there."

"And what about the dangerous roads?" she asked him. "The trip will take about two days."

"By the time it's nightfall, we will have passed the dangerous spots," he answered. "I'll get you there as fast as possible."

She almost hugged him, but held back. Instead, she smiled widely and thanked him.

"Wait here," she said to him and went to her tent to get a sleeping rug, a pillow, and a blanket. She arranged them on the floor for him. He thanked her profusely, and she left after they'd agreed to leave by five-thirty in the morning.

She hardly slept through the night. At about five o'clock, she hurriedly bathed, changed into a long kaftan and scarf, grabbed her purse, and left her tent. She entered the prayer tent and saw the driver was already awake.

"Are you ready to go?" he asked her.

She said she was, and they set out immediately.

Throughout the journey, Miriam slept on and off. They stopped at different towns to buy food and water. All through the trip, whenever she was awake, Miriam prayed, asking for God's help and direction. She still remembered Zainah's tiny town, but did not know her father's house.

They finally passed through the border into Mali. The driver thankfully knew the area quite well and with a few pointers from Miriam, found the road leading to Zainah's small community.

They reached the small town, Nira, just as the sun was rising. The driver stopped Miriam at the market, which was at the center of the town. Some of the traders had already come out with their wares, but there were still some empty stalls.

Miriam got out of the truck, waved goodbye to the driver, and then prayed silently again, asking the Lord to show her where to find Zainah and Leila. She looked around her, hoping the Lord would send some kind of sign. She didn't want to ask about Zainah and Leila as she didn't know what kind of trouble they might be in. They might be hiding out somewhere now, not wanting to be discovered. She was afraid that asking about them might put them in danger somehow. She continued to wait for a sign, but there was nothing.

A trader called out to her from his stall and asked if she wanted to buy something. She shook her head and began to turn away when the Lord told her to approach him. She obeyed and he asked her again what she wanted to buy.

"Nothing," she answered. "But I'm, umm… I'm looking for two women. Their names are Zainah and Leila." She began to describe their physical features to him and he nodded vigorously.

"I know Zainah. She is Karim Keita's daughter," the man said. "I heard that she and her friend are Christians, but will convert to Islam once they are married off."

Miriam's jaw dropped. "Married off? To whom? When?"

The man told her about the two men they would be married to and even gave her directions to Zainah's father's house.

Miriam couldn't believe what she was hearing. They were going to be forced into a marriage to men they probably didn't know. Worse, they would be forced to convert. Miriam knew what that meant. Zainah and Leila were dedicated Christians. They would never agree to convert. That meant that their lives were in danger. Her heart twisted in fear. She had to find them now.

The trader looked at her with suspicion. "And you… are you a Christian, too?"

Miriam turned around without answering and hurried away.

She followed the detailed directions the man had given her and found herself in front of a big house; it was bigger than any she had seen in the small community. There were some women dressed in bright outfits carrying platters of food in and out of the house. Some distance away from the house was a group of men, who looked like musicians, carrying their musical instruments. The whole area wore a festive mood. She quickly went to the back of the house, instinctively knowing that she had to make sure she wasn't seen by anyone until she'd found Zainah and Leila.

Lord, what now? she silently asked as she stood hidden behind a huge tree.

She suddenly remembered a man who'd come to the camp some days after Zainah and Leila had left. He'd said Faizan had sent him to give Zainah a message. When she'd told him Zainah wasn't in the camp, he had given her his card and said to call a number on it when Zainah came back, or if she ever needed help. She'd noticed a gun on him as he'd walked away and had kept the card in her purse. Maybe he would be able to help.

She dug out the card and her satellite phone from her purse, praying there was service here, and then breathed a sigh of relief when she saw there was. She quickly dialed the number on the card. She waited impatiently as it rang, knowing that Zainah and Leila's lives were at stake.

*****

Sienna bit her lip and shut her eyes as she listened to the final call to board the plane to Boise. She took a deep breath, stood, and went to board her flight. After her ticket and boarding pass had been checked, she followed the other passengers boarding the plane while asking herself if she was doing the right thing. However, she knew she was. She loved Bryan, but he'd broken his promise to her too many times. She couldn't keep living the way she was, with a heart full of resentment.

She watched as the people in front of her entered the plane and took another deep breath to calm her nerves. Just before she stepped onto the plane, a voice in her heart said firmly, "Sienna, don't go in!"

Her eyes widened in surprise and her heart raced wildly. An overwhelming sense of God's love settled on her and she started to tremble. She could barely manage to stand up. She looked up at the air hostess, who was gazing at her quizzically, probably wondering why she was just standing there instead of boarding the plane. She shook her head and immediately turned around. She walked away quickly and didn't stop until she was outside the airport. She stood behind a grove of trees and wept.

Waves of divine love swept over her, and she trembled in pleasure and guilt. And then she cried out, "Lord, why now?"

"You shouldn't punish Bryan by leaving when I'm the one you truly resent."

Sienna gasped. And then she realized that it was completely true. She'd taken out all the anger and resentment she felt toward the Lord on her husband. But it was God she was angry with. And her anger stemmed from the fact that He had spoken to Bryan about their moving to another country without ever speaking to her. In fact, she'd hardly ever heard God's voice, even though she constantly yearned to. Bryan, however, had heard the Lord's voice clearly and dramatically so many times that she was now actually jealous. She had never admitted that to herself until now.

Tears fell down her cheeks as she sobbed even louder. A minute later, she sniffed and said, "I just felt so angry when Bryan told me You wanted us to move. Yes, I was sad because I would miss my family, but I was resentful because I had to move and You told me nothing. It just felt like You didn't care about me as much as You did Bryan."

"You should have asked me, and I would have spoken to you as clearly as I spoke to him. It might not have been in the same way, but I would have spoken to you."

"I guess I thought you would not answer. It's always been like this since I met Bryan. He always tells me what's on Your mind and I obey. I think I got tired of it." She sniffed. "Poor Bryan. He'll be so worried about me. I need to go home as soon as possible." She smiled. "I'm so grateful that You stopped me, Lord. Most of all, I'm grateful that You spoke to me the way You did. You didn't have to, but You did anyway."

She walked away from behind the trees, engulfed in the love and presence of God. She was certain she wore a silly smile on her face, but she didn't care.

As she made her way to the road to get a taxi, her eyes widened as she spotted Bryan's car coming toward her. Her heart leapt with joy and she happily waved him down. She stuck her head through the window as he stopped. She was grateful for the bright streetlights that enabled her to see his handsome face clearly. "Can I get a ride, sir?" she asked, smiling.

He jumped out of the car and with lightning speed, reached her side. Sweeping her into a hug, he kissed her hair and said in a voice choked with emotion, "I thought you were gone. Thank God you are still here!"

"I'm so sorry, Bryan."

He pulled back and stared at her quizzically. "What are you sorry for, my love? I'm the one who should be apologizing, not you. I failed to keep my promise to you again."

She shook her head and wiped the tears from her eyes. "No. I've a lot to apologize for; like my impatience and jealousy."

"Jealousy?"

"It's a long story. I'll tell you when we get home."

He hugged her happily again and then they got into the car. He took her hand just before he started the car. "Sienna, I am truly sorry. I'll try to do better, but I can't promise that I won't come home late again. So, I'm also asking for your forgiveness when that happens."

She nodded. "I know, Bryan. You have to do the Lord's work. I've decided to start my own N.G.O. so I can have something productive to do while you are away."

He looked at her with a surprised expression. "When did you decide that?" he asked.

She laughed. "Just now."

He laughed along with her and then started the car.

She couldn't take her eyes off him as they drove home. Thank you, Lord, for stopping me from leaving.

She leaned in and kissed him on the cheek. When he turned and smiled at her, she grinned, and her heart overflowed with love for him. She knew they would face other challenges in the future. There would probably be times when she felt like leaving again; times when her old resentment would creep in. But she knew without a doubt that they had a love that was from God. The God who had brought them together in the first place would keep them loving each other, even through the hard times.

*****

Trisha banged her fist on the Kesslers' front door and then waited. She'd been knocking for a while now. She was sure Frank's parents were home because their cars were parked in front of the house. She was also certain they knew she was the one knocking, hence their refusal to open the door.

She'd been coming here for the past three days. Each time she came, she asked them where Frank was. They always refused to tell her. Today, they had just chosen not to let her in. But she'd promised herself that she wouldn't give up until they gave her the information she wanted.

She knocked on the door again and sighed. She was being obnoxious, she knew. But this was all she could think to do. Desperation couldn't even begin to describe how she felt. She had to talk to Frank and tell him she was sorry and that she wanted him. That she loved him.

She lifted her fist to knock again and then shifted back slightly as the door opened. Frank's mother peered at her with an angry look.

"Please, Mrs. Kessler," Trisha pleaded. "Please tell me where Frank is. Or give me his number."

The woman shook her head. "I've told you many times that I am not going to do that. Just give it up, Trisha. Leave Frank alone."

"I'm not going to leave this place until you tell me where Frank is."

Mrs. Kessler glared at her and Trisha stared back.

"Who is that, Mom?" a voice called out from inside the house.

Trisha gasped and her jaw dropped.

"It's no one important," Mrs. Kessler called out. She began to shut the door.

Trisha found her voice and pushed against the door. "That's Frank!" she cried out. "Frank, it's Trisha! Please, I have to speak to you!"

She struggled to push the door wide open so she could enter the house, while Frank's mother tried to shut the door.

Frank appeared and his eyes bulged as he stared at them. "What are you doing, Mom?" he finally said. "Please, let Trisha in!"

"Frank, it's not right. She shouldn't..." She gasped as Trisha took the opportunity of her distraction to push the door wide open. Frank's mother gave her a dirty look, sighed, and marched off.

"I'm so sorry," Frank said as he gazed at Trisha.

Her heart twisted as she looked up at him. His green eyes had lost the sparkle in them. She said to him, "I thought you moved to another country."

He raised his brows and looked quizzically at her. "Who told you that? I took a trip to several countries to clear my head. But I'd always planned to return."

She smiled sadly at him and said, "I guess everyone has been desperate to keep me away from you. I can't say I blame them."

His mouth dropped open and then he shut it. "To keep you away from me?" He searched her eyes and said in an emotion-laden voice, "You want to be with me?"

Tears filled her eyes and she said, "Frank, I know I hurt you so many times, and yet you kept on loving me. I have given so many excuses for why we can't be together, but you've loved me through them all. I don't know exactly when it happened, but your love has overtaken me. I can't fight how I feel about you anymore and I don't want to. I love you, Frank Kessler. And I'm so grateful for how long and how much you have loved me. If you will have me back,

I want us to be together… forever."

For a long moment, Frank stood staring at her without saying a word. Her heart beat fast as she wondered what he was thinking. The longer he said nothing, the more she began to believe he didn't want her anymore. And she wouldn't be surprised after everything she'd done to push him away.

Finally, he reached out and slowly took her in his arms. She hugged him tightly and sighed in contentment. She felt completely safe in his arms. She knew he loved her with everything in him and would protect her and Ruby even with his life. She stepped back from him and looked into his eyes. She smiled, not surprised by the tears shining in them. As always, he was gazing at her as though she was his everything. But in addition to that usual look, he had a smile so bright it could illuminate all of Boise. It made her so happy that he was happy.

"I love you so much," he said to her, his voice shaking.

"I know," she said, touching his cheek lightly. "I love you, too."

She jumped as he suddenly laughed out loud. "I always dreamed of this day," he said, his face full of unbelievable joy. "After you got engaged to Stan, I thought it would always remain a dream. But now…" he shook his head as he stared at her with a look that said he wasn't sure if this was a dream or if it was real. He finally asked, "Is this real?"

She giggled. "Should I pinch you so you know that it is?"

"No," he answered. "Only one thing will convince me that it's real. Something that has haunted my dreams since we were teens."

"What's that?" she asked, smiling.

"A kiss from you." He gazed longingly at her lips.

She nodded. "I am dying to kiss you as well." She wrapped her arms around him.

He gently took her face in his hands and then kissed her softly. He blinked as he moved back, and she laughed at the look on his face.

"Do you believe it now?"

He looked dazed as he said, "Just one more time, so I'm sure." He took her lips again and kissed her passionately this time. When they finally separated, he whooped and swept her off her feet. She hugged him tight as he swung her around and then put her down.

"You finally believe it's not a dream," she chuckled.

"Just one more thing."

She shook her head and smiled. "What now?"

Her heart jumped into her throat as he knelt before her. "I don't have a ring right now," he said. "But I can't let this moment pass me by." He looked her in the eye. "Trish, will you marry me?"

Without hesitating, she yelled, "Yes, Frank. I will marry you!"

He stood and this time he kissed her slowly and reverently. When he pulled back, he said, "Now I know it's not a dream."

He took her hand and led her to the sofa. They sat talking about their future, the wedding, and Ruby. Trisha gazed at him as he told her he couldn't wait for them to get married and start their lives together.

She said to him, "You waited for me for so long. You don't have to wait anymore. I'll marry you now if you want." She laughed as he ran outside and yelled for all to hear, "I'm getting married to the girl of my dreams!"

She sighed happily. She'd made a lot of mistakes in her life, but this wasn't one of them. Without a doubt, being engaged to Frank was the best decision she'd ever made. And she knew the Lord agreed, because she could feel Him smiling down on her.

TWENTY

Zainah forced herself to remain stoic as her mother and sister put the richly embroidered wedding dress over her head. They adorned her neck and wrists with gold jewelry and then placed a beaded white veil over her head. She could hear drums beating and the musicians her father had hired for the day singing outside the house.

She glanced round her mother's bedroom and noted all the women there looking at her in admiration. Everything in her had died after praying through the night and most of the day for deliverance and finding none. Her heart had stopped racing in fear and dread. Now, she was completely numb. In about an hour, she would be married to a stranger and forced to convert to Islam. She knew she never would. What she wasn't sure of was whether she would live to the end of the week or be kept in captivity until she did what her new husband wanted.

Sherifat, her stepmother, led Leila into the room. She was dressed in a heavily beaded blue wedding dress with a white veil. Her eyes were red from crying through the night. She looked as though she was about to pass out at any minute.

As soon as Leila saw Zainah, she began to weep again. "Zainah, do something!" she cried out.

Zainah shut her eyes as Leila's weeping suddenly broke into her self-imposed numbness. Indescribable pain settled in her chest as she thought about Faizan and the fact that she would never see him again. Her feet couldn't carry her any longer, and she staggered.

Her mother held her hand and steadied her. "Are you okay, Zainah?"

Zainah glared at her. She wanted to scream and ask her mother if she looked okay, but she stopped herself. There was no use. Even her own mother thought they were doing the right thing by giving her away to a random man.

They finished dressing her up, and her mother asked her to turn around so she could look at herself in the mirror. She flatly refused. Leila also refused to look when she was asked to.

"Suit yourself," her mother said.

Someone came to tell them it was time for the brides to come out, and Zainah momentarily shut her eyes. Panic began to overtake her and she prayed for peace. She would not deny the Lord. They could force her to marry a strange man as they didn't really need her agreement to marry her away. But they would never get her to deny her faith. If God intended for her die as a martyr now, then so be it.

The women led her and Leila outside together. Her father's men surrounded them, making sure she or Leila didn't try to escape. There were two huge canopies some distance away that housed the guests. Zainah's heart raced wildly as she was led toward the canopies. She shut her eyes briefly and muttered a prayer for help and calm. The tempo of the music increased as she entered one of the canopies and a loud cheer arose from the guests.

Her father appeared with two men in embroidered kaftans. Zainah immediately knew they were the grooms. They came near, and one of the men, much older than she even imagined, assessed her closely, as though he were inspecting a horse he was about to purchase. Her heart rate increased rapidly and she began to pray even more earnestly.

The women around her began to dance and her mother whispered in her ear, "Dance, Zainah!"

She ignored her mother. She stood in front of the crowd and immediately zoned out as people danced around her and Leila. Leila stood still beside her. Soon, they were left in front of the crowd. The man who had inspected her closely came to stand next to her. Their community imam, who looked much older than how she remembered him, walked under the canopy. He came to stand in front of her and the man she was to marry. Leila stood a foot away with the old man she was to wed.

Zainah bit her bottom lip, trying not to cry. Lord, this cannot be happening.

But it was. The imam started the wedding rites and she knew then that all her prayers for deliverance were not going to be answered. She would be married to the old man standing beside her in a matter of minutes. She would never see Faizan again and they would never have the chance to be together.

A soft murmur arose from the crowd, but she ignored it. The imam stopped speaking and frowned. Her eyes suddenly widened as a loud cry pierced the air followed by an ear-splitting bang that sounded eerily like a gunshot.

People began to scream, and Zainah turned around. Her heart jumped in fear as she saw half a dozen armed men enter the canopy. People took to their heels, screaming.

One of the armed men, who was wearing dark glasses, shouted, "Stop that wedding now!" He pointed his gun at the imam, who was now cowering. The armed man approached her and she swallowed. He said to her, "You are safe," and then stared menacingly at her husband-to-be. "Leave this place now or you will be shot!" He turned and said the same thing to the man that was supposed to wed Leila. Both men ran away with the imam.

The canopy was empty now, except for her, Leila, and the armed men. Zainah gazed at the men, wondering if they were angels sent from God to deliver her and Leila. But they looked too brutal to be angels. Everything felt surreal, as though she were in a dream. Her heart drummed as she looked at them in dread and haltingly asked, "Who are you?"

"We were sent by a friend called Jake," the man in the dark glasses answered.

Zainah shook her head, confused. She said in a trembling voice, "I don't know anyone called Jake."

"He told me to tell you he is Faizan's friend."

Zainah's jaw dropped and then without thinking, she cried out, and hugged the man tightly. He looked taken aback when she drew back. She smiled at him as all her fear vanished.

Leila followed her example and hugged the man. Tears flowed down her cheeks.

Zainah beamed and her heart soared. "Is Faizan here?" she asked excitedly, looking around her, wondering if Faizan would appear at any minute.

"No," the man said. "We need to go now."

Zainah nodded, ecstatic and slightly disappointed at the same time. She quickly followed the men. They led her and Leila to a black SUV. When she got in, she gasped in shock and exclaimed, "Miriam! What are you doing here?"

"It's a long story," Miriam answered, hugging her and then Leila.

The driver immediately started the car and zoomed off. Only the man in the dark shades got into the car. He sat in the passenger's seat beside the driver.

Zainah looked behind her and saw the other men were piling into another SUV. She turned around and she and Leila fell into Miriam's arms again. They both wept loudly with relief and did not stop until they were far away from Nira.

*****

Faizan sat in front of his computer, tapping his feet and waiting impatiently for Zainah's call. A week before, when Jake had called him with news that Zainah was about to be married to some guy in her community, he had been speechless at first. And then he'd blurted out, "It can't be Zainah! She isn't free to get married, and she wouldn't marry someone else even if she was."

Jake had told him on the phone that she and her friend Leila were going to be forced to marry men they didn't know and convert to Islam. He had gone into a rage similar to the kind he used to have before he'd come to Christ. He'd wanted the men who were trying to force her to get married dead.

"Jake, I know you can help. You have to send men now and invade that place. Get her out of there even if you have to kill in order to do so."

"I can't do that," Jake had said. "We are not allowed to interfere with—"

Faizan had cut in. "Please. I won't ask you for anything else. Please do this one favor for me."

For almost a minute, Jake had said nothing, and then he spoke. "Okay. I'll help. But you will owe me… and when it's the right time, I'll collect."

Faizan nodded. "Yes. I agree. Just please get Zainah out. And her friend Leila too." He felt the Spirit's conviction and said, "Please don't kill anyone, though. I take back what I said."

Faizan had waited anxiously for hours to hear back from Jake. When Jake called and told him they had retrieved Zainah and Leila and they were safely on their way to the women's camp, he finally breathed a huge sigh of relief. Jake promised Faizan would be able to speak with her soon. Today was the day they had decided he would speak with Zainah on Skype. He could hardly hold back his excitement and impatience.

He glanced at his wristwatch and saw it was a few minutes past two o'clock. Jake had told him the call would be at two. He looked at his computer again. "Come on! Ring now!"

He jumped when the doorbell rang. "Who is it?"

he said angrily.

He ignored the bell and continued to tap his feet, wondering why he hadn't gotten Zainah's call. Maybe something is wrong with the connection, he thought.

Someone banged on his door and he groaned. Why can't this person, whoever it was, just go away? He wanted to call out and tell whoever was at the door to stop disturbing him and go away, but he sighed loudly and stood up. The sooner he got rid of the person, the better. He walked to the door with his ears still perked up so he wouldn't miss Zainah's call. He would just tell whoever had come to visit that this wasn't a good time.

He unlocked the door quickly and glanced back at his computer before turning around again. And then his eyes bulged as he stared at the woman standing before him.

It can't be. Either I am dreaming or it isn't her.

She screamed and fell into his arms, and he knew he wasn't dreaming. And it was definitely her.

"Zainah," he croaked as he held her tight. "How come you are here?"

She laughed and pulled back to look at him. "Your friend Jake made it happen. I asked him not to say anything so I could surprise you." She pointed at the car on the other side of the road. Jake stuck his face out of the window and waved at him. He waved back and then focused on Zainah again. His heart raced madly as he gazed at her in wonder. She looked even more beautiful than the last time he'd seen her. He hugged her tightly this time. "I can't believe you are here," he said, his voice choked with emotion.

She laughed again and pulled back. The smile dropped from her face and her eyes searched his. The look of love in them took his breath away. His gaze moved to her lips, and he had to summon up all the willpower he had to stop himself from taking her in his arms and kissing her. But the way she was staring at him now didn't help at all.

Her eyes shifted to his lips and he knew he was in trouble. If she didn't stop looking at him like that, he wouldn't be able to control himself any... He gasped when she suddenly pulled him close and kissed him.

Everything around him disappeared, and time seemed to stop as he fervently returned her kiss. His hands tightened around her and he trembled with pleasure as he kissed her with everything in him, relishing her lips. He'd dreamed of doing this for so long, he couldn't believe it was actually happening. His dream had come true.

He kissed her nose, her hair, her chin, and then her lips again. Nothing else around him mattered, and he saw nothing and no one, except for her. And then, he suddenly came to his senses, and immediately pulled away from her.

He looked down in shame and confusion and said, "Zainah, you know this is wrong." He looked at her and sighed. "There is nothing more I want than to keep kissing you, but what about your vow of chastity? You know you can't break your vow to God."

Zainah giggled and he frowned. "What's funny?" he asked, smiling in spite of himself.

"I don't have to keep that vow anymore," she said to him.

"I don't understand."

She began to tell him about her dreams; the ones about him. She told him why she had made the vow and ended with the dream she'd had shortly after he'd left the women's camp. The Lord had told her that he'd never asked her to make that vow and had showed her they were meant to be together.

After she'd finished, he shook his head in wonder, and then the reality of all she'd told him dawned on him. He whooped, "That means we can get married!" He turned around and then realized they were still outside the house. "I'm so sorry, Zainah. I didn't even invite you in." He pulled her into the house and sat her down on the couch. He sat beside her and gazed at her as his heart overflowed with love for her and gratitude to God. "I can't believe you are here," he said again. "Most of all, we can be together." He folded her in his arms and kissed her again. The kiss became more and more passionate, and he knew he had to stop now. It took everything in him, but he finally managed to pull back from her.

"We have to get married as soon as possible to avoid a disaster," he said huskily as he trembled with unmet desire.

She nodded. Her eyes were glazed with desire, and he sighed deeply. He took her hand and kissed it, and then shifted to the end of the couch. He looked at her and said soberly, "Will you marry me, Zainah?"

She nodded. "Of course I'll marry you. I wish I could marry you right now."

He gazed longingly at her but resisted the urge to pull her into his arms and kiss her again. He knew if he did, they wouldn't stop until they had gone all the way. And that would be wrong.

"I love you, Zainah."

"I love you too, Faizan. More than life itself. I'm glad I finally found you."

"Found me?" he asked curiously.

"I've been trying to find you. That was why I left the women's camp and ended up in my community." She told him everything that had happened from the day she'd left the camp up until the day she was rescued by Jake's men.

He couldn't resist taking her hand in his. "I can't believe you went through all that for me. I will love you forever." He beamed at her. He couldn't help but lift his voice silently in thanksgiving to the Lord who had blessed him with such a beautiful and loving woman. She had saved his life and then changed it completely by bringing the gospel to him. Now she'd agreed to spend the rest of her life with him. He would devote his life to her, thanking her every day for everything she'd done for him, for loving him relentlessly.

A LOOK AT: FALLING IN LOVE

From a dusty, rural village in the Middle East to the quiet, leafy streets of Rosefield, Zainah has traveled the globe to be with the man she loves. Their union has provoked the wrath of her father and the disgust of her community, but her impending introduction to sisters-in-law Trisha, Audrey, and Sienna, might be the most nerve-wracking challenge of all.

But Zainah's problems are light in comparison to those of her best friend, Leila. The girl remains trapped in the women's refugee camp, desperate to find a way to return to her beloved Malik. Neither of the young women know that back home, Zainah's father has made a deal with the devil that will have devastating consequences for them both. And when Faizian receives a call from Jake, his CIA handler, a conspiracy is set into motion that will send Zainah, Faizan, Leila, and Malik on a collision course that will change their lives forever.

COMING MARCH 2020

ABOUT THE AUTHOR

Like the characters in her stories, Emma Easter juggles a range of identities.

In the low-income community where she works, Easter is known as a family medicine physician who treats patients of all ages and backgrounds.

College friends see her as an accomplished musician, having studied and mastered five classical instruments—but behind closed doors, she's just as comfortable rocking an air guitar to Creed. And when she isn't giving her heart, soul, and sanity to her three young children she's indulging in her most secret identity of all: meeting new characters, crafting fresh plots, and exploring every corner of her imagination.

Across all these different roles, one cohesive thread has tied everything together: her faith and love of Jesus Christ.

Find more great titles by Emma Easter and Christian Kindle News at https://christiankindle-news.com/our-authors/emma-easter/

Made in the USA
Monee, IL
07 July 2026

56551607R00177